PR
ANNA

MW00904971

Royal Hearts of Mondoverde Series

"BEAUTIFUL. Anna Dynowski embarks on another great series of Christian romances, this time involving the royal family of the tiny Principality of Mondoverde.

"Canadian reporter Sofia Burska is ticked-off with her assignment to interview the crown prince, until he turns on the charm with surprising results. She can't be falling for him. She's not 'princess material.'

"Dynowski's excellent writing and tricky plot makes this one a great success and it's only the first of four. I can't wait for more."
— Arline Chase, author of *Killraven, Ghost Dancer* and the Spirit series.

Moretti Men Series

"EXCITING! A romantic new series from popular Christian author Anna Dynowski. Her faith is strong, her heroines are sassy, her prose is inspired, and her heroes are an inspiration!"
— Arline Chase, author of *Killraven, Ghost Dancer* and the Spirit series.

Harmony Villiage Series

"THE DELIGHTFUL CUPID CAT IS BACK! This time he's urging the owner of a restaurant to follow her heart, and of course to keep the faith. You won't be disappointed."
— Arline Chase, author of *Killraven*

"5 STARS THE BEST ONE YET. Everyone will love this one—Christians, readers, and writers alike!"
— Arline Chase, author of *Ghost Dancer, Killraven,* and the Spirit Series.

"**5 Ticket rating** I *loved* returning to Harmony Village and catching up with all the folks there. Once again Cupid Cat is up to his match-making tricks. "
— Sherry Kuhn, *Love 2 Read Novels*

"**Love the way you write!** I was also excited to see that there will be a book 5!!! YEAH! Thank you again so much for the opportunity of reading *[On Wings of Trust.]* As always I love the way you so naturally weave the Gospel into all your stories. Great job!!! You better keep on writing!!!"
— Reader e-mail

"**One twist after another.** I kept wondering why Izabella and Ricci were married in such a manner in the beginning of the story. I loved the way the author made the reader wait... Anna Dynowski is a master story teller.."
— Sandra Stiles, *The Musings of a Book Addict*

"**If you ever** have been a prisoner of hate or if you know of someone who has, then, *A Pocketful of Hope*, is a must read. When you have been victimized how do you live with yourself? How do you ever learn to love and forgive again? This is a book you will not want to put down once you pick it up."
— Pastor Jim Hughes, author of *C Through Marriage, Revitalizing Your Vows*

"**4 Stars** This was a wonderful book... It touches on the issues of child molestation which can have an adverse affect on relationships in adulthood. Dynowski handled it beautifully. Her characters find out that with God, forgiveness can happen. "
— Sandra K. Stiles

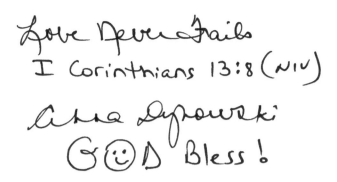

Love Never Fails
I Corinthians 13:8 (NIV)

Anna Dynowski
G☺D Bless!

Wanted:
Royal Princess Wife and Mother

ROYAL HEARTS OF MONDOVERDE SERIES, VOL. 1

by Anna Dynowski

Cambridge Books

an imprint of
WriteWords, Inc.
CAMBRIDGE, MD 21613

𝕮𝖆𝖒𝖇𝖗𝖎𝖉𝖌𝖊 𝕭𝖔𝖔𝖐𝖘 is a subsidiary of:

Write Words, Inc.
2934 Old Route 50
Cambridge, MD 21613

ISBN 978-1-61386-300-8

Fax: 410-221-7510

Bowker Standard Address Number: 254-0304

Dedication

To Yahweh, who has promised His presence and power in my life,

To Henry, my husband, the love of my life, my forever mate, my soulmate,

To my BFF and mom, Alba Caldarelli, whose unswerving faith in the Lord is a constant encouragement to me and an example for me to live up to.

LETTER TO THE READER

Dear Reader,

Nothing that happens to us is an accident. Not the family in which we're born. Not the neighborhood in which we live. Not the company that employs us. Not the setbacks that may befall us. Not the illnesses that may plague us. Not the victories that may encourage us. Nothing is an accident and everything rests beneath the powerful hand of Almighty God. With wisdom and love, He weaves together every circumstance of our lives, the good and the bad, the ordinary and the remarkable, the painful and the uplifting, into a beautiful tapestry of life. Nothing is an accident.

It was not an accident of birth that had Stefano born into the House of Graziani. It was the will of God for him. But nevertheless, born to reign and trained from birth, the Crown Prince of Mondoverde cannot shirk the responsibilities attached to his privileged position. He must lead as a wise ruler, one that recognizes that allegiance to God is the first requirement of an ideal reigning monarch and head of state. It is the first requirement of any position we hold: spouse, parent, son, daughter, employer, employee, friend, family.

Sofia fumes at her "royal" assignment, considering it a waste of her time, energy, and talent in light of the real, gritty, soul-stirring news events of the day she wants to cover. But, this feature article for her newspaper, is the will of God for her. As is changing diapers, washing dishes, mowing the lawn, shoveling snow, buying groceries, doing the laundry. We must take courage and become stronger, more cooperative, more eager in doing the Lord's will in our lives, even if we don't like it.

When we reach that point where we know, deep in our hearts, God is in control of all our situations, when we believe, deep in our spirits, in the presence and power of Almighty God in our lives, when we trust, deep within our souls, that the Lord our God will be with us wherever we go, we won't fritter away our physical, emotional, mental, and spiritual well-being through tension, stress, bitterness, and discouragement.

My prayer, dear friend, is that you will go boldly forward, knowing, believing, trusting in God's promise: "Be strong and courageous. Do not be afraid; do not be discouraged, for the Lord your God will be with you wherever you go."

God Bless!

Anna

Scripture

"Be strong and courageous. Do not be afraid; do not be discouraged, for the Lord your God will be with you wherever you go."
—Joshua 1:9 (NIV)

CHAPTER 1

He'd almost made it.

His fingers gripped the gold-gilded balustrade. The pit of his stomach tightened hard as though some invisible fist had closed around it. His eyelids pinched closed on one brief moment of frustration.

He'd almost made it, Stefano thought, heaving a rueful sigh, and glanced down at the Calico cat at his feet for help. After all, cats with Micia's coloration—a predominantly white coat with patches of ginger and black and a raccoon-striped tail—were believed to bring *buona fortuna*. And he could use a massive dose of good luck right about now. The green eyes staring up at him turned apologetic, the meow accompanying it sounded low and forlorn.

Stefano received the feline transmission loud and clear. *You're fresh out of luck.* On another sigh, this one resigned, he turned around to face the man standing in the glow of the lamp spilling softly into the carpeted corridor from the office behind him. Almost. He'd almost managed to escape without incident.

"A moment of your time, Stefano?" Alessandro Graziano, wearing a charcoal-colored suit with a pristine-white shirt, and a black-and-silver striped tie, asked in a casual, almost comforting tone in complete contradiction to the gravity glinting in the depths of his blue eyes.

Clenching his jaw and holding back the vehement *no* springing instinctively to his mouth, Stefano suffered no illusions studying his father's stately stance. How could he when the impervious arch of the other man's brow made any refusal denied?

Besides, when Prince Alessandro, the head of the royal House of Graziani, the head of the government of the micronation located in the Adriatic Sea, the head of the country's armed forces, the sovereign ruler of the Principality of Mondoverde, asked something of him, Stefano II, Crown Prince of the Principality of Mondoverde, hereditary heir to the throne of Graziani, couldn't imagine responding in any other way, even if he cringed at the suspected topic for discussion.

His father and his advisers had been pressing him more than ever over the last dozen months on an issue he'd avoided like one would evade a virulent disease. Releasing a quiet outbreath, he admitted they were right. He knew he couldn't delay this part of his duty forever. He was already one year overdue in fulfilling the obligations associated with his title. But still… Didn't his feelings matter, his opinions count?

"Come." Alessandro said the one word in a clear warning that had Stefano sighing in surrender.

Determined to play out the scene coolly and casually while Micia, the scardy-cat, pawed his leg in remorse before cannonballing for the stairs, he inclined his head. "Of course, Your Serene Highness." Following his father, he stepped into the plush office and closed the wooden door behind him with a decisive click. It sounded like the sliding shut of the heavy metal bars of a prison. A prison not of his making, but a prison he wouldn't be allowed to sidestep.

"We can dispense with the *Serene Highness*." His father's dry voice drifted back. "We are alone."

With the footfalls of his Armani shoes being swallowed in the *Tappeti Abruzzesi*, the antique velvet Italian rugs featuring a repeating floral pattern set over a burgundy field,

Stefano approached the stunning 18th Century style desk in cherry wood, and folding his hands together, he waited with deference for his father to sit before he took the chair placed to the right of the massive desk.

"What is it you wish to discuss, Papa?"

But Stefano already knew. Born to reign and trained from birth, he had always understood and accepted his life would never be his own. He had never shirked the responsibilities attached to his privileged position. He had never complained about his duties to the House of Graziani or to the Mondoverduvian people, at least not in public. But what was being asked of him now seemed most unreasonable. Especially for the twenty-first century. And most especially since his father, his grandfather, and his great-grandfather had all managed to navigate this particular stipulation with relative ease and personal happiness. So why couldn't he enjoy the same prerogative? He just needed a little more time to ensure he, too, could achieve the mandated end result.

Alessandro leaned back in his chair, steepled his fingers, and pinned Stefano with a look so sharp, it could have sliced through him. The *Corpo della Guardia*, Mondoverde's armed forces could take a lesson from his father, Stefano mused, a wry grin trying to break out on his mouth, but he managed to beat it back and firm his lips. Reclining in his chair, he crossed his legs, intertwined his fingers, and held his father's gaze with an unflinching stare of his own.

"Stefano, you know that I love you."

"And I love you, too, Papa."

"You know of our history. Why my grandfather left his home on the Italian peninsula and arrived on this island." Alessandro leaned forward, clasping his hands on the desktop. "How he created the constitutional *hereditary* monarchy." His imperial brow lifted.

Stefano stifled a groan. "From the day I was born, I was instructed in such matters." *Here it comes.*

"And from the day you were born, you were also given careful and consistent instruction in your duties and responsibilities as the Crown Prince of Mondoverde."

"And because of that...careful and consistent...instruction, Papa," Stefano responded, repeating his father's choice of words, "I have always understood my actions would reflect on this office, this government, this country..." The hesitation was deliberate before he added, "This throne." His lifted his chin a fraction. He kept his countenance dispassionate. He tried to ignore the tightening in his gut. "I have always acted in the manner worthy of my station in life." While his quiet and calm voice projected a confidence in his conduct and character and conversation, his beleaguered mind raced to string together a prompt and profitable defense.

For his one failure.

Alessandro rose from his chair, came around, and perching a hip on the corner, he leaned forward, resting a hand on Stefano's shoulder. Could his father feel the tautness lodged there? "There is no question, *figlio mio*, your behavior is exemplary. You do your mother and me and our country proud." He squeezed his fingers once in reassurance. "And your assistance to me in ruling Mondoverde has been invaluable these past five years. I have no doubt when it comes time for you to assume full reigning power and become the head of the Principality of Mondoverde, you will make an excellent sovereign ruler." He gave Stefano's shoulder a gentle double pat before lowering himself in his chair behind the desk and crossing his arms.

"Thank you for your vote of confidence, Papa." The muscles in Stefano's stomach relaxed, the tension pooling at the base of his neck flowed out, the grip of his fingers went lax. "I appreciate your faith in me." It looked like he'd been given a reprieve.

"However..." Narrowing his eyes, Alessandro tap-danced

his fingers on the desktop.

Stefano caught a ragged breath. It looked like he would not be given a reprieve. Shifting in the chair, he bit back a groan.

"It is the other matter of your duties that is giving me concern."

Stefano opened his mouth, sucked in a much-needed breath, and exhaled the one word, "Papa," as a groan.

"Stefano, you know—"

"That Giovanni Graziano established the provision for dynastic succession when he styled himself as His Serene Highness," Stefano interjected, scowling and warm behind the ears. "Yes, Papa, I know." He stubbornly set his jaw and squared his shoulders. "Just as I know that every Crown Prince of Mondoverde is expected to marry by the age of twenty-five—"

"As my grandfather, Prince Giovanni, and my father, Prince Stefano I, and I have done. We have upheld the tradition of our country to—"

"Immediately produce an heir to the throne, preferably of the male gender, thus ensuring the continued line of the Graziano family and royal House of Graziani. Yes, I know." He bit out the last three words.

"Just as Prince Giovanni, Prince Stefano, and I have done."

"I know." The two words, tersely spoken, hung in the air of the opulent office.

Alessandro exhaled a sigh, and leaning his spine into the back of the chair, he curved his fingers over the arms of his chair. "Then you also know you have reached the age of twenty-six and have yet to—"

"Get married." Stefano gripped the arms of his chair, his fingers digging into the soft leather. "Yes. I. Know."

"You understand the gravity of this situation?"

"Yes." How could he not with his father and his advisers pressuring him for the past year?

"What is the problem?"

Apart from the fact I want to marry for love like you and grandfather and great-grandfather have done?

"The search for a suitable bride is proving somewhat fruitless" was all Stefano said.

"I haven't exactly seen you looking," Alessandro drawled. "You had a more active dating life while you were in school."

"And since my return to Mondoverde five years ago upon the completion of my studies, and you invested me, officially, as Crown Prince, with the Coronet, I have been extremely occupied with the Cabinet of the Prince and all the royal social appearances, that I haven't had time to find a wife." There was a hint of defensiveness in his tone.

"Make time, Stefano."

Stefano stiffened. Then thrusting out a sigh, he uncurled his fingers, let his hands fall away from the arms of the chair, and bracing his elbow on his thighs, he lowered his head, shoving the fingers of both hands into his hair.

Make time? He hadn't even been able to carve one hour out of his ridiculous schedule in the last five months to take *La Principessa* out on the Adriatic Sea to unwind a bit under the warm sun. So how could he possibly have found time over the past five years to find a woman who would be willing to take him on, embrace the public life of a princess, accept her life would never be her own, right down to her very identity, and produce the required heir for the House of Graziani and the future ruler of the Principality of Mondoverde? Time? He snorted. Sometimes he didn't have five minutes to take a bio-break his schedule was so grueling.

"Stefano."

Huffing out a weary breath, Stefano raised his face, held his father's concerned gaze.

"Time is marching on and you are not getting any younger. Neither am I."

"Papa?"

A sudden, fierce weight pressing down on his chest, Stefano sat up, his spine ramrod straight, and let his eyes flash over his father's features. At fifty-two, the reigning monarch had just begun to gray at his temples. But his eyes were as blue and sharp as they always had been. There were no dark smudges under those intelligent eyes. His skin showed no pallor beneath the olive coloring inherited from his Italian ancestors. No lines of strain…or pain…appeared to fan the corners of his mouth. He didn't appear to have lost any weight. He still looked agile and strong and fit, but… Was there something, something serious, his father wasn't telling him?

"Papa?" He swallowed the lump that had formed in his throat. "Are—are you not well?" The lump he'd swallowed crash-landed at the bottom of his stomach. His father couldn't be sick. He couldn't…die.

Two dark brows arched. "Apart from worrying my eldest child and Hereditary Prince refuses to seek out a wife and make me a *nonno*?" he drawled, tapping together the fingertips of both hands.

Grandchild. His father wanted not just an heir to the throne, but he wanted a grandchild.

The breath whooshed out of Stefano, and slumping in the chair, he rubbed the back of his hand back and forth across his forehead. And swore. "You've just taken ten years off my life."

"Then you'd better speed it up and get married, hadn't you, *figlio mio*?"

"It's not that I don't want to, you know." Stefano surged to his feet. "I just haven't been able to find my soulmate like you and Grandfather." And he didn't want to settle for anything less than love, the true abiding love, the kind of love that would anchor him and his wife through the good and the bad and everything in between. Shoving his hands in his pockets and feeling his father's steady eyes on him, he paced the office, his gait not his usual self-assured one, but long-legged and agitated.

He'd resisted marrying for the sake of marrying.

9

But now with the pressure mounting from the House of Graziani and the Mondoverduvian people for him to find the Princess of Mondoverde and produce the much-anticipated royal heir, his chances of finding the love of his life rapidly diminished.

"Stefano?"

He halted, looked at his father.

"A word of advice?"

Stefano gave a perfunctory nod.

"Trust in the presence and power of God. In all situations." A pause, then, "Enter into your secret place of prayer and you will find God is in the midst of your situation. Pray for your God-appointed spouse. And for the wisdom to recognize her."

Prince Alessandro reached for a folder on his desk, indicating this meeting had concluded. "A wise ruler, Stefano, recognizes that allegiance to God is the first requirement of an ideal Sovereign," he reminded his son in a soft voice, and reaching for his eyeglasses, he slipped them on, and flipped open the folder. "Do not forget our country's motto."

In God we trust, Stefano mused, stepping into the corridor and shutting the door behind him.

He let his eyelids close as he leaned against the door.

Behind his lids Stefano saw his duty to the throne loom glaringly before him.

* * *

Standing outside the closed door, Sofia Burska felt the familiar claw dig into that area of her torso, somewhere below her heart and above her abdomen, cutting off her ragged breathing. Her diaphragm, her doctor had told her at her last physical. All she had to do, she reminded herself now, was relax, breathe in deep and slow, and reaffirm to herself she could do this. And she could. She could approach the man on the other side of the door and voice her...complaint.

He was, after all, just a man. An intelligent man with a living, pumping heart. A reasonable, rational man who could listen to her grievance without taking offence. She tapped at the door, resting her forehead against the panel while she waited. The man was her boss and he could fire her for what he would consider impudence.

"Come in," the voice roared from the other side of the door.

Sofia inhaled a stabilizing breath through her nostrils, repeated a silent *I can do this,* and turning the knob, she pushed in the door and entered the hallowed office of the editor of *The Polish Alliancer.*

Walter Kostecki, sitting in his tattered leather chair behind a battered desk stacked full of newspaper editions and printed articles submitted for his approval, flicked an irritated brow greeting at her and finished his call. Slamming the phone in its cradle, he glared at her and barked, "What do you want?"

His tone and expression formed a formidable combination, formidable enough to make Sofia want to surrender to her insecurity, spin around, and bolt into the outer office. Maybe hunker down under her desk. Better yet hightail it out the front door and fast-foot it home. Instead, she drew in a quick, shallow breath, linked her fingers together in a tight grip, gave her mantra a mental nod, willed starch into her knees, and planting her sneakered feet firmly on the plank flooring, she stood her ground. Or at least, she hoped she pulled off the appearance of standing her ground. "I'd like to talk to you, sir, about my job."

"Your job?" He narrowed his eyes in suspicion. "What about your job and make it snappy. I've got a meeting in—" He swiped his watch with a quick glance. "—ten minutes." He pushed back from his chair, lumbered to the beat-up credenza, and picking up the pot, poured coffee into a chipped mug. He brought the mug up to sip and grimaced. "Sit." When he lowered himself into his squeaking chair, he looked at her, scowling.

Sofia nodded once, and obeying the grouched order, she sat, clenching her fingers together on her blue-jeaned lap and trying to ignore the rapid tattoo of her heart.

"Burska," he said, patience straining when she remained silent, and drilled his fingertips on the desktop. "I really am busy here." He opened his laptop.

"Yessir." When she saw his irritated brow flick up, she said, "First of all, sir, I'd like to thank you for hiring me last year without any work experience."

When he leaned back in the chair, it squeaked its protest. Pushing it back from the desk, he looked at her through hooded eyes and pressed his lips together, as close as he ever came to a smile. "You showed potential during your 30 day work placement with us." He shrugged the shrug of a man who didn't care. "So why not?" He turned his attention back to the computer screen.

"I was at the top of my class in the School of Media Studies and Information Technology at Humber College." Sofia pinch-rolled the knotted twine bracelet on her wrist.

The editor grunted, then eyeing his mug with wariness, he picked it up, took a sip, and made a face.

"I've learned a lot, sir—here—at *The Polish Alliancer*."

"Good." Her boss gave his watch another glance, a very pointed stare, before transferring his gaze to her face. "Is there a point to this conversation, Burska?"

"Yessir." She continued to pinch-roll one of the knots in her bracelet, but when it drew her boss's attention, she made herself stop, rubbed her sweaty palms down her thighs, then clasped her hands to keep them from fidgeting. "I've appreciated all the assignments I've been given." And all of them frivolous, she thought with frustration, but kept her features deadpan. She was so sick and tired of covering the celebrity-gossip-designer-clothes-expensive-champagne *human interest* stories for the society pages of the newspaper.

"I've learned a lot," she added when he rolled his shoulders in a shruglike motion and assumed a pensive expression. "But, sir, I want to apply what I've learned in school—at *The Polish Alliancer*—and cover the real, gritty, soul-stirring news events. I know I can do it. I just need you to give me a chance to prove myself."

"You're still a rookie, Burska."

"I know that, sir, but—"

Walter Kostecki stopped her retort by holding up a hand. "You are not ready yet."

"But sir—"

"No, Burska." Tugging at the hem of his T-shirt, he gave her a speculative study. "I have an assignment for you. It involves some traveling."

"Traveling?" Sofia looked at him with new and slightly less hostile interest. She'd never gotten to leave the Toronto area before, so traveling to an assignment boded well for the advancement of her career. This was the break she'd been looking for. A way to prove to her boss she could handle the real stories and establish herself as a journalist of high caliber. *Yes!* "Where to, boss?"

"To an island nation in the Adriatic Sea."

She had no way of seeing her own face, but she suspected she looked as stunned as she felt. An island nation? In the Adriatic Sea? *Yes!*

"What is it you want me to cover?" She whipped out her small spiraled notebook and black pen from her jeans pocket and flipping open the notebook, pen poised to jot down points, she looked at the editor.

"A rising political dynasty." A slight hesitation. "In general."

Sofia wrote down the words. Island nation. Adriatic Sea. Rising political dynasty. Lifting her gaze from the notebook, she planted it on the editor. "In general, sir?"

Her boss swatted the air above his desk, the movement of the hand indicating exasperation. "You know. The usual.

Who are they? An overview of their history. Unless, of course, you find something there of news worthiness, then expound on it. Tie it in to how they got to be where they are. What is their vision for their island state? Their mission statement? Etcetera. Etcetera. Etcetera." Once more, he lifted the mug to his mouth for a sip, and grumbled, "I don't know why I bother drinking this stuff." Setting the mug down, he glared at the offensive coffee, but when he raised his vision to Sofia, his expression turned thoughtful. "But I want you to concentrate, not so much on the ruler of the country, but on his successor."

"His successor." After jotting the words in her notebook and putting an asterisk to the right of it, Sofia glanced up, her brows drawn together in a request for more information. "Who is this person and why is he—or she—a person of interest to our readership?"

Walter Kostecki leaned back in his squeaky chair, his hand moving across the bristly skin of his chin in slow back-and-forth strokes, giving Sofia the uncomfortable feeling he tried not to show his amusement. Something akin to a warning skittered down her spine.

"He is, as I said, poised to take over the reins. Not immediately, but he's in place, being groomed, operating in the highest levels of his country's government. Having said that, nobody knows much about the private man. He's never involved in any scandals. Never seen with women, at least, not in the last several years. He never agrees to an interview by the press, yet he is furiously sought for one." He shrugged, aloof. "Perhaps it's a simple case of interest being sparked from a refusal on his part to be interviewed. Or perhaps..." An impish light danced in his eyes. "It's because of *who* he is." He leaned forward, gave her a hard stare. "Your job, Burska, is to nail that interview for our paper. I trust I do not need to remind you our ratings are in spiraling-down mode and we need a booster shot. Fast."

"Yessir. You can count on me, sir. I'll get that interview." Sofia felt proud her voice sounded strong, certain, assertive. Her heart palpitated and her stomach trembled as insecurity tried to rear its ugly head. "If I...if I manage to get this interview—"

"Do you have any doubts as to your abilities as a journalist, Burska?" he demanded, annoyance evident in the furrow of his brows. "If you do, you best tell me now and I'll get another reporter—"

"No sir." Sofia felt a blush climb her neck and throb in her cheeks. She raised her chin, threw back her shoulders. Her heart kicked over a beat or two before resuming a steady rate. She could not show any sort of weakness. Not if she was to attain her goal. "I can do this, sir." Determination and defiance sounded in her words. She had to do this. She had to prove to her editor she could be trusted with the biggies. She had to prove this to herself.

"Good to hear it."

"Sir?" There was a pause, fragile and quivery, nearly tangible, but when her boss looked at her questioningly, she sucked in a breath, then plunged forward with, "If— *when*—I get this interview, I want you to assign me to the real stories, not the flighty stuff I've been doing." She angled up her chin another notch in challenge. And purposed not to fidget.

He gave another of those could-mean-anything shrugs. "Agreed."

She wanted to punch the stale-coffee scented air in the office with the victory fist of her right hand. But the light of challenge in his eyes made her stomach free-fall in panic.

He pulled the note pad toward him and picked up the pen. He scribbled something on the paper, tore it off from the pad, and slid it across the desk toward her. "That's where you're flying to tomorrow and that's who you are going to interview."

She glanced at the paper and forgot her panic. "Prince?" The one word from her mouth held a world of irritation.

"That's right. I want you to interview Prince Stefano II, Crown Prince of the Principality of Mondoverde, the heredity heir of the House of Graziani. And I want the feature story for the society pages of our paper."

"But, sir—"

"This is not a debate, Burska. If you don't want the job, I have other reporters who'll jump at it."

"I'll do it," she told him, grudgingly. "But I want that promotion."

"When I have your article, we'll have further discussion."

"Fine." It was Sofia's turn to scowl at the editor. Her stomach churning, she shoved notebook and pen into her pocket. *Prince.* Gritting her teeth, she rose. *Another flighty story.* "You'll get it." She felt her hands curl into fists and turned to leave, anger and frustration burning hot and bright inside her. Deliberately, she blew out a long breath and unfurled her fingers.

"Burska. One more thing."

Her hand on the doorknob, she flung a look over her shoulder, not making any effort to disguise her irritation.

"Stefano Graziano is, from what I hear," her boss said, his tone dry, "a good-looking, wealthy prince."

"So?"

"So produce the article of interest but don't make the mistake of falling —" Walter Kostecki rolled his eyes. "—for the prince's charm."

She stared at him, incredulous.

Her? Sofia-with-her-feet-planted-firmly-on-the-ground-Burska develop an infatuation with the prince?

She allowed herself a silent snicker. Like that would ever happen.

"Don't worry, sir."

"Good." He managed a flicker of a grin and turned his attention back to the computer screen.

16

She let herself out of the office, closing the door behind her with a quiet thud. Her? Fall for Prince Stefano? This time she did laugh, out loud. Not likely.

If pushed, Sofia would admit she wasn't the looking-for-marriage kind of girl. She wasn't a fairy tale kind of girl, either. And she definitely wasn't princess material.

CHAPTER 2

Royal headlines sell papers.

Three days later, her editor's words still rang in her ears when Sofia turned her rental car onto the *royal* driveway and came to a stop at the *royal* palace gate to check in with the *royal* security guard.

They also ensured she remained employed which, in turn, guaranteed her pay check, which subsequently meant she could —

A discreet clearing of the throat drew her back to the present and to the guard with his white-gloved hand extended through the open window of the security booth.

After handing over three different forms of ID plus her newspaper badge to the stoic-faced man in the guard booth to verify and reverify and verify again — he probably checked her against RCMP, FBI, and MI-6 databases, and just for the fun of it, ran her through Interpol to make certain she was no terrorist intent on the demise of the *royal* family — she was instructed in an impassive voice, once clearance was given, of course, where to park her car and which palace entrance to take. Her documentation was handed back and the massive iron gate swung open to admit her onto the *royal* grounds.

Still chafing at having to write the society column for her newspaper and still ticked off at her boss for making her rub elbows with arrogant royalty, she followed the curving, cobblestoned driveway, her eyes widening despite her best intentions to not be impressed. *So this is how the other side lives, is it?*

The front of Bellaterra Castle faced an enormous square where she assumed the changing of the guard took place. In the center of the square stood a towering bronze statue, the plaque identifying him as Giovanni Graziano, Mondoverde's pioneer prince. Behind him, soaring high into the sky, stood a giant, purple cross with a white dove set against the cross beams. The same white dove emblem graced the palace facade. The House of Graziani flag, a miniature of the purple cross and white dove with the words, *In God We Trust* encircling it, flew from the tower on the south end, while a huge round clock with black Roman numerals and currently indicating the time as ten o'clock in the morning, adorned the north end tower. In carefully landscaped gardens, under the protective branches of the majestic palm trees, lilies of the valley waved in the air alongside tulips, daisies, and other flowers Sofia didn't recognize, but when she stepped out of the Fiat, the scent of lilac, fresh and clean and sweet and innocent, greeted her senses.

So this is how the other side lives, she thought again, walking toward the palace guard standing outside the main entrance, dressed in a white uniform, purple shirt, white helmet, and — *dear God, could it be real?* — a rifle. She hadn't done anything wrong, she had every right to be here, but for some crazy, unexplainable reason, as she moved past the guard, she suffered through a flash of guilt.

Not so unexplainable, she admitted to herself, nodding to the poker-faced guard, and climbed one of the two semicircular staircases rising to the main entrance. Being a girl and the youngest of the Burska siblings, and as a result, overshadowed by three overly protective and successful brothers, she'd always felt she had to try harder to break free of their sheltering and sometimes stifling auras and their let's-take-charge-of-our-baby-sister tendencies, and at least, trail after them at an acceptable distance while pursuing her own aspirations and agenda. Not an easy feat to accomplish with three big brothers always looming overhead, watching her every move. She loved her brothers. Knew they loved her, too. But sometimes, though they didn't mean to, they made her feel…insecure.

Adam, at thirty, was a married school teacher and father of a 4-year-old precocious daughter. Gabriel, at twenty-six, was a married politician with a spirited infant son. And Simon, at twenty-three, the restaurateur of the popular *Café Polonez*, just got married.

Though her parents were as proud of her as they were of her brothers and her father had always encouraged her she could do whatever she put her mind to, still she struggled with this sometimes strangling insecurity. No matter how she worked to eradicate this constant need to prove herself, it always managed to keep pace with her, shadowing her, smothering her. An inherited flaw in her character from a long-ago ancestor, she decided, blowing her bangs off her forehead. A clinging flaw.

A clinging flaw energized by fear.

Fear of the unknown. Fear of being out of her depth.

She was a commoner, a working commoner. Stefano Graziano, the subject of her article, was, well, he was a rich royal.

So what did she know about rubbing elbows with the ruling monarchy of this micronation?

Not that she would have cause to fraternize with any member of the House of Graziani. She came here to land an exclusive interview with the heir to the throne. Not to rub elbows with him. Not that Prince Stefano II would want to rub elbows with her.

Nevertheless, what was the proper protocol for greeting the Crown Prince of Mondoverde?

She wished now she had done her research on the prince, but she hadn't wanted to form preconceived ideas about the never-before-heard-of prince in the never-before-heard-of principality with anything she might have read about him on the Internet. But now she found herself with a dilemma.

Sofia gnawed at her bottom lip. How was she to address him? Did she curtsy? Did she speak or sit or stand first, or did she wait for his prompt?

"Thank you." Sofia gave a tentative smile at the two guards who opened the massive front doors for her and came to a grinding halt.

"Ohmygod," she whispered, astonishment dancing through her veins and popping her eyelids wide open.

So this is how the other side lives.

The circular foyer of Bellaterra Castle was stunningly beautiful with sparkling chandeliers, marble floors, and delicate sculptures. Ornate tables, strategically positioned, held heirloom vases overflowing with fresh flowers picked, she presumed, from the numerous flowerbeds on the palace grounds. Though she didn't see the lilacs, she picked up their sweet scent hanging in the air of the luxurious, but soothing entrance hall and she did a slow pivot, taking in her impressive surroundings.

"Wow."

"May I help you?"

Sofia spun around and slammed solidly into the man. He put a hand on her shoulder to steady her, but the hand, warm and strong and solid, lingered too long.

Feeling the heat of his fingers scorch through her navy blazer, she took a hasty step backward, breaking the searing connection. She drew in a sharp breath, and adjusting the purse strap over her shoulder, locked her gaze on the man. *Some butler.* The words floated into her startled brain.

Tall. Sofia, wearing 3-inch shoes on her five-foot-five-inch frame, had to tip her head back to look at him. He was tall. At least six feet of well-honed body. And all of that encased in an expensive black suit, crisp white shirt, and black-and-white patterned tie. His dark brown hair, olive skin, and sharp cheekbones gave him a certain magnetism, combining power, intelligence, and masculinity. His scent, sexy but not overpowering, wrapped around her senses. But his eyes… His eyes imprisoned her. Darkly blue. Sensual. Arrogant.

"Are you lost—" He glanced at her left hand clasping the purse strap, but when he lifted those blue eyes to her face, they glittered with something she couldn't identify. "—*Signorina*?"

Her heartbeat pounded in her chest, her neck, her wrists. Her cheeks were on fire. "L-lost?" She heard a roaring in her ears and she was breathless—all because of a casual encounter with the butler? Oh, she was so pathetic.

Remembering the purpose for her being here, she put some starch in her spine and lifted her chin up a noticeable notch. "I am looking for His Serene Highness, Prince Stefano, Crown Prince of Mondoverde," she informed the *royal* servant with what she hoped came across as a matching hauteur.

One dark brow lifted. Of course, it would. She grimaced, working the purse strap with her thumb and forefinger. Of course, the butler would know Prince Stefano was the Crown Prince. She didn't have to spell out the full title, name, and position to an employee of the palace. Her cheeks were already aflame, but that didn't stop the heat of a fresh blush crawl up her neck to stain the skin of her face, but she made herself hold the man's probing gaze.

"What business do you have with…Prince Stefano?" Though he spoke in a modulated voice, the air around them quivered with a strange energy.

"I am here to interview His Serene Highness."

If she'd ever get past all the *royal* red tape. She banked down, hard, on a fresh wave of irritation at the *royal* runaround she'd been given for the past couple of days. When she'd finally managed to connect with the prince's public relations representative, after a zillion failed phone attempts from her hotel room, all he would say was His Serene Highness never gave interviews, but he was scheduled to hold a press conference at the palace on Monday morning at eleven, and as a member of the press, she was welcome to attend.

"Are you now."

"'Scuse me?" When she zoned back in, she found the butler surveying her with a lazy appreciation. "Am I now what?" What had they been talking about before she'd side-tripped into a replay of her frustration?

"Here to interview the Prince." The man gave her one of those not quite there smiles.

Oh-oh. Tread carefully.

"Yes." Sofia never lied, but though her answer was truthful, she felt another slap of heat on her face, and wished she hadn't said the word quite so fast. As if it was a weapon to be wielded to swashbuckler her way into the official residence of the Mondoverduvian royal family.

She upped the angle of her chin another inch. She was here to interview the prince, the fact she hadn't been able to set it up notwithstanding. She had a job to do and she would do it, come hell or high water. But she had no intention of thanking her boss for this assignment. She felt no gratitude at the prospect of having to rub elbows with an arrogant, elusive-to-the-media royal.

"And you have an appointment, *Signorina*?" Mischief sparked like blue fire in his eyes as he looked into her face, and maybe right down into her soul where she stashed her deepest secrets.

Oh boy.

She swallowed, willed her thrumming heart to beat at a normal rate. She'd thought she could fake her way in, secure that interview, and then hop on the next flight out of Mondoverde. She bowed her head and concentrated on breathing, and trying to detach herself from the insecurity that popped in for its regular visit. She reached deep within her. Like she always did. And fingering the purse strap, fought back the plaguing emotion.

She would not lie. Even to get the interview. Even if she lost her job. Even if it meant she would be unable to meet her obligation. Lying did not fit who she was. She raised her head high. And hoped he did not see her fear. She stood, rigid on the outside, trembling on the inside. She swallowed again, forced her throat to work. "No." Her heart tripped as though it were on a downhill nose-dive.

The man ducked his head briefly in a half-decent attempt to hide his grin of enjoyment. "And without an appointment, *Signorina*, how did you expect to arrange such an interview with the...very busy prince?"

Sofia blew out a breath. The butler was going to throw her out. No, he was much too well-trained for that. He would simply take hold of her elbow in a firm grip, walk her to the front door with purposeful steps, open it with exaggerated pomp, and propel her out with a strong shove. "I figured I'd work out the details as I went along."

Her comment surprised a laugh out of him, rumbling through the foyer, which surprised her.

"*Cara*," he said when he'd stopped chuckling, "what newspaper do you work for?"

"*The Polish Alliancer.*"

"You're from Poland?" His chuckle had downgraded to a lady-killer smile and she turned beet-red.

She was having some serious trouble ignoring her unexplained attraction to this man. "No." At the quirk of his brow, she added, "I'm from Toronto — that's in Canada."

"I may...work here, but I do know where Toronto is, *Signorina*," the butler replied, his tone dry.

Sofia bit down on her bottom lip. It would not do to alienate her one possible helper. "*The Polish Alliancer* is located in the "Little Poland" district of Toronto known as

Roncesvalles Village. It's a quaint, little family-friendly neighborhood. It has a cool, yet small-town feeling and features the remnants of the Polish Guard." She knew she rambled and bit down on her lip again.

"How long have you worked for the newspaper?"

"One year," she responded in a dull voice. *And all of it doing trivial reporting like this assignment.*

"And you are how old, *Signorina*?"

"Twenty-one." If she raised her head any higher, she'd be pointing her nose in the air at the man presumptuous enough to ask far too many questions. Surely the butler didn't enjoy such privileges, did he?

"Ah," he said, a wealth of meaning in the one word.

"What exactly does that mean?" Her feet were firmly planted on the marble floor and her fists were bunched atop her hipbones.

"It means—" He dipped his gaze to her name tag, then pinned her with a somewhat knowing glance and a wicked grin. "—Sofia Burska, that you are too young and too inexperienced. Otherwise you would know no one, and I mean no one, sees the Prince without an appointment. Why don't you call his public relations—"

"I did that." Her harsh words landed with a thud between them. Furious tears of frustration and failure pressed against the back of her eyes, but she refused to let them fall. "And got the royal runaround for my trouble."

"I see." The butler rubbed a hand across his chin. "And you struck out, yes?"

"Yes," she gritted out, "I struck out. Look." She waved a frantic hand at him. "You work here. Can't you do something? Can't you talk to the prince and get me that interview?" She was begging now. But she was desperate. She didn't want to think how quickly the first of the month would roll in. And the ramifications of it if she failed. "I really need to get that interview for my paper." She couldn't hide the panic that underlay each word.

A buzz of tension charged the atmosphere. Her heart thundered in her ears.

Would he agree to help her?

The butler's forehead furrowed with lines. The fingers of his right hand rubbed at his cheek.

Sofia found herself wondering how those fingers would feel caressing her cheek. *Stop it!*

He dropped his hand, leaned forward, eyes intense. Her heart bumped up a couple of degrees.

She didn't understand this crazy attraction to the man — the butler of the prince she was supposed to interview — but she had to *stop it!*

She had to control this — this — absurd reaction to this — this — stranger. Yet despite her silent, self-addressed order, her pulse tripped into a dangerous zone.

"You already understand, Miss Burska, the prince never gives interviews."

"My newspaper, Mr. — I'm sorry I don't know your name."

"You may call me…Alberto."

"Alberto," Sofia repeated, nodding her head. Was he softening in his inflexible the-prince-never-gives-interviews stance? Would he try to help her by speaking to the prince on her behalf? She had to make him understand, this ally. At least, he looked to be a potential ally. Or maybe it was just wishful thinking on her part. She took a deep breath and made her sell. "Alberto, my newspaper, *The Polish Alliancer*, is not a tabloid newspaper, I assure you. We are a respectable, if small, newspaper servicing the Polish community in Toronto. We don't print schmuck."

The butler frowned. "Schmuck?"

She made an impatient sound. "Alberto, we both know in the newspaper industry, information is routinely slanted to encourage hype. Truth is frequently stretched to excite interest. Headlines are usually exaggerated to endorse sales —"

"The very reason the prince does not entertain one-on-one interviews with journalists." His gaze was sharp, his voice soft, yet implacable.

She was losing. She couldn't lose. She couldn't afford to lose. The discharge from her obligation was at stake.

She gripped the strap of her purse. "But my newspaper isn't like that. *I'm* not like that. We only print the truth after we've researched its accuracy."

"Be that as it may—"

"Alberto, please." She looked away, looked back. She had to get through to him. "I must see the prince. It's imperative."

"You will see the prince." The butler's voice came as a warning. Then he smiled, slow and easy. "Along with the other representatives of the international press. In the Press Conference Room. Straight through that door." He aimed an imperial forefinger at a door. "In—" He consulted his gold watch. "Ten minutes. Sharp." When he returned his gaze to her, his smile didn't fade, but something dark and dangerous crept into his expression.

She wanted to argue. She wanted to cry. She pulled her lower lip through her teeth.

"If you hurry, *Signorina* Burska…" He brushed his finger across her lower lip, sending shivers through her. "You may yet get a seat close to the front. Near the prince," he added, his voice a sensual purr.

With a lingering look and a slow turn that spoke of arrogance, the butler left her standing alone in the foyer, his walk slow and easy, loose-hipped and sexy.

What just happened here?

Sofia lifted a shaky hand to press her fingertips to her lips, staring wide-eyed at the back of the departing butler. What just happened here, she wondered again, watching him disappear through another door without a curious glance back at her. She scrunched her eyes tight to try to jiggle away those feelings of warmth she'd felt at his touch. Of contentment. Of forever.

Stop this craziness and get a grip, the remote and rational nook in her brain ordered. Shaking her head in the hopes of dispersing the fuzziness that had rolled over the rest of her brain, she inched toward the Press Conference Room, her fingers rebelliously stroking her bottom lip.

The spacious, marble-tiled room, lit up by four gigantic crystal chandeliers, was rapidly filling up with members of the media. Sofia made her way down the aisle, the heels of her shoes clicking on the floor, and snagged one of the chairs in purple velvet fabric. Slipping the purse strap from her shoulder and settling the purse on her skirted lap, she gave the Press Conference Room a quick, assessing glance. At the front, on a raised dais, sat the podium in a solid wood finish with the Coat of Arms of the Principality of Mondoverde emblazoned on the front. Beyond the podium, she saw one single chair in a red velvet fabric with gold-adorned arms. Directly behind it, two Mondoverduvian flags stood in their gold bases, one on either side of the chair. And on the wall, hung the portrait, in Italian woodwork and gold trimming, of the progenitor of the Graziano Dynasty.

Would the current ruler of the micronation—and his successor—bear a resemblance to the patriarch, Sophia mused, watching the other journalists take out their laptops. Once again, she wished she'd done some internet research. Reaching into her purse, she pulled out her trusty notebook and pen. Archaic in the 21st Century it may be, but she felt more in control, more competent with the conventional manner of jotting down remarks and annotations. She would use her own computer to assemble her scribbled notes into a cohesive, coherent report on Prince Stefano. An exclusive interview with the elusive prince, where she could ask pertinent questions, would have been much preferred. She sighed, opening her notebook to the blank page and poising her pen over it, but that didn't look like it was going to happen any time soon. She had to admit it. She had *struck out*, as the butler had pointed out with audacious impunity.

The fingers of her right hand tightened on the pen. And shadowing her obvious failure would be serious ramifications. Of the financial kind.

The sound of a door opening interrupted her morose musing. The room hushed and all heads tilted toward the door at the front right side of the room. Anticipation hummed in the air. Security had already secured the room before the prince arrived, but now the palace watchdogs swept in first, followed by the royal. He paused in the doorway, scanning the room with quick and intelligent eyes, blue eyes she knew though she couldn't see them from this distance, and her stomach sunk like a stone.

Ohmygod.

The butler. No! The prince!

She thought she could hide behind the standing assembly, but to her chagrin, he found her, pinning her with an intense look that had her breath coming too fast. After a couple of seconds, or maybe it might have been hours, Sofia had no way of knowing, he disengaged his gaze from her, walked to the center of the stage, and climbed the steps to the podium, his gait every bit the same as earlier in the foyer. Slow and easy, loose-hipped and sexy.

She'd been talking to the prince and hadn't known it. Oh, what a fool she must have looked to him. Remembering his assessment of her, she felt a blush pulse in her cheeks. *You are too young and too inexperienced, otherwise you'd know.* He was right. She had to agree with his opinion. She couldn't argue with facts, with the shaming proof. She pinched her lids together and willed away her insecurity, in vain. She was too young. Too inexperienced.

Too stupid.

Otherwise she'd have known she'd been speaking to the Crown Prince of Mondoverde.

And she, fool of fools, wanted to prove to her editor she was a reporter of high caliber, a reporter he could count on to get the breaking news. *Yeah, right.* She cut off the bitter laugh and swallowed miserably, audibly, wishing the marble floor would gape open beneath her and plunge her down into the shadowy bowels of the castle where she and her humiliating stupidity could die an obscured death.

"Thank you, ladies and gentlemen, for coming to this press conference today. For those of you who may not know—" He paused, sought out her flaming face. Sofia could have sworn she saw a glint of humor dancing in his eyes. "—I am Prince Stefano." Smiling, he waited for the chuckles to die down before all business and solemnity, he launched into his agenda for the press conference.

Sofia scrambled to compartmentalize her inferiority and embarrassment and concentrate on the prince's opening remarks.

"The purpose of kingdoms and governments should be to bring order, peace, and prosperity to their countries. Ideally, they will look out for the well-being of their citizens."

And for the next hour, the heir to the throne of Graziani shared the monarchy's hopes, desires, and intentions for the people of Mondoverde and their country's prospective relationship with the international community. With a "Thank you again for coming," he concluded the press conference, but he ignored the questions from the journalists. Descending the stairs, he looked in her direction, his eyes holding hers a moment too long. Then, encircled by the palace security guards, he exited through the same door he'd entered.

Sofia slipped pad and pen into her purse, slid the strap over her shoulder, and had just risen to her feet when a man, dressed in a dark suit with the Mondoverduvian crest over the right breast of his blazer, stopped by her chair. "Miss Burska?"

She frowned. "Yes?"

"Miss Burska, I am Tonino Masselli." He inclined his head. "The official representative of the royal House of Graziani."

Her heart thumped against her ribcage. The hair on the back of her neck stood up. Her skin prickled with unease. "Yes?"

"Come with me, please."

"Why?" Her gaze darted from the man's shuttered expression and skittered over the emptying room before returning to the *official representative of the Royal House of Graziani*. "Where are you taking me?" Her imagination might be taking flight, she silently acknowledged, chewing down on her bottom lip. Stress and lack of sleep could easily explain it going haywire. But this burly man who looked to be well trained in martial arts and could probably commit murder in a dozen different but effective ways—with his hands alone—never mind the silver weapon she'd gotten a glimpse of when he'd extended a hand toward one of the closed doors and his blazer parted, would be a more accurate explanation for her sudden fear.

"Come with me, please," he repeated, this time his fingers curled over her elbow in a don't-mess-with-me hold.

Sofia sucked in a breath, rubbed one temple with the fingers of her right hand to forestall a tension headache, and wondered if Bellaterra Castle had a tower of execution or a dank and dark dungeon underground for pesky reporters—no, not plural, just one—one pesky reporter who needed to be silenced.

* * *

"Your Serene Highness?"

Ah. How is it they say? It is show time.

Stefano got so few opportunities to have some fun he would thoroughly enjoy this one. The woman made it easy for him to enjoy an entertaining diversion from his life of constant pressure and stress, of negotiations and diplomacies, of considerations and concerns. A life always ruled by the clock and the duty. A life not of his own.

Now, stifling the smile of amusement and assuming the dominant, formidable inbuilt air of confidence that went hand-in-hand with his position, he turned from the window, his mouth disciplined into a straight decisive line, his gaze landing on the woman he'd met earlier in the foyer and picked her out with incredible ease during his press conference. Dressed in a navy blazer atop a white dress—not the usual attire for female journalists, he mused—with navy spikes for shoes and matching blue purse slung over her shoulder, she stood just inside the Palace Office. There was something stiff about her posture. Her face was unreadable.

"Miss Burska is here," his aide announced.

"*Grazie*, Tonino. That will be all."

The aide gave him a slight bow, and backing out of the room, he turned and closed the door, leaving Stefano alone with Sofia Burska.

"*Signorina* Burska." Stefano gave her a brief bow, elegant and fluid and ironic. "I am Prince Stefano, Crown Prince of Mondoverde."

"You might have said that earlier." Brown eyes snapping at him, she made a ridiculous attempt at a curtsy. "You said your name was Alberto." His name twisted on her lips until it sounded like a curse. "You deliberately lied to me."

His brows lifted at the barely repressed fury in her voice. "I did not lie, *cara*. Alberto is my name. One of," he corrected with wry amusement. "My full name is Prince Stefano Alberto Emmanuele Alessandro Graziano, Crown Prince of the Principality of Mondoverde." He executed another bow, delivering it with his best conciliatory smile.

"You deliberately withheld your true identity." The accusation was cross and impatient, nearly making his grin widen.

"Everyone knows my identity." He chuckled and met an ice wall.

"Not everyone," she gritted through her teeth. "You made me look like a fool." Hurt vibrated from her every word.

A little trickle of guilt worked its way in as he saw the red-face expression of humiliation. "My apologies, *Signorina*." He moved closer, his footsteps silenced by the plush carpet. "It was not my intention to make you look like a fool." He stopped in front of her, in her personal space, and had to suppress a smile when she took a hasty step backward. "I was merely having some fun."

"At my expense," she said, eyes narrowed, hands on hips, elbows jutting.

"Yes," he admitted on a sigh. "Again, I ask for your forgiveness, Sofia Burska. You will forgive me, yes?"

She hesitated, then nodded her head.

"*Bene*. We will begin again. Welcome, Sofia, to Bellaterra Castle. My home." *And prison.* "I am Stefano."

He thrust out a hand. Again she hesitated, but when she shook it, he clasped his other hand over hers and held it exactly one second past friendly. One second where a jolt of adrenaline shot through him. Her eyes flashed with surprise and he stared at her in the same stunned disbelief she felt. But he didn't let go of her hand. When she tried to discreetly pull hers away, he held onto it, lifting his to run the back of one knuckle down her rosy cheek and watched her eyes darken to midnight black.

"You are warm?" he asked, sounding only a little strangled. *What is this?* He felt so on fire he marveled the sprinkling system hadn't been activated from the blazing heat generating between them. He had never had such a reaction to a woman before. Such a strong, visceral reaction. Resisting the vibrations sizzling between them, he released her hand and smiled, a tight fierce movement of his lips. Something told him this woman was going to drive him mad.

She was young. Too young. A mere twenty-one-year-old. An innocent. A babe barely out of the cradle.

He, on the other hand, though only five years older, had already lived a lifetime. He had grave responsibilities resting on his shoulders. He'd known from the time he was old enough to understand, this was his destiny. His hands clenched at his sides. Not the least of his responsibilities to the Graziani throne was to procure for himself a suitable wife and present to the people of his island nation the royal heir. He forced his fingers to relax, but the feeling of exasperation raced through his veins.

Stefano had no legitimate reason for asking his aide to escort Sofia to the Palace Office where he'd be waiting. But he wanted to see her. Wanted to talk to her. He did not want to examine the reasons.

"So, Sofia, how are you enjoying Bellaterra, our beautiful capital?" he asked, his tone casual, his eyes dropping to her mouth, his brain wondering how those lips would taste beneath his own. A shot of desire surged down his blood vessels, elevating his body temperature into the red hot zone. *What is this?* He clamped his hands together. A health and safety precaution. He moved backward a couple of steps. Another health and safety precaution.

She flicked him a mutinous glance. "I'm not."

His heart dropped. She did not find their city attractive? How could that be? Mondoverde had it all. Greek and Roman ruins. Olive groves and vineyards. Their coastal strip was a tourist haven. Bellaterra, as the capital, had museums, cafes, fashionable shopping districts. What was there not to enjoy?

His skin tightened over his face. His mouth thinned. "Why, *Signorina*?" he asked her austerely. "What is wrong with our city?" National pride rose like an avenging angel.

She glanced toward the window. She seemed like she fought to breathe. Fought to speak sensibly. She looked back at him.

"Sofia?"

"Nothing is wrong with your city," she blurted, dragging a hand over her forehead and into her bangs.

Stefano felt the sudden irresistible urge to thread his fingers in her blond-bronze chin-length strands. Would her hair feel as silky soft as it looked? "Then?" he returned, his tone brusque and his manner inflexible, determined, formidable.

He didn't move, but she must have sensed a reaction in him so intense she took an involuntary step backward. Steadying her breathing and her voice with an effort that clenched her fists, she answered, "I only arrived a couple of days ago."

"That is sufficient time to tour our beloved city." He forced his voice to come out level and without emotion. His insides churned. Why was he making such a big deal about this? Why did he care if this woman, this stranger, did not feel an affection for Bellaterra? For Mondoverde? For…

She unclenched her hands to spread them out in front of her. "Not when you spend those two days huddled in the hotel room, with the phone glued to your ear, and getting the royal runaround from *your* public relations department."

"Ah. I see." Stefano scrubbed a palm across his lips to hide a grin.

"Do you now," Sofia replied, acid in her tone. "How royally smart you are, Your Serene Highness."

"You are upset."

"The Prince is so astute."

His brows hiking at her tone, he said in a soft voice, "*Signorina*, if you are trying to ingratiate yourself to me, I am saddened to inform you that you are failing."

She huffed out a sigh. "It's not the only thing I'm failing at." Her eyes held shadows he hated to see.

"You are referring to the exclusive interview you want for your paper which I never give any member of the press."

"Yes."

He studied her in silence for a moment and saw a lot more than she would have wanted him to notice. He saw the slight slump to her shoulders despite she tried to keep her posture erect. He saw the slight quaver to her bottom lip despite she tried to firm it. He saw the youth of her years despite she tried to appear a veteran in her field.

He felt a sudden crushing wallop to his gut and had to turn away despite he had reasons, excellent reasons, for not granting interviews to reporters. Summoning from deep within him for his signature fluid grace and inherent dignity, he moved to the desk and turning around, he perched against it. Scanning her face, he felt a distinct uneasiness crawl through him. Worse was the thought that pierced his brain. Had he been set up on a path that would change his life?

Get a grip, Stefano told himself silently, wondering where his usual generous allotment of self-confidence, not to mention his convictions, had gone. "Sofia, I don't engage in private talks with reporters." His voice sounded odd in his ears and he frowned.

He didn't have time to reflect on this anomaly assaulting him. He was too busy being mesmerized by the transformation in the young woman standing before him. He watched as she fought some internal conflict. He watched as she pulled herself up, threw back her shoulders, angled her chin. He watched the light of battle shine in her brown eyes and her mouth move up at the corners into something he would never call a smile.

He watched her move toward him, her manner predatory.

And he thought of Mondoverde's emblem. The lion.

His great-grandfather, Prince Giovanni, had chosen the lion as the symbol of his island nation for three reasons.

The first, the lion represented the triumphant Jesus Christ, the descendant of the tribe of the Kings, the tribe of Judah, and served as a reminder to the Mondoverduvian people that Jesus, as the Savior of the people, protecting them, loving them, was King of their country.

Secondly, the lion indicated the monarchy would rule the nation with benevolence, honesty, and strength, and promised the Mondoverduvian people any Graziano sitting on the throne would exercise wisdom and justice and honor to protect and lead and defend the subjects of his country.

And thirdly, the lion symbolized the Mondoverduvian people themselves who had the courage to state their dissatisfaction with the results of the referendum of the motherland and demonstrated that same courage with faith in God, in Prince Giovanni, and in themselves by settling in this country.

And now, Stefano watched Sofia approach him, the heart and soul of courage in every line of her body. And he felt admiration and respect and—he frowned—an uneasiness in the pit of his belly.

"Your Highness—"

"Stefano." He needed to breathe. "Call me Stefano." He loosened the knot in his tie. "We are alone." He drew in a breath and inhaled her scent, feminine and soft and tantalizing.

"Stefano," she acceded with a nod of her blond-bronze head.

He had to clasp his fingers together again, tight, to prevent him from following through on the second unexpected and very impulsive urge to tangle them in her tresses to discover if they indeed felt as feminine and soft and tantalizing as they looked. He needed to breathe, desperately, but he feared he would lose all control and lean forward to dip his face in her neck to take that breath. Tugging hard at the knot in his tie, he stood, and with every ounce of dignity and grace he possessed, he skirted the desk and lowered himself into the chair. With the massive furniture between them, he should be safe from this very un-Stefano-like reaction.

"Like I said before," Sofia began in an earnest voice, stepping up to the edge of the desk, planting both palms on the desktop, and leaned in.

So much for safe distance, he mused, darkly, and leaned his back into the chair, but it was too late. He'd already inhaled her unique scent that was destined to drive him mad.

"*The Polish Alliancer* does not publish schmuck. We just want to do a write-up—an honest write-up—on—"

"On me," he finished for her in a tone that should have told her she was trespassing.

Should have. But didn't, it seemed apparent when she continued her sales pitch.

"You're the world's most eligible bachelor." She lifted her hands in the air, the word *dah* embedded in the motion.

"And the press has to sell newspapers and magazines," he said cynically, irritably. If the newspaper business or magazine circulation suffered, anything that increased sales and kept those numbers up had to be done. Including pursuing royalty. Without any remorse for intrusion on private moments. Or frightening small children.

"Arrogantly handsome royalty are always good for a headline, I admit." Sofia straightened, adjusted the purse strap that had slipped down her arm. "But people, and not just here, but all over the world, are especially interested in you, Stefano, and in particular, when it comes to love and marriage."

"They are interested in gossip." Stefano lifted one clenched fist and slammed it down on the desk, startling Sofia and she jerked backward. "When I was younger, I was resentful of the *paparazzi*," he told her in his best cool, judicial voice so at odds with the hand on the desktop still curled into a fist. "As an adult…" He gave a dismissive shrug of his shoulders. "I have learned to use the media for advancing my agenda for Mondoverde." He gave her a sharp look. "But I do not give interviews so that my life can be dissected and minced and shredded for the public's entertainment."

"But I'm not like that, Stefano. I wouldn't—" She made a lackluster slice of the hand through the air. "—dissect and mince and shred your life."

"No, you will not." Although barely a muscle moved in his face, he couldn't have made it more plain that she had overstepped the mark in pushing for the story, his story. "Because I do not engage in interviews with reporters," he said between his teeth. Why did he have Tonino bring her here? He knew she was a reporter. He knew what all reporters wanted from him.

His soul.

"But, Stefano—"

"Did you not get enough material for your write-up from the press conference?" he asked harshly.

"I want—need a personal slant to my article," she said, the words raw and desperate on her lips.

"The answer, *Signorina*, is no." He delivered his words precisely, as icy as he knew his eyes to be. "Now." He pushed back the chair and stood, towering over this woman, and regaining the advantage over his see-sawing emotions she provoked, he offered her a cool smile of dismissal. "If you will excuse, *Signorina* Burska, I have a meeting to attend." He did not, but she need not know this. He needed some quiet. He needed some aloneness. He needed to settle his agitated spirit.

He needed to figure out why he felt like he had been set up on a path that would change his life?

"Thank you for indulging me with your time." With an autocratic point of the finger, he indicated the door, signaling the conclusion of the conversation.

Sofia gave a small, strangled scream of sheer and unadulterated frustration and stomped to the door, banging it shut behind her with barely controlled violence.

Stefano sank into the chair. He felt a pang of something sharp and forlorn, bleaker than loneliness, but not quite qualifying as anything he had ever felt before.

Chapter 3

"Oh!" Sofia grabbed the other woman's arms in an instinctive move to steady her. "I'm so terribly sorry."

"It is all right." The petite woman with dark friendly eyes and dark hair pinned into an attractive twist smiled. "No harm done."

"I wasn't paying attention to where I was going." Sofia flicked daggers at the closed door behind her. "I—I was—I didn't mean to bulldoze you. I'm sorry."

The woman, dressed casually but elegantly in a pair of black pants topped with a white satin blouse and accented with discreet pearls on her ears and around her neck, studied her for a long intense moment, skimmed her gaze to the closed door with *Palace Office* emblazoned on the brass plate, brought her appraising eyes back to Sofia. "I hope Tonino has not upset you, *Signorina*." The woman pointed a manicured hand at the door. "As Bellaterra Castle's official representative, Tonino can be—how do you say?—intimidating, yes? I beg your pardon if he has been a little too…forceful."

"Oh, no—" Sofia gave a surreptitious glance at the woman's left hand, saw the gold wedding band and sparkling diamond on her ring finger. "—*Signora*, I have no complaints with *Signor* Masselli," she insisted, not wanting this palace employee to report the man to…to whomever had authority over him. "Only with…"

"Only with?" the woman prompted when Sofia let her voice trail off.

WANTED: ROYAL PRINCESS WIFE AND MOTHER

"No one."

The woman found the response amusing. A hesitant smile teetered around her mouth. "I do not believe *no one* had you charging out of that office," she replied, her tone sardonic. "Nor did *no one* cause you to glare at that door with murderous intent." One well-shaped eyebrow arched. "Who has upset you?" Still when Sofia remained silent, chewing on her lip, the woman coaxed, "Come now, *Signorina*, you must tell me."

"I—it isn't important."

"Miss Burska." Tonino Masselli materialized on the carpeted corridor and approached, clipboard in hand. "Your meeting with Prince Stefano has concluded?"

"Y-yes, th-thank you, *Signor* Masselli. I'll be going now—"

"Prince Stefano?" The woman shot out a restraining hand, hindering Sofia's escape. The fingers coiled around her wrist were soft, but unyielding. "You were in there with Prince Stefano?" The words were delivered in an impassive tone underlined with a keen interest.

"Yes, *Signora*." Sofia caught the alarmed expression on Tonino's face and frowned, grinding her teeth in worry and frustration. What? What had she done wrong?

She felt heat blossom on her cheeks.

Heat she attributed to the remembered awareness zigzagging between her and the prince. Heat from the too-difficult-to-forget waves of sensation that had pulsed through her body, sensations she neither expected nor wanted to experience. Heat from her failed mission and the Prince's abrupt and arrogant dismissal.

"I'll be going now," Sofia told the two palace employees, her voice flat, and made a discreet attempt to release herself from the other woman's grip.

"Shall I escort you out, Miss Burska?" Tonino snapped at attention.

The woman's clasp tightened, making Sofia wonder if

she'd be sporting bruises there by morning. "That will not be necessary, Tonino. You may go now."

Tonino offered the woman a slight bow. "As you wish, Your Se—"

"*Grazie*, Tonino." One eyebrow dipped. There was an odd inflection in the woman's voice, but Sofia didn't have time to ponder it. Tonino gave Sofia a little bow also, knocked once on the closed door, awaited the Prince's bellowed "Come," and disappeared into the Palace Office.

Feeling somewhat despondent, Sofia wanted to do a disappearing act, also, only she wanted to disappear right out of the palace. But how did Sofia tactfully but firmly break the woman's iron grip? "Well." She took a fortifying breath. "I'll be going now. I know my way out. Thank you." And once again, using subtleness and diplomacy, she tried to free herself from the human restraint.

"Not so fast, *Signorina*." Though the tenacious fingers looping Sofia's wrist slackened, they slid down to link with Sofia's digits. "Please spare me a few moments of your time and join me for refreshments."

"Thank you, I appreciate it, but it's not necessary."

"Trust me, *cara*, it is very necessary," the woman contradicted, flashing her a confident grin before tugging on her hand. "Come." As autocratic orders go, this one brooked no argument, demanding compliance.

With no other recourse, Sofia had to comply, and was forced by the inflexible grip of the woman's fingers on hers to follow the woman down the long carpeted corridor. For a petite person, the woman moved like lightning. They went through a closed door and along a maze of crisscrossing corridors that totally disoriented Sofia. If left on her own, she'd need GPS to find her way around the palace. When they stopped at yet another closed door, this one displaying the coat of arms of the Principality of Mondoverde, the woman keyed in a code on the reader beside it and when it buzzed clearance, she pushed open the door, and they entered what Sofia surmised to be a private staircase. They climbed two flights of marble stairs, walked half way down the wide carpeted corridor to a closed gilded door. The brass plate read *HSH The Prince Alessandro and Princess Cristina of Mondoverde.*

Sofia's stomach muscles clenched. Whatever she had done wrong, this woman had hauled her right up to Prince Alessandro and Princess Cristina, whoever they were, for an account of her misdemeanors.

Once again, Sofia wished she'd done her homework and berated herself for her obvious display of unprofessionalism.

And if she'd gotten the royal runaround from the palace staff over the weekend, if she'd gotten the royal refusal from Prince Stefano a little while ago, she was about the get the royal kick-in-the-butt from whoever held court behind that closed door. Would the palace guards be summoned to consign her to the castle's dungeon? she mused, part in jest, part in dread.

A dark, dank dungeon.

A dark, dank dungeon infested with rats.

Rats had an affection for dark, dank dungeons.

Sofia Burska had no affection for rats. Or for dark, dank dungeons.

"Come in, *Signorina*." The woman preceded Sofia into what looked to be a private drawing room, big and furnished with a Victorian taste. "Will you not sit down?" the woman invited, motioning to the ornate sofa as she herself took the opulent chair opposite, sitting with such an impressive manner, Sofia felt certain she would garner the royal approval of the ruling monarch.

Inhaling the soft scent of lilacs fragrancing the room, Sofia obliged and sank onto the sofa, not because she'd been told to sit, but because she felt her knees buckle. If she wouldn't be escorted down into the cellar by the palace guards, she would certainly be shepherded to prison by the island police.

She could her see her own headlines now.

Canadian Reporter Gets Busted For Undisclosed Contravention of Mondoveduvian Law

Allowing herself an internal moan, she gave a cursory study of the room, all the while conscious of the woman having picked up the phone and saying into the mouthpiece, "Please come into the drawing room." Her nerves jangled and mangled, she continued her nervous perusal of the room, and had her attention snagged by a large painting in a place of honor on one of the walls.

A man, looking to be thirty-five or forty years of age, with olive skin, brown hair, and a sexy, smiling mouth, sat in a wingback chair, legs crossed, hands folded. But it was his eyes. The striking, penetrating blue had a laser-like quality to them and seemed to look down at her with commanding power. And hold her captive.

The clothes, though impeccable and classy, spoke of another time, maybe the 1940s or 1950s, but other than that obvious dating of the picture, Sofia would have sworn the man in the portrait was...Prince Stefano.

"Prince Giovanni Carmine Graziano."

Sofia snapped her head to the woman, and blushing, gave her a slight nod, not wanting to admit she had no idea who Prince Giovanni Carmine Graziano was. Other than the obvious. The plague on the statue out front proclaimed him the first prince of the royal House of Graziani. She could take some credit, not a lot, but some, that she displayed some intelligence, not a lot, but some, and had taken the time to read the plaque.

As if the woman could read minds, she offered, "Prince Giovanni founded the sovereign Principality of Mondoverde. Our history, both as an island nation and a constitutional, hereditary monarchy, is quite extraordinary." With an impish glint in her eyes, she suggested, "Perhaps you should ask Prince Stefano, as a proud Mondoverduvian and hereditary heir to the throne, to share the story with you."

"Like that's going to happen," Sofia muttered and caught the other woman giving her a long, steady smile that had a hint of a smile fading.

"Ah, Luciana," the woman addressed the maid who entered the drawing room and curtsied, leaving Sofia wondering why one staff member would curtsy to another. Turning to Sofia, the woman asked, "*Cara*, what would you prefer? Coffee or tea?"

She'd prefer to make a run for it. "Coffee. Thank you, *signora*," she replied, frowning when she intercepted an aghast expression on the maid's face. Now what?

"Luciana, bring us a pot of coffee, *per piacere*. And a plate of *biscotti*, yes?" she asked Sofia, who shrugged. The maid nodded, bobbed, and left. "It has occurred to me, *cara*, we have not been properly introduced." A perfect brow lifted.

Aware she'd been manhandling her purse strap, Sofia released it, and settled her hands in a demure clasp atop the purse. "My name is Sofia. Sofia Burska." Why did she have the strange feeling she waited for the proverbial shoe to fall?

"I am pleased to make your acquaintance, Sofia Burska." A hesitation long enough to embolden the earlier hint of humor to reappear in her eyes. "I am...*la Principessa* Cristina." She halted long enough to smile at Sofia's gasp, then added, "Prince Stefano's mother."

The shoe fell.

* * *

What Stefano said was law.

He sat, leaning forward, resting his forearms on his thighs, fingers interlaced, hands suspended between his knees, and raising his eyes only, watched his trusted and devoted assistant enter the Palace Office.

As the hereditary prince and next in line to the Throne of Graziani and one who already carried a good deal of the duties and responsibilities of ruling Mondoverde, Stefano was accustomed to being in control. He was accustomed to having people fear him, to having people awed by his station in life, to having people intimidated by his power.

What he said was law.

No one dared to question him. No one dared to make suggestions to him. No one dared to initiate a discussion with him. No one dared to argue with him.

What he said was law.

"Your Serene Highness?"

Straightening in the chair, Stefano rubbed his neck with both hands to stretch the tight muscles. Yet the young slip of a girl had done all that and much more.

Sofia Burska had challenged his irrefutable law of not engaging in interviews with the press.

Sofia Burska had been exasperating, maddening, incredibly sexy, and profoundly a breath of fresh air.

Sofia Burska had feared him, was awed by his title and position, intimidated by his power, but she'd also refused to bow to those feelings. He'd watched her reach deep within her for the strength, the determination, the will to crush down her fear, her awe, her intimidation.

And argue with him.

As if who he was mattered little to her.

And *Dio mio*, he found himself respecting her.

He found himself reluctantly wanting to trust her.

He found himself fearing her, of being in awe of her, of being intimidated by her.

Fear. Awe. Intimidation.

Because she'd managed, somehow, in a few short minutes, to drill through his armor of protection.

He needed to be reserved. He needed to be self-possessed. He needed to be in control.

Not simply because it would ensure his emotional safety, but because he would one day become the ruler of Mondoverde.

His character, his conduct, his conversation would earn him the trust and love of the citizens of Mondoverde. It would also keep him from being embroiled in the scandals plaguing other European monarchs. Stefano knew as a royal and a member of public office, everything he said and did was subject to media scrutiny.

Sofia Burska was a member of the media and he *knew* he should keep her at a distance. He *knew* she stripped him of his usual strength, his usual resolve, his usual sense of duty. His *knowing* what was appropriate and proper.

Yet he couldn't extricate himself from the thought he'd met his equal in life.

And what a beautiful equal.

Not a Hollywood kind of beauty.

Not a painted-on kind of beauty.

But a pure, natural, genuine kind of beauty.

The kind of beauty that would not disintegrate with the passing of years. The kind of beauty that would not require cosmetic surgery to keep her looking youthful and attractive because her kind of beauty flowed from within her being, her heart, her soul.

How had he known that? He shook his head.

He'd felt himself drawn to the woman. He scrubbed a hand across his jaw. As if he had been drifting in the Arctic Circle, nearly dead from exhaustion and frozen from cold, and finally catching a glimpse of the promise of the warm gilded light of a blazing fire in the distance, he'd felt himself drawn.

He needed to guard against this insanity! He needed to raise up his shield.

The future of his island nation rested solidly and solely on his shoulders, as he was the immediate successor to his father, Prince Alessandro's, throne. That was enough incentive to steer clear of the press.

And he needed to remember she was a member of the press.

Seeing him as too stern, too serious, too remote, the press would delight in catching him in the worst possible moments. To impale him, if they could, with some salacious scandal. And if they could not, then the next best thing would be to exaggerate the truth. It was the sizzle that sold newspapers and magazines. And he had the dubious honor of being that sizzle.

Stefano sighed, a weary sound. "Yes, Tonino?" He stood, grateful for a rare afternoon with no appointments scheduled. He would return to his personal apartments, change into his swimming trunks, and enjoy himself by doing a few lazy laps in the pool. Alone.

"Your presence, Your Serene Highness," Tonino began in his formal manner, "is requested in the Cabinet of the Prince's meeting room where His Serene Highness, Prince Alessandro, has assembled the ministers."

Stefano's brows drew together. "I do not recall a meeting being scheduled for this afternoon."

"I believe none was originally scheduled, Your Serene Highness, but your father has asked me to notify you to join them at your earliest convenience."

"You mean *right now*, do you not, Tonino?" Stefano asked, his tone dry.

"It is as you see it, Your Serene Highness."

"You are always very diplomatic, are you not, Tonino?" Stefano adjusted the knot in his tie and buttoned his blazer.

"Yes, *Principe*."

"Have you any ideas why the impromptu meeting has been called?"

"Prince Alessandro did not inform me. He only instructed me to locate you and advise you to attend."

"Care to speculate?"

"It is not for me to speculate." Tonino tacked on *Your Highness* to emphasize the wide chasm between their stations in life.

"*Grazie*, Tonino." Stefano strolled to the doorway where his assistant still stood, erect and straight-faced. "I shall relinquish your office back to you." In a very un-royal-like manner, he pressed a hand to the other man's shoulder.

Tonino looked startled by the action. As startled as Stefano felt and he hoped he still had the appearance of a royal in control. He managed to hold in the snort. In control? He feared he stopped having control since a certain woman practically collided with him in the foyer. "I appreciate its usage and your help earlier in bringing Miss Burska here to see me."

"I am here to serve you and the royal family."

Stefano nodded and left the room, quietly closing the door behind him. It was odd for his father to call a meeting with the council and not discuss the matter with him first. Making his way to the meeting room, he searched his memory for *any*thing that could be considered a situation, an urgent situation demanding an emergency meeting. But nothing came to mind. Except…

"Except the face of one slip of a girl who had made me want, almost desperately, to explore all that energy crackling between us," Stefano said in a haunted whisper. He gave himself a mental shake, admonishing himself to remember Sofia Burska was a member of the hated press.

* * *

Sofia felt the color drain from her face. "Ohmygod." The moan tore from her lips. "Twice in one day," she groaned, her fingers raking through her hair before she covered her mouth and nose. "This can't be happening." Her trembling fingers muffled the words.

Now she understood—red hot heat slammed into her cheeks—the stunned looks on both Tonino Masselli and the maid's countenances.

She'd brutalized the breech of royal etiquette and very incorrectly addressed Her Serene Highness with the very simple title of…*signora.*

"I am so sorry, Your Serene Highness."

"Whatever for, *cara*? Oh, *grazie*, Luciana." The princess watched the maid set the tray on the coffee table.

"Shall I pour, *Principessa*?"

"No, thank you, Luciana. I can manage."

"Very well, *Principessa*." She performed another curtsy, and left the room.

Picking up the pot, Princess Cristina poured coffee into two heirloom cups.

Sofia took the coffee offered, but some sixth sense warned her to wait for the princess to settle back into her chair and lift the cup to her mouth to sip first. Then, with a little moan of beleaguered thanks, she raised the cup to her mouth with both hands, praying she wouldn't do something foolish, like spill the coffee over her white dress, or worse, over the costly furniture, or worse yet, break such a delicate and expensive teacup. She managed to carry the cup to her mouth, managed to take a sip, and—thank God—managed to not choke on the coffee. With exaggerated care, she set the cup on the table, and folded her hands primly on her lap.

"Please try the *biscotti*. Our chef makes them. They are a favorite with my children." A sly smile. "Especially Stefano."

"Ah...thank you...*Principessa*, but I—"

"You will try one and not offend our chef, yes?" The princess held out a plate of enticing *biscotti*.

Did protocol demand she take a cookie even if she was ninety-nine percent positive she'd choke on it? Oh, the crumbs. Surely she would litter the sofa and carpet with crumbs no matter how careful she'd be?

"Come, *cara*, just one," the other woman cajoled. "It will not harm your lovely figure and it will make our chef very happy. I, too, will be pleased."

When put like that... Sofia reached for the *biscotti*, the fresh-baked scent teasing her nostrils, again waited for the princess to chew off a piece first, then she sank her teeth in the hard cookie. The taste sent a soft moan of pleasure falling from her lips. "My compliments to your chef, *Principessa*."

The woman inclined her head in a regal acknowledgment of Sofia's flattering remark. "He will be very pleased to hear you enjoy his creations. Now, Sofia, please tell me..." A slight frown marred an otherwise perfect forehead. "What did you mean earlier when you said, 'Twice in one day'?" Concern threaded through the words.

Sofia had just chewed off a piece of *biscotti* and began to cough.

The princess jumped to her feet, took Sofia's cup, and sitting beside her on the sofa, handed her the coffee. "Here. Take a drink. Better?"

Eyes watering, cheeks flaming, Sofia nodded. "Y-yes," she rasped out. Coughing to clear her throat, she set the cup down, slid her index fingers beneath her eyes to catch any moisture, and tried to find her voice. "Thank you."

Instead of returning to her own chair, the princess draped an arm around Sofia's shoulders, a very un-royal-like gesture, Sofia would have thought. "What happened between you and my son? You may speak freely." When Sofia made a moaning sound in her throat, the princess added in a dry tone, "I will not have you beheaded, I promise."

"No, you'll just have the palace guards throw me in the dungeon." Sofia's hands flew to her mouth. Eyes wide with contrition, she apologized. "I beg your pardon, *Principessa*."

The last thing Sofia expected was for the woman's laughter to tinkle into the room. It was a beautiful sound, rich and full of amusement. "We don't have a dungeon here, *cara*." When her laughter downgraded into a smile, she asked again, "What happened?"

A sigh came out of Sofia. While she explained her newspaper assignment and her weekend full of dead-end phone calls to the Palace Office, the princess commiserated with a nod of understanding. But when Sofia recounted her mistaking Prince Stefano for a butler, his mother started chuckling. The minute Sofia said the prince compounded her error by not revealing his true identity, his mother's chuckles turned into laughter. Sofia made light of her mortification in the Press Conference Room when she realized who he really was, added her *concern* when *Signor* Masselli appeared at her side to escort her out. To where, she did not know.

"*Signor* Masselli did not offer me any information." Sofia stopped short of telling the princess her blood pressure probably zoomed off the charts.

The princess's sober expression masked the weight of the throne on all the royals' shoulders and said quietly, "No, Tonino would not." She sighed. "He is a devoted assistant to not just my son, but to my husband, Prince Alessandro. To the entire house of Graziani, in fact." The last was accompanied by a lifting of both hands into the air for emphasis. "Tonino is the soul of discretion and his tendency not to engage in gossip is a sterling quality. He is also one of our most loyal and ardent protectors. You understand?"

Sofia nodded. "He laid a firm grip on my arm as he ushered me into the Palace Office where…"

"Where Stefano sat waiting," his mother guessed, her lips twitching.

"Yes." Sofia cleared her throat, searching her mind for words. Finally she settled on, "We had a quick conversation. When it concluded, he dismissed me." She was proud she kept her voice steady, almost unemotional, but she dared not glance into the princess's eyes. Sofia had the feeling the woman saw too much.

"I sense there is more to the story, yes?"

The woman was very intuitive, too. When she turned to look at her, Sofia saw Princess Cristina had narrowed her eyes on her.

"Talk to me." The princess's hand stroked up and down Sofia's arm. "He is my son, but I can remain objective." She made a wry face. "It is part of the inborn, or in my case, taught, discipline to remain calm, clearheaded, and completely in control of the emotions. So you may speak freely." She let out a gentle laugh. "Remember, we have no dungeons here. And I promise, I will keep your confidence."

She smiled in a secretive way and zipped her lips with her fingers.

Rubbing the back of her neck, Sofia took a deep breath and admitted, "I really need that interview with the prince. I need to prove to my editor I can be trusted to do real journalism, not cover the society pages." Disgust oozed from her mouth along with the words. "Oh!" She slapped a hand over her mouth. Why didn't she simply yank her tongue out of her mouth today? "I'm sorry, *Principessa*. I did not mean to infer you—your family—are in any way trivial."

The princess patted Sofia's knee. "No offence taken, *cara*. Do not worry."

"My editor promised—" *sort of* "—if I produce the special interest story on the Prince, he would give me a shot at some real reporting. I would then have the opportunity and means to show not just my boss, but the readers, I am a woman of depth not…not…some flighty female who dreams of being Cinderella and being galloped to the castle to live happily-ever-after."

She stared down at the cookie in her hand, but instead had the uncomfortable vision of Prince Stefano mounted on a proud-looking horse, riding fast toward her, bending at the waist to scoop her off her feet, settle her in front of him, holding her against his rock-hard chest in a vice-like grip, and galloping with her toward Bellaterra Castle.

The cookie in her hand powdered beneath the tautening of her fingers, scattering the crumbs over her lap and onto the antique Aubusson rug. "Oh! I'm so terribly sorry."

"It is nothing." The princess curled one gentle hand on Sofia's arm and with the other, she swept the crumbs off Sofia's lap and onto the carpet, causing Sofia's eyes to widen in shock. "Do not concern yourself over a few crumbs," she said and chuckled, the sound warm and affectionate. "You must see what the room looks like when all four of my sons are gathered together."

How was Sofia to respond? Since she had no clue, she

chose discretion and forced her lips to curve into an even-tempered smile.

"You do not believe in marriage? In a *loving* marriage?" The woman's gaze bored through Sofia, seeking and searching something.

"I do, *Principessa*. My parents have such a marriage. Very loving. All three of my brothers have married their soul mates." Sofia lowered her vision to her clasped hands.

"Yet, you do not believe in such a possibility for yourself?"

Sofia felt the woman's gaze on her, relaxed and relentless at the same time, and tingles of trepidation prickled at the base of her neck. "Perhaps," she allowed with caution, stretching the word over three syllables. "I—my priority is to establish a respectable career."

And pay off the huge debt she'd amassed through student loans. The first of the month, when payment was due, loomed before her, huge and hostile.

She would make that payment. She would whittle down the outstanding amount to a zero balance. She would extricate herself from the albatross.

But did she want to marry? Sure. Some day. But as she'd not met anyone she'd like to marry, it was a moot point.

"You do not believe in fairy tales, then?" The princess slid her heels off and tucked her stockinged feet under her, rubbing them with her hand. Yet another un-royal-like behavior.

"Fairy tales?" Sofia looked up and her mouth curved with laughter. "When I was a little girl, I read all the classics. *Sleeping Beauty. Beauty and the Beast. The Twelve Dancing Princesses.* And of course, the classic of classics. *Cinderella.* But I'm an adult now. And I have my feet firmly planted on *terra firma.* So, no, I don't see me in a fairy tale with a happily-ever-after." A vision of the attractive prince slid into her mind. A peculiar melancholy slid over her chest. She chuckled, but there was a rawness to the sound.

"*Cara*, God is the Architect of love and marriage and romance and…fairy tales." Princess Cristina laid a hand on Sofia's arm as if to emphasize her next statement. In a tender voice, she said, "God is sovereign over everything. He is also very creative when it comes to bringing couples together. Believe me. One day I will tell you how Prince Alessandro and I met, yes?" She gave Sofia's thigh a sympathetic pat. "Trust in the presence and power of God, Sofia, and do not underestimate His ability to give you your…prince."

"Right."

"You must have faith, little one," the princess chided, with a shadow of a smile. "Faith is not simply believing God can, but that He *will* do it."

"Your Serene Highness, please don't concern yourself over my love life." *Or the nonexistence of one.* "You have much more important concerns." She bit her lip. Should she say it? If she did, it would be the height of brazenness. Impudence. Audacity. She could take comfort no dungeons existed in the palace. Nor the rats that infested them. But her cheeky courage—or her sassy stupidity—could earn her a private encounter with the island prison. With a barely imperceptible move of her shoulders in a shrug, she added, "Like Prince Stefano."

The princess released a heartfelt sigh and swung her feet to the floor. "And that ridiculous Mondoverduvian tradition." Her mouth firmed into a rigid line of disapproval. "Just because Prince Giovanni happened to meet and marry the woman of his heart by the age of twenty-five. Yes, Prince Alessandro, also, managed to fulfill the requirement," she acknowledged with another sigh, "but in both those cases, it was love." Her tone turned vehement. Lines darkened her pretty face. Her eyes glowed with the fierceness of a lioness protecting her cubs.

Sofia's brows met in a frown. "You refer, *Principessa*, to Prince Stefano having passed that age requirement." That much she did know from what her boss had told her. It was supposed to be a part of her ill-fated article on the heir to the throne of this little-known principality. At least, little-known in North America. She presumed it not to be the case here in Europe.

"They are insisting he take a wife for the growth and prosperity of the Graziani dynasty." The princess shoved her feet into her shoes. "Yes, he is the firstborn. Yes, heaven has picked him to rule Mondoverde. Yes, it is an enormous responsibility being the sovereign ruler and head of the Principality of Mondoverde and the head of the government, having to ensure the peace and prosperity of our citizens." She began to pace the room, her steps fast and furious. "But must he be forced into a marriage of convenience and produce the mandatory heir like there was some kind of urgency? My husband is only fifty-two. He is still young. He is still healthy. He is not going anywhere." She halted in front of Sofia and made a snarling sound in her throat. "*Dio mio*, can my son not be afforded time to find his princess? To find the *right* wife? His God-appointed helpmate?" Her eyes glowed with a hint of anger. "I want grandchildren, too, just like everyone else, but not at the expense of my son's happiness."

"*Principessa*." Sofia couldn't believe she was about to say what she would. She needed her head examined. Certainly her boss would ask for her resignation. Ask? No. He'd terminate her employment without further notice. But in listening to the cries of a mother, of a royal mother, in witnessing her worries over her son, the one *heaven has picked* to rule this micronation located in the Adriatic Sea, and possibly wind up in a loveless union for his trouble, she had to say it. Her conscience demanded she say it.

"It's probably not a good idea for you to…to…share such personal details with me."

"Why not?" The woman looked stunned.

"Because I—I can't be trusted. I'm a member of the press.

You know. Anything you say can end up on the first page of the newspaper." *There goes my career. Career? Forget that. How am I going to pay off my twenty-eight-thousand dollar loan without a job? A* debt the Statistics Canada survey suggested would take fourteen years to pay off based on an average starting salary of $39 thousand dollars. And she didn't come close to earning that kind of a salary at *The Polish Alliancer*. Because she was a rookie. A rookie not allowed to earn more money by covering real stories. She almost let loose on a growl of frustration.

A brilliant smile erupted on the princess's face. "*Cara,* you are the most trustworthy person I've met." She picked up her coffee cup and took a sip of her now-cold coffee. "You are going to be just perfect."

Perfect for what?

The half-formed question echoed in Sofia's head but it would not come out of her mouth.

CHAPTER 4

When Stefano approached the meeting room of the Cabinet of the Prince, the two members of the Royal Guard, in their traditional attire of white uniform, purple shirt, white helmet, with their weapons discreetly shielded, saluted him, then in perfect sync, reached to open the double oak-paneled doors. Nodding at them, Stefano stepped into the marble-floored room with gold trimmings and accessories and displaying a cross hanging on the wall with a painting of Prince Giovanni beneath it and two Mondoverduvian flags standing sentinel on either side.

His father and ruler of the Principality of Mondoverde, Prince Alessandro, in a dark gray suit, pristine white shirt, and charcoal tie, sat on one side of the wide oval conference table. The ministers of government, a total of eight members making up the Crown Council, not including himself, sat on the other side. As the State Secretary and Minister of Internal Affairs, Stefano took his seat, sitting directly across from his father and next to his brother, Prince Cristiano, who held the position of Minister of Finances, Tourism, and Sports.

"Thank you, Prince Stefano, for joining us." His father sat back, the shift in his body indicating he had crossed his legs, his hands curled around the arms of the gilded chair, his expression royally inscrutable.

"My apologies for my tardiness." Stefano held his father's gaze for a moment before skipping it over the faces of the ministers on either side of him and bringing it back to his father. "I did not realize a meeting of the Council had been scheduled until Tonino advised me." Leaning forward, he clasped his hands on the oak surface of the table, and sent his father a telepathic message. *What is going on?* "And I came at once."

"There is no national crisis," Prince Alessandro reassured him and the other council members. "Nevertheless, I called for this meeting to discuss a number of items, not the least, to have a summation of your press conference."

In Stefano's chest, relief warred with disbelief.

Relief that no catastrophic crisis had arisen demanding their tact and diplomacy, their sharp wits and quick actions to defend their citizens and uphold their sovereignty.

Disbelief his father would have ordered a spur-of-the-moment meeting of his cabinet with no apparent and creditable reason.

An update on the press conference failed, to Stefano's way of thinking, to warrant the ad hoc meeting.

Suspicion mixed with the disbelief.

One side of his father's mouth crooked up slightly, but the expression in his eyes remained solemn, even a little stern. "The press conference?" Prince Alessandro repeated, adding a regal hike to his brows.

Stefano searched his father's face for a clue. Talk about finding the Graziano needle in the Mondoverde haystack. He drew in a deep breath, released it in a heavy sigh. When his father would be ready to disclose his real motives for the meeting, he would. And not one second sooner.

"The press conference went very well," he told the gathered group. "The conference room was filled to capacity, as I had hoped. *Il Messaggero di Mondoverde*, of course, was represented, as were journalists from Italy, France, England, even—" *a slip of a girl* "—as far away as Canada."

"Canada?" Prince Alessandro looked surprised. "I had no idea we were known outside of Europe."

Stefano lifted his shoulder in what he hoped came off as an easygoing shrug. "Perhaps my promoting Mondoverde abroad is beginning to pay off international dividends. In any case—" He shrugged again. "—you Canadians were sufficiently intrigued by the Graziano royal family and the Principality of Mondoverde to have dispatched a reporter." *One who had absolutely no idea who I really was. How refreshing. One who resented reporting for the society pages of her newspaper. How intriguing.*

When he realized he grinned, he fixed his face into a sober mask. "In any case, I expounded my desire to better the lives of our people. We may have a population of only five hundred fifty-four, but every one of those five hundred fifty-four persons deserves our best. And I want to give them our best. Not just in building state-of-the-art hospitals and high-tech schools, but actually creating excellent paying jobs all over our thirty square mile island. We need to bring in business to Mondoverde. Prince Cristiano." He shifted his head to his right to address his brother. "Consider hiring a public relations consultant."

"Public relations consultant?" Cristiano sported a baffled expression. "We have the Palace Office that handles any public relations concerns."

"No. No. No." Even as Stefano shook his head, he swerved his body so he could give his brother a face-to-face stare. "We need a professional in the field that will know how to promote Mondoverde as the perfect place to spend tourist dollars and invest business ventures."

Cristiano remained silent a moment, considering. "I'll look into it," he finally said with a nod.

"Good." Maybe, Stefano mused, belatedly, he should have given Sofia Burska that interview. She, representing her Toronto paper, could prove to be an extraordinary conduit for advertising and promoting. Being in North America, her article could easily be picked up by newspapers in the United States. He rubbed a thumb across his chin as he considered it. No, he decided. She was a member of the press and he did not give interviews. Period. But for the good of Mondoverde?

"Prince Stefano."

Roused from his scattered thoughts, Stefano diverted his attention to his father.

"There is one matter still to discuss, though not in the urgency category, yet, still it is of grave importance."

Stefano intercepted the groan building in his throat and willed his facial features into bland lines. He willed his body to relax. He should have seen this coming. Prince Alessandro Constantino Taddeo Stefano Graziano, ruling monarch of the Principality of Mondoverde, was like a tenacious pit bull. He would not let go of his pet peeve. Stefano's hands fell to his lap. His fingers curled into tight fists of resentment.

* * *

"Your editor expects you back in Toronto soon?"

Sofia eyed the princess watching her with a speculative expression. If royalty stood, did protocol demand she stand too? Her muscles contracting in her stomach, Sofia realized she had actually forgotten this woman, this mother, was Her Serene Highness, Princess Cristina of the royal House of Graziani, and she made her home in the luxurious Bellaterra Castle.

How could she have forgotten such a station in life? Such an obvious proof, a vivid reminder that she, Sofia, not only a commoner, but a foreigner, did not belong in this world. Had no business being in this world. A world of pomp and ceremony.

A world of power and position and privilege.

Even if she had been dispatched here on assignment, she had no business staying here.

Now, as she got to her feet, her movement clumsy, she wished she'd been coached in the proper protocol. She hated the idea of offending such a lovely woman, even if out of sheer ignorance.

A sadness fell on her.

In other circumstances, Cristina Graziano and Sofia Burska could have been friends. In these circumstances, the Princess of Mondoverde, the royal wife of the ruling monarch of the Principality of Mondoverde and a working girl from a middle class family with a debt on her shoulders to pay off could have no common ground to encourage friendship.

"Since I failed in obtaining an interview with His Serene Highness, Prince Stefano—" It would be best if Sofia remembered *his* station in life, remember the man was a prince and not simply a man. A man who rattled her sensibilities. A man forbidden to her. "—I'll have to make arrangements to fly home as soon as I return to my hotel room." Why did it bother her that Prince Stefano was forbidden to her? What did she expect? He was a prince, she a pauper. There was probably some decree, stamped into law with the royal seal, forbidding royalty and commoners from…from…

"I would ask you, *cara*, to remain on our beautiful island for a few more days, to take a tour of it, enjoy our many splendors."

"Oh, Your Highness, I would like that very much. Prince Stefano mentioned the Greek and Roman ruins."

Sofia heard the longing in her voice. The wistfulness. She'd only been here three days, and though most of that holed up in her hotel room, there was something about the island that called to her, called to some deep, secret place within her soul. She'd been unprepared for the enormity of emotion that had risen up inside her. She'd felt something, of magnitude proportion, stir within her heart when she'd landed at the quaint Bellaterra airport and had descended the steps from the airplane to the tarmac.

Some kind of…connection. She'd wanted to drop to the ground and press her lips to it in gratitude, in joy. As if…she'd finally come home.

Which was ridiculous.

Her home had always been the Roncesvalles Village district of Toronto where her family resided. She'd been born and raised there. She'd never ventured outside her neighborhood. And except for this assignment, she had never wanted to venture outside. That was her *home*. So why did she feel this…this…peculiar bond to this island nation?

A face burst onto her mind. Olive skinned. Roman nose. High cheekbones. Laser blue eyes.

"Then it is settled. You will stay and visit the ruins."

"I'm afraid not, Princess Cristina."

"Why not?" The princess sounded genuinely baffled. "You just said you would like to see the ruins." But it was a regal brow that arched.

Sofia made a face. "While my editor would agree to pay for legitimate expenditures like my hotel bill and meals and car expenses *if* I came home with the article, he would definitely not accept the incurred costs of an extended stay in your charming country while I traipse around the ruins sponging up the history and beauty of Mondoverde."

Much as she would like to. With a certain male tour guide with olive skin, Roman nose, high cheekbones, and laser blue eyes.

"You will not need to depend upon the benevolence of your employer." Her face set in determined lines, the princess walked toward her, placed her hands on Sofia's shoulders. "You will stay here, at the palace, as my guest."

Sofia's mouth dropped open. She closed it. Tried to speak. "I—I can't do that."

"Why not?" The imperial brow rose again.

"Because—because…"

"It is settled." The princess wore a triumphant expression. "You shall return to your hotel and pack your personal belongings. I shall send my personal chauffeur to escort you back here tomorrow morning. I will arrange for your rental car to be returned." She took a step back and folded her hands together. "Will you be contacting your employer to advise of your...change...of plans or shall I?"

Astounded, Sofia shrieked, "You?"

"Yes." The corners of Princess Cristina's mouth tipped up. "I know how to use the phone."

"But—but you are a princess!"

"Yes, I know that, also."

"But you have servants to do things for you."

"It is true the palace employs..." The princess paused, then said, "staff, but we are not—how do you say?—snobs."

Oh. My. God. "I did not mean to infer..." Sofia's voice trailed off. The heat of embarrassment stained her cheeks. She had just insulted the royal princess, the wife of the ruling prince. If this alone did not prove she didn't belong in this magical world of princes and palaces, she had no idea what would.

The princess chuckled, patted a palm on Sofia's shoulder before slipping her fingers around Sofia's elbow. "Do not be alarmed, *cara*. We are also not—how do you say?—stuffy." Her laugh rang out at Sofia's groan. "Well, except for Stefano. He is stuffy. But he has to be. He is poised to be the supreme leader of our country, the head of state, the commander-in-chief of Mondoverde's armed forces." A troubled sigh escaped her. "It is inevitable like it was for my Alessandro, but I so pray my son will find himself a wife who will keep him young and happy and relaxed despite the considerable weight of his duty." She pierced Sofia with a pensive and precise stare. "And as my guest, I am inviting you to attend the state dinner here tomorrow night that we are hosting for visiting dignitaries."

"State dinner?" Sofia rocked backward in astonishment. "I—I can't."

"Why not?"

"Because—because—" Sofia lunged on the first excuse to come to her stunned brain. "I don't have anything suitable to wear to a state dinner." She was a commoner! She was a working girl! She was a nonentity! She didn't do ball gowns and jewels. She didn't *own* ball gowns and jewels.

"That is not a problem. I will take care of every detail. I am good at taking care of such details." A glint of humor entered the princess's eyes. Humor and something else Sofia could not decipher. "I will instruct my maid to escort you directly here to my private apartments when you arrive tomorrow morning. We will have coffee and pastries first, then I will take you myself to your room."

Alarm skipped up and down Sofia's spine. "But I know nothing of royal protocol." But she would have the opportunity to see and talk with Prince Stefano again. Excitement zipped in to elbow out the alarm.

"Do not worry, *cara*. I will have an advisor prompt you tomorrow during a quick palace orientation." With her hand still curled around Sofia's arm, the princess rested her other hand overtop it, and walked Sofia to the door. "Among the dignitaries," she continued, her tone casual, "will be some young aristocratic ladies who will do their utmost to snag Stefano's eye and try to make what they will hope will be a lasting impression upon him. It is no secret, you understand, that my son requires a wife." A secretive smile curling her lips, she opened the door leading to the corridor where a maid waited to escort Sofia to the front entrance of the castle.

Sofia felt the faintest pang of jealousy. "No, it is no secret," she replied in a wooden voice.

Princess Cristina looked at her with a deep and stripping thoughtfulness into her eyes, then said, "*Ciao, cara.*" The princess dropped a kiss on Sofia's forehead. "I will see you tomorrow." To the maid, she instructed, "Please show *Signorina* Burska out."

The maid curtsied and said, "This way, *Signorina.*"

Young aristocratic women who will do their utmost to snag Stefano's eye and try to make what they hope will be a lasting impression upon him.

She recalled the princess's words with a touch of envy.

She was not well-bred. She was not upper-class. She was not blue-blooded.

It seemed like something went very still in her.

She followed the maid down wide corridors and marble staircases.

What was she doing here? Why had she accepted the princess's invitation?

She couldn't allow herself to enjoy this fairy tale world.

She couldn't allow herself to enjoy the company of the hereditary prince.

She couldn't allow herself to invest her time, her heart, in unrealistic hopes and dreams.

Because suddenly she yearned for something more than her journalistic career.

She, Sofia Burska, who had never deliberately searched for the happy-ever-after for herself, felt a swift overwhelming desire to claim it for herself now.

The hopes and dreams. The fairy tale and castle. The prince destined to rule.

At the front door to the palace, she thanked the maid, and stepping through the door, she used her palm to shield her face from the powerful glare of the sun. "Don't get carried away with the ambiance," she muttered under her breath, scurrying toward the parking area where she'd left the rental car.

"You're invited to the dinner because the Princess feels sorry for you for not getting that interview with her son."

Not because she thinks you have a chance to snag Stefano's eye.
"That's Prince Stefano to you, my girl."

She unlocked the driver-side door and slid in. "You don't have to worry about making a lasting impression on the prince." She slipped the key into the ignition. "You've already made one."

She turned the key and the engine fired to life. "You are firmly and eternally etched into his mind as a reporter." Checking her mirrors, she backed out of the parking spot and drove toward the gate, flashing her gaze to her rearview mirror for a last glance at the castle.

"And he dislikes giving interviews to reporters. He obviously dislikes...*me*," she added, her voice a forlorn whisper.

Sofia reminded herself to not look for unrealistic hopes and dreams. She always kept her feet anchored on *terra firma*. She never permitted her head to ascend into the clouds. And she would not do so during this charming interlude on this charming island nation with its charming hereditary prince.

Because Sofia Burska knew who she was, what she was. She was not princess material.

* * *

"We still have the matter of our tradition to discuss." Prince Alessandro spoke the words with all the authority invested in him as the ruling monarch. The hereditary monarchial authority passed down from the founding royal, Prince Giovanni Carmine Graziano, to his heir and firstborn son, Prince Stefano Amadeo Filiberto Giovanni Graziano, to his son and successor, the current sovereign of Mondoverde, Prince Alessandro.

The silence in the room was thick, almost cold, with discomfort.

Of course, the ministers felt an awkwardness despite the fact they all agreed with Stefano's father.

Stefano understood the tradition. Stefano understood the

duty. Stefano understood he would fulfill the mandate.

But Stefano would embrace it when the time was right. He gritted his teeth. And the time was not right.

Making a supreme effort, he dug deep for his strength and serenity, and in a flat voice, said, "We've discussed the matter ad nauseam."

"Apparently not enough," his father contradicted, folding his arms across his chest, "otherwise you would not be one year late in satisfying your duty to your country." Unfolding his arms, Alessandro leaned forward, gripping the table with his right hand, the ring bearing the royal crest clearly visible. "You, Prince Stefano, are my successor to the throne of Graziani. And for the good of Mondoverde, you must marry and produce heirs."

"I understand," Stefano argued, his control over his temper becoming fragile, "my duty of progeny. I will fulfill my duty to my country, but what about *my* life?" He shoved back the chair and surged to his feet, his hands curled into balls at his sides. "Am I not allowed to marry for love?"

"Prince Stefano." His father's tone carried a warning. A warning Stefano chose to ignore.

"Prince Giovanni married for love. Prince Stefano I married for love. *You* married for love." Stefano chose to ignore the glint of caution in his father's eyes. He had to. His heart hung in the balance. He could not allow it to be trampled over. He had to fight for his own happiness. A vision of Sofia Burska stormed his mind. He gave his head a vicious shake. "For the good of the country, would it not make sense for me to marry for love also? It would make for a stable throne. A stable rule. A stable *country*." Not to mention, a stable family. His! Once again, Sofia Burska occupied his thoughts.

"Prince Stefano." His father paused, his tone and manner, though affable was undergirded with power. And authority. "Please sit down."

Stefano wanted to yell his refusal to sit down and make

his opinion loud and clear on what they could do with the tradition of the country. Stefano wanted to spin around, march out of the meeting room, and head for his private apartments. Stefano knew who he was, what he was, he'd known it from birth, had been trained for it from birth, and he pulled all his inner strength together to tamp down his anger, his frustration, his desperation, and ignoring the mammoth headache pounding in the center of his forehead, sat down, and to calm himself, he rehearsed his own personal mantra.

Have courage. Have faith. Stand tall. Remember your birthright of power. Hold your head high, even in times of conflict. Conduct yourself with dignity. Show your authority, but lead others with a loving heart. When it comes time to defend what is dear to your heart, defend it fiercely. And never forget the national emblem of Mondoverde. The lion.

Stefano did not feel calm.

"Now." Alessandro gave the flaps of his blazer a tug before pressing his spine into his chair. "As I said earlier, this matter of you finding a royal wife and producing a royal heir is not in the critical category, yet. I do not need to remind you, though, every day that passes without a royal wedding serves to undermine the integrity of the crown, the stability of the country, and the confidence of the people of Mondoverde."

"I understand the seriousness of the situation, Your Serene Highness." Stefano held his father's astute and penetrating gaze without flinching, and felt more than saw out of the corner of his eye his brother squirming. "I assure you I do not make light of my marital status."

"I am confident you do not."

"I also assure you, Your Serene Highness," Stefano continued, aware of both the grinding in his stomach and his father's narrowed gaze, "I will make every effort to find a woman who is willing to take me on, embrace the public life of a princess, and produce the required heir." *But I will not marry unless it is love that binds us.* Once again, his mind was abducted by the vision of Sofia Burska.

"*Bene,*" his father said with a nod of approval. "Prince Stefano, as you endeavor to find such a woman, never, never forget the living God is with you. He has already chosen your wife. Get down on your knees and pray for God's guidance to lead you to her and wisdom to recognize your God-appointed spouse when you find her. Then get up on your feet and make it happen. Fast. For your country." A pause. A wry expression. A sardonic tone. "For your mother. You do understand she desires *nipoti*?"

Stefano replied. "I understand." A pause. A wry expression. A sardonic tone. "As you desire grandchildren and your father, Prince Stefano I, and Princess Alessia desire great-grandchildren."

"Yes. You understand very well." Assuming the royal demeanor, Alessandro concluded the meeting by standing. All the ministers, stood, bowed, and save Prince Cristiano, exited the room. Alessandro came around the table, laid the father's hand on the son's shoulder. "Have the faith, Stefano." And with that, he left his sons.

Cristiano sunk into his chair and exhaled an embellished sigh of relief. "Thank God it's you and not me, *big* brother, who carries the HSH title and legacy that goes with it." He directed a brotherly smirk at Stefano. "*Buona fortuna* in finding your royal princess wife and mother of your children."

Luck had nothing to do with it, Stefano thought grimly as he left the room. But why did the vision of Sofia Burska hound him?

* * *

When moving down the receiving line, the members of the royal family will address you first. You will then curtsy. The royals will extend their hands to you in greeting and exchange a few pleasantries. You will call them 'Your Serene

Highness' upon first being introduced, then 'Sir' or 'Ma'am' afterward. As a general rule, stand when royalty enters a room, sit only after they have sat. Speak only when spoken to. They will dismiss you. When you have worked your way through the receiving line, you will be ushered to your table. Remember these simple rules and you will do fine. I will be back for you, Miss Burska, at exactly 6:45 this evening to escort you to the Great Ballroom. Please be ready. We do not keep the royal family waiting. Ever.

Recalling the male adviser's prompt during her palace orientation earlier that afternoon, Sofia sank onto the bed, and pulled a steadying breath. Almost at once, she popped off the king-size brass bed, her hands flying to her mouth to muffle the cry of distress.

How could she have sat so...so disrespectfully on the white spread dripping with Italian lace? Her gaze lifted to the gauze canopy sheltering the bed, drifted over the Queen Anne antique furniture decorating the bedroom, scanned the dusty-rose-and-silver carpet matching the chintz throw pillows on the two cushioned love seats on either side of the coffee table, the Tiffany lamps, the white-gilt writing desk. The room had decidedly feminine touches.

The room had decidedly feminine touches fit for a princess.

But Sofia Burska was no princess.

Sofia brought her arms to fold at her waist, and drawing her bottom lip through her teeth, she considered her blessing.

Perhaps, just this once, she could indulge herself and enjoy the blessing bestowed upon her. Perhaps, just this once, she could roll with the scene unfolding before her and allow herself to be pampered. Perhaps, just this once, she could permit herself to let go of her usual no-nonsense attitude toward life and pretend.

Pretend she was Cinderella going to the ball. Pretend Prince Charming would sweep her off her glass-slippered feet and carry her off to their Happy-Ever-After Castle.

Pretend she was royal, or at least, noble, like the aristocratic women who'd be vying for Stefano's eye.

Her chest tightened and she felt a blush coming on. "That's *Prince* Stefano to you. So stop thinking of him in casual terms. There is nothing casual about the man. He's a prince. You're an ordinary working girl. He's not now, nor will he ever be, interested in you in a romantic way."

Sofia felt her blush deepen, yet she lifted her chin. "So stop being as flighty as the readers of the society pages." She would go take a shower and wash her hair. She would take extra care in applying her makeup. She would wear the ball gown the princess had sent to her room. She would act in a gracious manner and attend the state dinner in the Great Ballroom.

And she would make certain she returned to her bedroom in Bellaterra Castle before the stroke of midnight, before her carriage could return to its rightful appearance of a pumpkin.

And she would make flight arrangements, as soon as possible, to return to her rightful world, the world of a working girl with a debt to repay, of a girl hailing from a middle class family in a middle class neighborhood, of a girl who so was not princess material.

"And you'd best remember that," she admonished. "Better yet, stop these fanciful dreams you're all of a sudden conjuring up." She decided the castle with all its glamor and grandeur played havoc with her down-to-earth mindset. The sooner she returned to normalcy, the better. "Oh," she gasped, when stepping into the private bathroom, she saw the charming claw-foot tub and a sink with a skirt. Unable to resist, she peeked beneath and saw exposed plumbing. Raising her head, she stared at her reflection in the mirror hanging over the sink. "This is all so surreal," she whispered, shaking her head.

And it got more surreal when a maid arrived to help her dress in the gown, satin high-heeled sandals, and what had to be Mondoverde's royal family's jewels.

Sofia stared at herself in the full-length mirror, her eyes and lips rounded in wonder.

"Oh, miss, you look beautiful." The maid's words held a reverential tone.

Sofia shifted her astonished gaze from her reflection to the maid. Their eyes met and held in the mirror. "Who *is* this person looking back at us?"

The maid giggled. "She is the belle of the ball, miss. I will get that," she added in response to the knock on the door to her suite.

Sofia continued to study the *belle of the ball*, in total shock.

How she dazzled and shone in the ravishing evening dress in the color of soft mauve. The v-neckline bodice had thick straps and shimmered with a decadent array of eye-catching rhinestone and crystal adornments. The full-length skirt, fitted at the waist, gradually flared, floating to the floor in a stunning silhouette look. The only jewelry she wore were the rhinestones on her ears and a matching bracelet on her wrist.

The benevolence of Princess Cristina. Sofia's throat thickened, closed tight. What had she done to earn the benevolence of Princess Cristina? To be given this once-in-a-lifetime shot at being…a princess, a make-believe princess, but nevertheless, a princess.

"Miss?" The maid had reentered the bedroom and now handed Sofia the clutch purse. "It is time."

With a slow nod of her head and something coursing through her veins, whether fear or excitement, she didn't know, she followed the maid into the sitting room where the adviser stood waiting, his hands clasped in front of him.

His deadpan expression altered. A gradual smile worked his mouth. Admiration lit his gaze. "*Bellissima*," he breathed, and held out his arm. "Shall we go, Miss

Burska?"

Fortified by his approval, she took his elbow, and within minutes was delivered at the Great Ballroom. But when the two palace guards, standing sentinel on either side of the tall double doors of rich walnut, moved to open them for her, Sofia clutched at the adviser's arm, feeling her stomach tense.

"*Coraggio*. Be brave." He patted her hand before disengaging himself. "You will do fine, Miss Burska." In her ears, he murmured, "They may have position and power, but they are human beings created by God who serve God in their position and power." On those words of wisdom, he winked and turned and retraced his steps.

With the double doors held open, Sofia sucked in a breath, and when she stepped into the ballroom, the breath she held swooshed out of her mouth at the grandeur of the white-and-gold walled room. Her awestruck eyes flitted everywhere. *So this is how the other side lives?*

The fading sunlight streamed through the twelve floor-to-ceiling arched windows. The Italian marble floors shone to a brilliance. Thousands of Swarovski crystals sparkled from the three huge chandeliers hanging from the frescoed ceiling.

Men, in the austere black and white of formal evening clothes, radiated power and prestige. The women, in haute couture ball dresses and priceless tiaras, earrings and necklaces, glittered beneath the light from the gilded chandeliers.

The differences between them and herself were clearly defined.

And in the receiving line, the princely family of Mondoverde stood, very regal, very resplendent in their royal attire, and with a calm confidence that came from wealth, from position. Princess Cristina wearing a glittering tiara and a magnificent gown in emerald green. The man beside her, her husband, Prince Alessandro, in a black tuxedo and black bow tie. Their four sons, likewise in formal dress. All breathtakingly handsome. But none could supersede Prince Stefano II, Crown Prince of the Principality of Mondoverde.

He was simply gorgeous.

Sofia wished she didn't find him so attractive. To date, she had never gone goo-goo-eyed at any man, no matter how good looking his face was, no matter how well built his body was, no matter how sexy his aura was. She didn't like she found herself succumbing to his potent male charms.

She didn't like it one little bit.

In his black tux and purple sash, Stefano looked exactly what he was. A prince born to position, power, and prestige. A prince born to rule the country one day as its sovereign ruler. A prince in need of a royal princess wife and mother.

Sofia did not belong in this venue. She needed to get out of here. Now.

But before she could make good on her escape, she heard Princess Cristina say, "*Signorina* Burska, you have arrived."

In her peripheral vision, she noticed Stefano whip his face to her, his eyes cold and shuttered.

CHAPTER 5

"Prince Alessandro," Stefano's mother said with a wink at Sofia. "This is my *cara amica* from Canada, Sofia Burska."

"Good friend?" Stefano spluttered. Since when? When had his mother and the reporter met? And why didn't he know about it? Why had Tonino not informed him? Clamping down on his jaw muscles, he made a mental note to question his trusted servant at the earliest opportunity. Even if that meant immediately following the state dinner. Whether Tonino was off duty or not.

"Sofia." His mother broke with protocol by stepping out of the receiving line to come stand alongside Sofia, causing Stefano's brow to arch in disbelief. "I would like you to meet my husband, Prince Alessandro, the ruling sovereign of the Principality of Mondoverde." Then she further astonished Stefano by resting a hand on Sofia's shoulder.

His mother never, ever, touched another person in public.

No royal touched another person in public in such an open display of familiarity. Ever. It...just wasn't done. Ever.

And the shocks just kept on rolling in.

His father scanned Sofia's face with astute, penetrating eyes, watching her make a clumsy curtsy. "So you are the young lady my wife spoke to me about?" He held out a hand in greeting, an indulgent smile on his lips as Sofia hesitated, obviously uncertain as to protocol. "I am very, very happy to meet you, *Signorina*."

His father was *very, very happy* to meet her? Stefano's brows met together in the middle of his forehead in a frown. His perplexity only intensified when he witnessed his father take Sofia's fingers in his and raise her hand to his lips for a continental kiss.

"Welcome to *Castello di Bellaterra*." Prince Alessandro did not release Sofia's hand, but held onto it like a patient and loving father. In public!

"Thank you, Your Serene Highness."

Stefano heard the hesitancy in Sofia's voice, the formality. And he found himself hating both.

"I understand from my wife you mentioned to her my son here—" Alessandro spun his gaze to Stefano standing at his side. The wicked gleam shining in the blue depths made Stefano's blood pound in every part of his body. "—has recommended you visit our ruins." Addressing Sofia, he went on, "We have both Greek and Roman ruins. They are—" He brought the thumb and both the index and middle fingers of his free hand together to his mouth in a noisy kiss.

His father, His Serene Highness, Prince Alessandro of Mondoverde, the *ruling* prince of their island nation, just made a kissing sound? In public? Had the man gone mad? He made that sound in public? A royal, his father well knew, stayed a royal forever, and was watched and dissected without restraint. A prince…or princess…couldn't be born or die without the multitudes in attendance. The royal family was always held under a microscope. Especially at a state function. And his father just made that kissing sound? In public?

"—magnificent. You must see them. In fact—" Alessandro turned to Stefano, the gleam in his eyes becoming more pronounced. His father didn't bother to make even a token effort at disguising his amusement. "My son will clear his appointments for tomorrow and he will do Mondoverde the honor of escorting you, *Signorina*, a *cara amica* of my wife, on a grand tour of our lovely country, will you not, Prince Stefano?"

Stefano wanted to argue. He wanted to yell a resounding 'no' to the request. Request? Try a subtle order. He wanted to shout, *The* cara amica *is a reporter! And I don't do reporters. Unless I have carefully choreographed the press conference to my specifications.*

"Oh, no, Your Serene Highness," Sofia gasped. "Prince Stefano is a busy man." A blush painted her cheeks, but she refused to look in Stefano's direction.

Which annoyed him. An unexpected, uncalled-for flare of desire swept through him, irritating him all the more. He wasn't supposed to be attracted to *this* woman. She was a reporter.

"He—he can't just drop everything to take me sightseeing." Now her worried gaze did fall to him before rebounding on his father.

Stefano didn't want her afraid of him. But neither did he want to spend any considerable time in her presence. *He* was afraid of *her*? The strange and irrational thought broke onto his brain and his irritation grew, tensing his jaw muscles.

"Yes, he can," his father replied, in an equitable tone. "Though it is true, as the hereditary prince, he has many obligations and serious responsibilities he will have to shoulder for the rest of his life, it is also true, life happens and scatters all the carefully planned appointments into the Mondoverduvian sky for the wind to toss and tumble at will. What I say is true, is it not, Prince Stefano?" His eyes crinkled with amusement.

"Yes," Stefano forced the word through his tight jaw, and gave a curt nod.

"And you—" His father smiled down at Sofia's pained expression. "—are a life happening, as a good friend of Her Serene Highness, Princess Cristina." He sent Stefano a mischievous glance. "So you will conduct your mother's good friend on a personal tour tomorrow, yes?"

"Yes, Your Serene Highness." Stefano's jaw ached from

the pressure of grinding his teeth. Tension had now settled in his shoulders and began to stiffen his entire body.

His father's brow arched at the formality, but he made no comment. "Good. It is settled." Alessandro patted Sofia's hand and finally released it. "I want to hear your impressions of our country." Turning to his wife, he suggested, "Perhaps an intimate family dinner tomorrow night, *cara*? What do you think?"

Princess Cristina did another no-no for royalty in public. She slipped an arm around Sofia's waist. "I think that is a wonderful idea." She beamed a smile at Alessandro.

When Sofia was allowed to move on, she stood, with a tension-filled expression on her face, in front of Stefano, and made another inelegant attempt at a curtsy. "Your Serene Highness," she said, unable to keep the stress from her voice.

A tense silence hung between them.

He greeted her by meeting her eyes and holding her gaze for a long time. Everyone else broke with protocol. So... He took her hand, bowed over it, and kissed it. And felt an intimate warmth fill him at her soft, barely audible gasp. What were all these conflicting emotions he suffered all of a sudden? A sigh. Then in a low voice, he said, "Miss Burska, I hope you have an enjoyable evening."

"Thank you, sir, I shall." She looked like she wanted to add something else. She seemed to be entertaining an inner battle. But in the end, she reached some resolve and merely attempted a barely there quirk of the lips that quickly faded as a shadow of tension slid over her features.

He bent his head in an autocratic nod, signaling she may move on. And when she did, his annoyance knew no bounds as a coil of anxiety and anger mingled in his stomach. He drew his brows into a scowl and he tried to battle back the tightening in his stomach, but watching his brothers, one by one, bend over Sofia's fingers in a kiss drove him to jealousy.

Jealousy!

He, the Crown Prince of Mondoverde, felt jealousy.

Because of his brothers. Because they had kissed her fingers in a very European manner. Innocent kisses. And yet, he felt the jealousy.

It burned deep within him where no one else could see.

He had no right to feel this raw, almost painful longing, for this woman. An exclusive longing for this woman.

She was as off-limits to him as a woman could get. She was a reporter. And he would be wise to remember the pertinent facts.

Stefano clung to his irritation while he silently watched Sofia work her way down the receiving line, freely giving her smile to everyone.

To Cristiano, Lorenzo, and Maximillian, his brothers. To Princess Milana, his aunt. To Prince Stefano I and Princess Alessia, his grandparents. To Princess Daniela and her brother, Prince Giorgio, his great-aunt and great-uncle.

But she'd had no warm smile for him.

He forced his gaze away from her in an effort to maintain his equilibrium.

Maintain his equilibrium?

Now there was a royal farce if ever Stefano heard one.

* * *

She shrieked a laugh, causing every head to turn.

Including Stefano's.

He'd been trying to ignore Sofia all evening. But he'd been acutely sensitive to her presence. He'd refused to let his gaze find her at her assigned table during the seven-course dinner. But he'd been enormously aware of her presence. He'd overruled his inclination to follow her whereabouts on the shining marble floors as she whirled passed on the arms of besotted men. But he'd been keenly conscious of her presence.

He'd employed all his inner reserves and had managed to ignore her all evening.

But now, her spontaneous and infectious laughter ringing out into the Great Ballroom, he whipped his head in her direction. With grim amusement, he watched her chuckling at something her current dance partner—his own brother, the incorrigible and charismatic youngest brother, Prince Maximillian—said. The stem of Stefano's wineglass almost snapped beneath his irritated grip.

Max was only twenty, but his reputation with the female population was legendary. Unlike Cristiano who was serious about his governmental post, unlike Lorenzo who was serious about his horses, Max was serious about women, young and old and everything in between. And now he appeared to be seriously flirting with Sofia. While his eyes narrowed to slits and his lips firmed to a stern line, Stefano forced his clenched fingers to relax, one by one, and set the glass on the table with a controlled thump. And out of harm's way.

"Prince Stefano. Prince Stefano!"

The voice irked him. But drawing on a lifetime of training, he schooled his countenance into a passive yet pleasant expression, and turned to the woman seated beside him. And frowned.

"Prince Stefano, you have not heard a word I have said." The woman, poured into a skintight, low-cut cocktail dress and wearing a mountain of makeup which gave her a ghastly guise and whose name he could not wrench from him memory banks no matter how he searched, laid a red-tipped hand on his forearm, obviously not apprised of the royal rule to never touch a member of the monarchial family in public, and like a chastened recalcitrant child, pouted.

Heard what she said? He could not hear anything over the fury creating a buzz in his ears. "I apologize, Miss…?"

"Miss?" The woman looked affronted, which, in Stefano's opinion, much improved her facial appearance. "I am Lady Charlotte Beresford of Great Britain." She angled her chin, flicked him a censorious stare. "Your Serene Highness," she added in an equally censorious tone, as if to say, *If I can respect you by knowing who you are, you should afford me the same courtesy.*

"I apologize, Lady Charlotte." Stefano returned his scrutiny to the dance floor. Within a microsecond, he located Sofia, still in Max's arms. When she glanced over his brother's shoulders and their eyes met, and held, he felt something almost tangible pass between them. He couldn't explain it, but it sent a sudden rush of warmth racing through his body. And he found himself unable to break the visual connection. "I have much on my mind."

"I perfectly understand, Your Highness," Lady Charlotte said, sounding mollified and somewhat willing to overlook his faux pas, at least, this time. She gave him a shoulder pat, let her hand linger and trail across his back. "A man with your title and position has many maddening distractions."

"Not many." Stefano rubbed his lower lip with the pad of his thumb, staring at Sofia through shuttered eyes. "Only one."

In a sultry voice, Charlotte said, "Allow me, Stefano, to help you relax, then." The hand on his back moved to his neck. "Oh, you are so tense, Stefano." She began what she thought to be a seductive kneading of his muscles. It was, in fact, grating to the nerves and Stefano executed great effort to not allow his body to shake in recoil. When he failed to respond to her attempts at seduction, she leaned closer and purred in his ear, "Do you want to dance?"

"Hmm? Dance? Yes." He made the split-second decision.

The risk was too great.

He knew that. He knew he had to keep an emotional distance from her. He knew he had to tamp down this almost untamed attraction he felt for her. He knew following through on this crazy idea he had would set him up for trouble. Big trouble. He knew that.

He stood, adjusted his gold cuff links with the royal seal engraved on them.

There was little room in his world for spontaneity. His world was highly structured and carefully planned. His world consisted of a schedule of appointments and royal obligations that sometimes stretched years in advance. His world was guarded and protected against real and projected threats.

He knew this risk was too great.

He recognized it with his head.

His heart, it seemed, entertained another agenda.

One he felt would be infinitely more enjoyable considering the flare of anticipation zipping through his veins at the thought of wreaking havoc on his perfect and stressful and lonely world.

"Yes, I do believe I wish to dance," Stefano murmured.

He heard Lady Charlotte say, "Wonderful," in a thrilled tone. He saw Lady Charlotte rise to her feet in a graceful movement. But it wasn't Lady Charlotte he wished to dance with.

"If you will excuse me, Lady Charlotte." He turned and stalked toward the floor of dancing couples.

One very small part of his brain registered Lady Charlotte's expressions. At first, confusion. Then shock. Finally anger.

The rest of his brain registered the overwhelming urgency he felt in extricating Sofia Burska from his brother's charming comportment and enfolding her within the protective band of his arms.

Yes, the risk was too great.

He could lose his life.

But what a way to go, he mused, stepping up to his brother and clamping a firm, nonnegotiable hand on Max's shoulder.

"I am cutting in." His voice was just as firm, just as nonnegotiable.

As the youngest and most spoilt son of Prince Alessandro and Princess Cristina of Mondoverde, Max understood, like they all did, as a royal, everything he did, everything he said, at an official function, was a matter of interest to the press and to the populace and reflected back on their parents and the throne. Now, with inbred grace and ingrained glamor, he bowed to Sofia, but scowled at him, and with a neat spin on the heels, he strode away, leaving Stefano and Sofia staring at each other.

"Shall we, Miss Burska?" He held out his hand, palm out. When her fingers slid against his, he fitted his against hers. He tugged her closely, wrapping one arm around her waist, and lifted her hand to his lips to press a kiss to her palm. He heard her quick indrawn breath. He felt her stiffen. He felt the distinct hum of attraction through his veins. "You are...*bellissima.*" He heard the words fall from his lips, rough and ragged.

Her brown eyes rounded with surprise, she whispered, "Th-thank you, Your Serene Highness. But—but this isn't me."

His lips twitched. "If you are not Sofia Burska, who are you, then?" he asked, leading her across the floor in an effortless, seamless waltz, and very much cognizant, from the speculative glances cast their way from both the men and the women, that the lady in his arms spiked interest.

She certainly spiked his interest.

There was something about her. He could not identify it, but something about her drew him to her.

Now would be a good time to remember the risk is too great, his head warned.

Now is a good time to let go of all the restraints and enjoy the world, his heart volleyed back.

Stefano may yet regret his decision, but he chose to

listen to his heart and continued dancing with this woman, holding her against him, and thoroughly enjoying the feel of her in his arms.

It was madness. Exquisite, delicious, compelling madness. Heat rushed through him. He should put an end to this madness and step away from her. He should step away from her with a fluid grace and inherent dignity. He should. He did not.

"Do I need to call security? Or will you kidnap me before I can alert the palace guards of the breach in security?" Though he grinned down at her, he was too conscious of their bodies touching in the rhythmical dance, too conscious of her sweet, soft scent swirling around him, too conscious of the fact she fit so perfectly in his arms, like she was tailor-made for him. Too conscious of his fast-growing fascination with this woman.

Too conscious of this temptation.

Maybe he should signal for the *Corpo della Guardia*. It was their duty to protect the royal family. And he was in desperate need of protection. His hand at the base of her spine applied subtle pressure, persuading her body into a closer fit with his. Odd, but it was like he could not get close enough to her, could not get enough of her. Odd, very odd.

"N-no, of course, you don't have to call in your watchdogs. You're safe with me, Your Serene Highness."

"Safe?" Stefano said, his teeth clenched, his blood pressure climbing toward quadruple digits. Somehow Stefano doubted he was safe.

"What I meant to say was I don't wear haute couture dresses and expensive family jewelry. I don't have haute couture dresses and expensive family jewelry," she added, matter-of-factly. "Your mother—I mean, Princess Cristina—she…" Sofia gave him a careful, guarded look before glancing down at her clothes, her cheeks turning the color of a fine rose wine. "It was the Princess's idea to invite me tonight. I tried to dissuade her, really I did, but she is very—"

"Determined," Stefano finished for her, grinning.

"I would have said politely, diplomatically…" Sofia drew her bottom lip through her teeth, the blush on her cheeks deepening.

"Determined, as I said, particularly if she believes she is one hundred percent right in whatever she is thinking." His grin broadened. "It is a vice of the royal family." He lifted his shoulders and added, "We always get our own way."

"Yes, I see that." Her words held a wry resonance. She took a breath and plunged on. "Your Serene Highness, I apologize my presence here has caused you any discomfort."

His blood pressure spiked another ten points. "Discomfort?" His voice sounded deeper than normal and raw with emotion. And desire. And with his unsuccessful attempts to shove that desire down. Had she guessed at the crazy machinations of his mind?

Mind? his brain launched an immediate defense. *Not me. I tried to warn you, but* you *listened to that traitor, the heart.*

I am not a traitor, the heart countered. *I know when something or some*one *is right and I go for it.*

Sofia nodded fiercely. "In—in the receiving line, you looked…"

Stefano bored her eyes with his. "What, Sofia? You do not dare to stop now. Tell me." When she remained silent and hesitant, he said, "If it will make you feel better, then I order you."

"You what?"

"I order you to speak your mind."

"Order me?" she spluttered. "You can't order me. I'm not one of your subjects."

"You are in my country. Therefore I can—and will—order you."

"You say that with the certainty of one who has the power to change reality, who *always* has his own way."

"I am Prince Stefano, Crown Prince of Mondoverde. I *do* have power. And I *always* get my own way. I have already explained. It is a vice of the royal family. Now." He grinned at her, but there was a churning going on in the pit of his stomach.

He was so afraid he would do something he should not. Like kiss her. Right here, right now. No, he would not give in to the temptation. He could not give in to the temptation.

Because he knew one kiss would not suffice. He would want more. So much more.

And because he had not dated in five years, not because he wanted to remain celibate, but he had not had the time to be with a woman. His royal responsibilities had precluded any dalliances.

And right now, this woman, this very beautiful woman was in his arms and their almost intimate dancing reminded him he was a man. A man with needs. His body reacted with a fierce intensity to this woman and his need of her.

No, he will not touch her. No, he will not kiss her. No, he will not entertain any lustful ideas about her.

He was raised to be noble and a real Christian man.

He *will* treat her with respect, with dignity.

"How did I look in the receiving line?" he gritted through his teeth.

Sofia hesitated, chomped down on her lip, something Stefano noticed she did quite often. When she felt nervous. He made her nervous. He wanted to make her feel other emotions, not nervousness. Other emotions. Like…passion. He raised his hand, the one threaded with hers, to his chest, and pressed her palm against his erratic-beating heart. The passion she stirred in him with such innocence, he wanted to whisk into an inferno in her with such doggedness. And that lip she mutilated… He wanted to brush it with his own lips, lick it with his tongue, nip it with his teeth…

All he had to do was dip his head just a fraction and he could taste those lips.

He kept his neck muscles rigid and forced his eyes off her mouth. Her scent, soft and sexy, understated yet elegant, proved harder to avoid.

Would he survive the rest of the evening?

The rest of the evening? He let his eyelids drift closed. How about the next few minutes?

He was a dead man.

He opened his eyes, took in her features. Her blond-bronze hair cut into an attractive chin-length pageboy style. Her brown eyes peeking up at him through her bangs. His mother's jewels glinting in her earlobes. He took a breath, breathed in her soft scent. His fate, he feared, was sealed.

He was a dead man.

Possessiveness swelled in him.

Could a dead man feel possessiveness?

He let go of her hand on his chest and raising his, he stroked the knuckle of his index finger against her mouth. "How did I look?" he rasped. "You may speak freely, Sofia." Why did her name sound so right on his lips? "I will not have you thrown in the dungeon for the rats to devour you."

"You don't have a dungeon. With or without rats."

"No." But he did have a bedroom with a king-size bed where *he* could devour her. *Stop this! Stop this madness! Right now!* Fiercely he tried to stifle his wayward thoughts. "So speak," he ordered, his voice thick and throaty.

"You looked…mad." Sofia looked away, looked back. "At…me."

"No." Stefano laid his hand back on hers resting against his chest, twined their fingers together. "No, I was not mad. I was…" He sucked in another steadying breath. Something he noticed he was doing quite often this evening.

"I was…surprised," he continued and coughed to clear the huskiness in his throat. "Surprised at seeing you here tonight. Surprised at you being my mother's…*cara amica*." Surprised at his parents forgetting the established protocol with commoners and especially in public. Surprised at his vehement dislike of his brother's playful teasing and harmless flirtations. "I did not know you were acquainted with my mother, much less her...*dear friend.*"

He was surprised to discover how difficult it was to remember he was noble and a good Christian man and to act like a noble and good Christian man.

This woman made him forget a lot of things. A lot of important things. Like he was destined to rule this nation and to act like the future ruler in search of the perfect princess wife and mother.

This woman made him want a lot of things. A lot of important things. Like...kissing this woman. *Stop this madness!*

When had he grown vulnerable to this woman? It was an odd feeling, not entirely comfortable, and one that caused his blood to heat to an alarming degree. His gaze dropped to her mouth, then slid up to meet her eyes. His blood pulsed harder in his veins.

"How did you meet my mother?" Was his voice destined to remain hoarse?

Sofia turned a pretty shade of pink. "I—I...ran her down."

"You ran down my mother?"

"Yes." She whirled on him and the mortification that had been in her eyes flashed away in fury. "When I stormed out of the Palace Office. After you refused to give me my interview." She took a moment to calm herself. "I wasn't looking where I stomped and I collided with her."

"You collided with Princess Cristina of the Principality of Mondoverde?" Stefano asked in mock horror.

Dropping her forehead on his shoulder, she groaned, "At the time, she failed to introduce herself as the princess." She speared him with an accusatory glare. "Obviously a trait that runs in the family."

Her witty little voice made him grin. "And when *did* she reveal her identity?"

"Later in her apartment." The pink on her cheeks deepened to a crimson. "I'd mistaken her for…"

"Let me guess." He grinned. "You thought Princess Cristina was…staff."

"Well, you guys don't exactly act like reserved and haughty royalty. At least, not when it suits you," she muttered.

"You guys?" Stefano lifted his haughty eyebrow and firmed the twitch threatening his royal lips. "Such disrespect," he mock-chided. "It is a well-known fact, Miss Burska, when a person insults a royal, they are disciplined in a variety of ways. For example, King Henry VIII had his second wife, Anne Boleyn, arrested and taken to the Tower of London and executed. You, Miss Burska, need not worry," he reassured her in a dry voice. "We do not have such a tower here on Mondoverde."

"Lucky for me."

He tsk-tsked. "Still showing your disrespect?" He released an exaggerated sigh. "You leave me, then, with no alternative, Miss Burska, but to have the *Corpo della Guardia* arrest you and throw you in our dungeon."

"You don't have a dungeon," Sofia singsonged at him.

"I do not?" Stefano worked his forehead into a pretend-frown.

"No, you do not."

"You are certain?"

"Yes, I am."

"How?"

"You admitted it yourself minutes earlier. Plus—" A sensual smile broke out on her soft pink lips.

The need to kiss those lips reared up again, more powerful, more demanding. Stefano didn't think he would be able to stop himself from taking advantage of the tempting situation. His noblest intentions were being defeated, fast.

"—your mother told me." Her eyes danced with humor.

And something, more powerful, more demanding than his need to kiss this woman rose up within him. He grinned, then chuckled, then laughed, in public.

An amazing sense of wonder filled him. He could scarcely remember what his life had been like before this commoner, this Canadian had arrived at Bellaterra Castle. His laugh downgraded back to a chuckle, reduced to a grin. Then the grin fell off his face.

As they stared at each other, the awareness between them pulsed into life. The air between them buzzed with electricity. Some strange energy swirled around them. He saw the alarm enter into her beautiful brown eyes. Alarm that had to find its reflection in his own eyes.

"It's—it's late, Your Serene Highness," Sofia breathed. "I think I shall return to my room. I—I have—your mother—Princess Cristina gave me the—the Boaz and Ruth room. Here—I mean up—upstairs. Good night, Your Highness."

"Stop right there." His autocratic tone arrested her from her flight of escape. "First, stop calling me that."

A frown wrinkled her forehead. "Your Serene Highness?"

"That right there. Do not call me *Your Serene Highness*. Call me by my given name. Stefano. And a second thing, Sofia." Her name whispered off his tongue. "I shall escort you back to your room."

"That's not necessary, Your—I mean, Stefano. I can find my way."

"That is what is not necessary. You finding your way when I will take you. Do not argue with me, Sofia," he warned her, his tone stern. He crooked his arm, raised his brow, and gave a smile of approval when she slipped her fingers around his elbow. "*Bene.*" He led her along wide corridors, up marble steps back to her room. Outside her door, he said, "I will come for you at nine o'clock tomorrow morning for our excursion."

"Y—Stefano, please, don't feel obligated to take me out on a tour of your country."

"I do not feel obligated, *cara*," he murmured. "I feel honored."

"Thank you. I look forward then to seeing your charming island."

"I must, however, insist on one rule." He couldn't help himself. He had to touch her. He stroked a fingertip down her cheek. Soft. Just as he knew it would be. Her skin was soft as satin. "Tomorrow you will pretend to not be a journalist."

"But—"

"You will leave your reporter instincts here in this room. There will be no—how did you say it? Ah, yes—exclusive interview." He wound a finger through a lock of her hair, and pulled her toward him with it. Yes, it, too, was soft, soft as spun silk. "And anything we will talk about is not to find its way into your newspaper. Agreed?"

She puffed out her cheeks. "Agreed," she answered on a frustrated exhale of air.

"*Bene*. Good night, Sofia."

"Good night, Stefano," she whispered. "And thank you for tonight. I felt like Cinderella at the Ball."

Sofia bit her lower lip, then suddenly stepped close and slipped both her arms around his neck. He went rigid. She planted a kiss on his mouth, too quick and too light and before he could think what to say or do, she pulled back and dashed into her room.

He stood where she left him for a long, long time.

The woman messed with his head. Stefano had tried to exercise control. But the woman messed with his head. He blew out a ragged breath. The woman messed with whatever brain cells were still functioning in the bloodless zone of his brain. His heart, meanwhile, beat an ecstatic tattoo against his chest wall.

CHAPTER 6

Dawn's first light awoke Sofia with a sense of expectancy. And why not? Today's blessings would continue on the heels of yesterday's.

Unable or unwilling to rein in her excitement, she shouted, "Good morning, Abba Father! Good morning, Lord Jesus! Good morning, Holy Spirit! This is the day You have made and I shall rejoice and be glad in it." And she would have absolutely no problem in rejoicing this day. A satisfied smile curling her lips, she slid deeper in the satin sheets, and folding her arms at the back her neck, she stared at the gauze canopy overhead, her gaze reflective, dreamy.

Last night, not only had she worn a beautiful ball gown and the royal family's jewels, not only had she danced with the very handsome Prince Charming, alias Prince Stefano, in the Great Ballroom, not only had her carriage not turned back into a pumpkin at the stroke of midnight, not only had her prince—her prince?

When had she started thinking of the Crown Prince of Mondoverde as *her* prince? Her smile trembled on her mouth, a frown drew her brows together, then by a sheer act of her will, she smoothed out her forehead and made her lips reclaim the smile and continued with her delicious memories.

Not only had Prince Stefano walked her to her room, but outside her bedroom door, he'd affirmed it was his honor—his honor!—to escort *her* on a tour of his country. Her, Sofia Burska, the commoner and foreigner.

And then the kiss.

Sofia let her eyelids drift closed. She felt a blush heat her skin at the exquisite memory. She had no idea what had come over her last night. She hadn't been under the influence of the expensive Italian wine that had flowed freely because she'd only had a few sips. She pressed a hand to her mouth, suppressing a giggle. But one second, she'd been her usual no-nonsense-feet-planted-firmly-in-reality Sofia Burska. Okay. She's been a little starry-eyed at her surreal surroundings, she admitted. And the next, she'd morphed into a bold and brash woman, a so very un-Sofia-like woman, one who without thinking, went up on her toes and kissed — kissed! — the prince.

She laughed, a chiming sound, joyous, and no getting around it, brazenly bold and brash.

She felt so alive. So amazingly alive.

All those dazzling women in designer gowns and glittering diamonds last night, and she, Sofia, would be the woman to spend today, the entire day, with Stefano. The giggle bubbled up her throat and escaped through her lips.

In a flash, a cloud rolled over the morning sun, dimming the sunshine.

In one fell swoop, a cloud glided over her heart, stealing her happiness.

She trod on dangerous ground here, so she'd better perform a reality check, and fast.

Today's excursion was simply Stefano mollifying his parents. Stefano entertained no romantic aspirations toward her. Stefano was royalty.

She…an ordinary person.

And worse. Much worse in Stefano's estimation.

An ordinary person making — or, at least, trying to make — a living at what Stefano considered the ignoble profession of sensational, and if possible, scandalous journalism.

Nothing, *nothing* can come out of this, she scolded herself as she threw off the white, lacy spread and swung her feet to the carpeted floor. Something twinged in her chest. Something she could not—or would not?—identify.

She'd best remember Stefano's station in life and her own. Two worlds set far apart, as different as spring blossoms on the trees are the antithesis of branches weighed down in ice and snow.

A morose mood pursuing her, Sofia trudged to the ensuite bathroom. She eyed the charming tub with longing, but opted for a brief shower instead, hoping the pulsing jets of water striking her head, her chest would beat back the uncalled-for and unwanted gloom assaulting her.

She had no reason to feel this somber mood.

She adjusted the water to an invigorating cool. She hadn't come to Mondoverde looking for romance, and certainly not for the happy-ever-after of the Cinderella fame. She may have worn the appearance of Cinderella last night, but she suffered no illusions. She knew who—what—she was. And she was no princess.

She was no princess who'd stolen the prince's heart.

And she'd left no glass slipper calling card behind to identify her as Stefano's forever princess.

Sofia stepped beneath the pulsating cascades and sucked in a startled breath. What was this sudden and peculiar obsession she had for Stefano? For…the magical world he promised? Tilting back her head, she let the water strike her face with stinging hits. It must be the residual effects of the glee, the glitter, and the glamor of the fairy-tale night, she reasoned. She'd come to Mondoverde looking for an interview. With Stefano. That's all. Nothing more. And indeed, not anything along the line of the fairy-tale-ish. No.

Her aspirations for utilizing this interview to spring board her, catapulting her into a more distinguished class of journalism, had died a mortifying blow with her failure to secure the one-on-one with Stefano. She knew, with absolute certainty, her editor would rant and rave at her for failing in the simple assignment to produce the article of interest on

Stefano like any respectable news correspondent worth his or her weight in journalistic gold would.

Still she had no reason to feel this solemn mood.

She was a committed Christian who read the Bible daily, who attended church services weekly, who communed with her Lord in prayer continually, who grew and wanted to keep growing in her spiritual maturity.

She had even less reason to succumb to the sepulchral mood.

Stretching out her hand, she turned off the showering water and stepped out of the glass-and-brass stall. Bending at the waist, she turbaned her hair, then reached for another ultra-soft, oversized towel. She wrapped the exquisite and superthick towel around her, toga-style, tucking it beneath her armpits, and moaned at the ultimate in pampering, the sumptuous in post-shower experience.

Sofia might not be princess material, but she could enjoy this decadent indulgence for as long as it lasted.

She had no illusions.

After today's sightseeing trip, she'd be booking her flight back to Toronto. And face an irate employer. Perhaps a demotion, like writing the obituaries. She pulled a face. Maybe the disciplinary action would take the form of a dismissal, and she'd be joining the ranks of the unemployed.

Her front teeth biting down on her bottom lip, she moved to stand at the sink to give her reflection in the mirror a critical study.

"Do not worry about the loan repayment," she ordered out loud, aware, painfully aware her heart beat at an increasingly alarming rate. "Worry, any sort of pace-the-floor, can't-sleep-at-night worry is not useful because it changes nothing. Right, Lord? Worry doesn't solve a single problem."

Dropping her chin to her chest, she squeezed her eyelids shut. "I know You're stretching my faith muscles, Lord. I know You're a big God who can do big things. I know I should take my physical eyes off my financial problem —

one of those 'cares of this world' that You said would choke out the Word in my life, and look to You with my spiritual eyes. I know it's not only a sin to not trust You, but it's unbelief. I know by worrying, I'm actually saying You are incapable of helping me, incapable of looking after the practical details of my life. I know I should be saying, 'Let's see how You plan on dealing with this situation.' I know all this, but I gotta tell You, Lord, I'm kinda wavering here."

In order to pursue her post secondary school education, Sofia had applied for and received a student loan from the Canadian government. But when the six-month non-repayment period ended following her graduation, the Student Financial Assistant Branch of the government wanted its loan repaid.

The government was not compassionate. The government was not flexible. The government was not interested in anything other than getting their money back, with interest, and on time.

She knew, if worse came to worse, she could go to her parents, her brothers for a bail out. But, it was a matter of pride. Not in a bad sense. But in a I-want-to-feel-good-about-achieving-my-own-goals-by-my-own-efforts. Was that so wrong?

Sofia opened her eyes, lifted her face, stared at her reflection. "Help me to believe, Lord. I'm human. I need help. Help me to trust You," she whispered. "To trust You to take me through my stormy boat ride to the other side, to safety, to victory." *To the next rung in my faith ladder.*

In the silence that followed her prayerful plea, she heard the whisper to her heart. Remembered words. Timely scriptures.

Therefore I tell you, do not worry about your life...Consider the ravens: They do not sow or reap, they have no storeroom or barn; yet God feeds them. And how much more valuable you are than birds! Who of you by worrying can add a single hour to your life?...Consider how the wild flowers grow. They do not labor or spin. Yet I tell you, not even Solomon in all his splendor was dressed like one of these. If that is how God clothes the grass of the field, which is here today, and tomorrow is thrown into the fire, how much more will he clothe you...your Father knows that you need them. But seek His kingdom, and these things will be given to you as well.

"'But seek His kingdom,'" she repeated, her reflection throwing back a thoughtful gaze. "I'll try, Lord, I'll try," she promised on an exhale of air and reached for her makeup bag.

Pausing in the act of unzipping the bag, she let her eyes roam over the image in the mirror, and debated with her inner woman. The one who urged her to paint the barn. To make herself attractive.

Why? her brain grilled.

Because he's the prince, her heart cooed.

So? persisted her brain.

We want him to notice, her heart explained, the personification of patience.

Like he'd really notice a commoner, her brain replied, mockery lacing the words.

"Stop!" Sofia covered her ears with her hands and started to hum. But the voices grew louder, became more insistent, more determined to be heard. And have the last word.

He's not blind, her heart piped up.

He's also not stupid, her brain shot back.

Sofia grabbed the eyeliner, her only concession to makeup today, and with a couple of quick strokes darkened her eyelashes, her brown eyes widening when the tune she hummed registered.

"The Look of Love."

* * *

Stefano swore.

"Your Serene Highness must be very upset this morning

to use four languages to express your...displeasure," Tonino intoned, his expression impassive.

Stefano clutched the cup of coffee with his left hand and jammed the file folder bearing the gold embossed seal of the Mondoverduvian Coat of Arms beneath his arm, trapping it to his side, before sending a glare at his trusted servant. Using his free hand, he threw open the glass doors to his private balcony overlooking the east end of the palace grounds, and charging through them, he drank in air like water.

It was too bad he only spoke four languages, Italian and English, the official languages of Mondoverde, and French and the Sabine dialect of L'Aquila. Five languages if he counted Latin. He slammed the file folder on the small wrought iron table and cursed again when the hot coffee sloshed over the rim to scald his hand. Had he spoken more languages, he fumed in silence, setting the cup down and drying his fingers on the napkin he pulled out of his pants pocket, he would have expressed his *displeasure* in any and all languages known to man. He tossed an irritated glance over his shoulder at Tonino, correctly interpreting the gleam of humor in his eyes. His irritation growing, he strode over to the stone balustrade, and slapping both hands on it, he stared down at the floral garden below and the lush green lawn beyond. But it wasn't the garden and the lawn he saw.

Stefano saw a face. A woman's face. The same woman's face that had haunted his night. The woman's face that had stolen his sleep. The woman's face, that after making him toss and turn during the long, sleepless hours, had greeted him good morning when he'd lifted open his eyelids, given up on trying to sleep, and gotten out of bed, before even the birds had awakened and begun chirping.

Stefano saw the face of Sofia Burska. And scowled.

Anger. He felt anger toward her. He spun his gaze to

Tonino, and saw the twinkle in his eyes become more pronounced. The anger he'd felt at being treated to a sleepless night doubled.

"Your parents were somewhat…" Tonino considered his words with care. "…intrigued you did not return to the Great Ballroom."

A harsh laugh caught in Stefano's throat. He hadn't bothered to return to the Ballroom because the evening had ceased to interest him after Sofia had left him standing in the hallway outside her bedroom door feeling… needy…desperate…confused.

Grunting some unintelligible response, he stormed to the table and slammed his body into the chair. He downed the hot liquid in one, long gulp, hoping it would scald his throat, thereby giving him something else to occupy his mind, something that would chase a certain woman's face from his sleep-deprived brain.

"The ladies…" Tonino cleared his throat with a delicate cough. "…were understandably upset at your, shall we say, disappearance, Your Highness." Ignoring Stefano's bad-tempered shrug, Tonino intoned, "They had hoped to…win your affections last night." At Stefano's heated mutter, Tonino's lips twitched once, then firmed. "Or at the very least, be photographed with you."

"Wishful thinking," Stefano muttered under his breath. "And enjoy the prestige of having their names matched to mine," he spat out, grabbing the file folder. "And spinning stories about our *association* so far from the truth it would be laughable if it wasn't so disgusting." He wrenched open the folder and shuffled through the report.

"There is always speculation about princes, even when there is no basis for it, Your Highness."

"I am well aware of that, Tonino," he said through clenched teeth. Painfully. "But it does not mean I have to like it." And he did not, even though he knew it came with the royal territory. "When I was younger, the… attention…

was appreciated." He gave his aide a mocking grin. "It has grown very tedious," he continued, losing his smile, "to open a newspaper and find a picture of myself with some woman, and no matter how innocent the association, some fantasy story has been spun way out of bounds." He ground his teeth together with such force, his jaw ached.

"Then, sir, you might want to look at this." Tonino held out the *Il Messaggero di Mondoverde*, then quietly bowed and left Stefano alone.

He felt the grinding leave his mouth and plunge into his stomach. Cautiously, carefully, he unfolded the newspaper. His eyes narrowed and a muscle in his jaw tensed. There on the front page was a full blown picture of him at the State Dinner last night, dancing with Sofia. It looked less like they were dancing and more like they were connected in a passionate embrace. The photographer did a superb job at capturing their expressions.

"*Dio mio,*" he rasped out, studying their faces. Their eyes. Their desire-filled eyes.

He slammed the paper face down on the table and yanked himself upright in his chair. He shoved to his feet and strode to the balustrade with barely contained fury, gripping it so hard, his knuckles showed white. Damage control. Damage control was needed. He had to do damage control.

The picture was bad enough.

But the headline.

"*Dio mio,*" Stefano whispered, remembering the headline with absolute and fearful clarity.

A Commoner and a Foreigner— Has She Stolen the Heart of our Reluctant-to-Marry Prince?

* * *

Sofia glanced at her watch. Nine o'clock. "The Prince is punctual," she murmured, swiping suddenly damp palms over her jean-clad thighs, her heart thudding to a halt in her chest. Taking in a bracing breath, she smoothed down her short-sleeved blouse, and went to answer the knock on her door. When she opened it, that same breath caught in her throat.

Stefano stood looking like a Roman god in his blue jeans and black T-shirt. "*Buon giorno.*"

The morning greeting, delivered with an Italian accent, and this morning sounding very, very seductive to her ultra-sensitive ears, sent a swift shaft of feminine awareness racing through her, followed by an even stronger bolt of panic.

He stepped inside, causing her to take several hasty steps backward, caught the edge of the door in his hand, and pushed it shut behind him.

Was it proper for the prince to be with her in her private suite, alone? Surely, it must challenge some royal protocol, shouldn't it? It certainly challenged her heart which jackhammered in her chest so hard Sofia thought it would crack her wide open and vault out to skip, spring, and soar. And abandon her to her own defenses. Like she had any. She back-stepped, reminding herself to not act a total nerd.

"G-good morning, Y-your High-highness." Great. She sounded like a total nerd. "I—I'm ready." And she gave new meaning to nerdery.

Stefano moved to her side, his look slightly uneasy, as if he was unsure of himself. Or maybe it was fear she saw splashed over his countenance. Fear that her nerdiness might be contagious.

Before she could register the move, he snatched her hand, and bending gallantly over it, he kissed her fingers. Shock rolled in, disrupting her brainwaves. The earth stopped rotating on its axis. Beneath the intensity of his gaze, her skin tingled and her lungs collapsed, making breathing difficult. Then her heart—evidently it still remained in her chest—began to trip and thud and thump against her ribcage with a ferocity that assured her this time it would break free from her body. And do a joy-jig. She pulled her hand away and jerked back another step, and ordered herself to stop fantasizing that there was something more behind his kissing her knuckles than there actually was. It was simply a European display of chivalry. But his lips had lingered on her skin too long for comfort.

Those same lips, she saw now, twitched, causing her breath to catch. He was doing crazy things to her equilibrium without her consent. To her utter dismay, ragged breaths exploded from her, shaking her. While Stefano moved forward one step, she back-pedaled two, and turning a quick circle, eyes wide, and maybe a little wild, said, a little too brightly, "I'll just get my blazer. Just in case it gets windy. Or cold. Or…I'll be right back," she ended, aware she'd been babbling, and feeling downright nerdy.

He's just a man, she reminded herself as she stumbled to the sofa where she'd draped her jacket over the arm. She had to stop fretting about him being a prince. She had to stop seeing him as a prince. He *was* a prince, but still, she didn't have to get hung up over it. Yeah, right. She picked up the blazer by the collar. She'd pretend he was…

Sofia would pretend Stefano was one of her brothers. Yeah, that's what she would do. Pretend he was just like Adam or Gabriel or Simon. Another big brother. What's one more brother to add to her list, right?

Her heart wasn't buying into it. It was kicking up a mad tattoo against her chest. Somehow she managed to fight back the urge to turn around, roll up onto the balls of her feet, and touch her mouth to his, keeping the contact light and brief, just like she had the night before. Her heart screamed, *Light and brief? Not good enough. Not this time. I want more. So much more.*

Pinching her eyelids shut, she berated herself for thinking foolishness, admonished herself to *grow up*, pulled in a breath, and gathered her poise. And lost the poise the moment she turned around.

Stefano had followed her to the sofa and now stood in her personal space. Her heart almost stopped in her chest.

Too bad the groan didn't stop in her throat. She groaned out loud.

"Are you okay?" Stefano didn't smile.

"No! No, I'm not okay," Sofia wanted to shout, rapidly losing the ability to keep her hands to herself. She so wanted to grab fistfuls of his T-shirt and drag him toward her, drag his mouth to hers. What was this insanity? Instead, she forced "Just peachy" from her lips.

"Peachy?" A frown marred his forehead.

"Yeah, peachy." Then realizing he didn't understand her colloquialism, she explained, "I'm great."

"Great," Stefano tried the word on his mouth. The frown lifted. "Yes." His head moved in a slow up-and-down motion. "Yes, you are...great."

Her body tingled at the hoarseness of his voice.

Brother! Think brother! her brain yelled.

Brothers don't sound husky around their sisters, her heart singsonged with glee.

Remember who and what he is. Remember who and what you are. Sofia gave herself the silent warning. She'd almost regained her equipoise. She was just starting to congratulate herself. And then...

And then Stefano had the audacity to grin a way-too-gorgeous grin.

Oh, this was so not fair, Sofia panicked, mauling her bottom lip with her front teeth, and feeling the effects of his grin tingle all the way to her toes, anesthetizing all two hundred and six bones in her body, not to mention annihilating altogether the gray matter in her head. It was so not fair he would use such a devastating weapon on her already enfeebled state.

And how was Sofia supposed to survive this day and comport herself like a responsible, reasonably mature woman and disregard being made to feel tingly by a man she'd just met, a *prince* no less, if he would smile that lazy, sexy smile at her?

He had no right to have this effect on her. She shouldn't be so excruciatingly attracted to the man. But she shouldn't beat herself up for being a normal, feeling, living woman, either. Of course, she felt tingly around him. He was a gorgeous specimen of a man.

As a prince in a formal tux, he'd looked like a Roman god, all dazzling and delicious. As a prince in jeans and a T-shirt, he amped the dazzling and delicious *way* up and fulfilled every normal, feeling, living woman's idea of a dream. A dazzling and delicious dream.

So who wouldn't feel all tingly near him?

He probably had this effect on every member of the female race.

A hot stab of jealousy shimmied up her spine, making her wince.

She had no right to feel this sudden, tight-fisted possessiveness. He was a royal prince. She…definitely not princess material. *Remember you station in life, Sofia.* She had no claim…no hope…no right to dream the impossible dream.

Sofia turned around, ostensibly to slip on her jacket, but in reality, to try to regain her composure and foster the appearance that Stefano's many, many women on his arm and in his life, women who were beautiful, poised, and titled, didn't bother her. She wasn't beautiful, poised, and titled. She could never compete with the beautiful, poised, and titled women who lived in his world.

She didn't live in his world. She never would. So she silently told herself to stop acting like a nerd.

A surprised gasp sounded from her mouth when a masculine hand reached past her, took the jacket from her fingers, and shot her attempt at composure into exile.

"Allow me." Stefano held the blazer open for her to slip her arms into the cotton-lined sleeves.

He was just being a gentleman. It was nothing personal. It was his well-bred manners he would have displayed toward any woman. It was nothing personal. Her breath hitched in her throat.

As he pulled the jacket to her shoulders, he paused, and though Sofia didn't dare glance over her shoulder at him—she was too busy trying to control her erratic breathing—she got the distinct impression he'd lowered his head to inhale her scent. Which was absolutely ridiculous. And it only went to show the crazy collusions her brain contemplated.

But she could have sworn she'd felt his warm breath caress her neck.

"Sh-shall we go?" Sofia jerked herself out of his personal space—since Stefano made no move to remove himself from hers—sounding breathless, sporting a blush, and feeling like all kinds of a nerd.

"Are you all right?"

She blinked once, then twice, then gasped, "All right?" Did he have any idea what he did to her when he looked at her like…like…like she was the only woman in the world, the only woman in the world who mattered to him? "Yeah," she croaked out. "Of course, I am." The hoarse affirmation heated up the color in her cheeks, but did little to dispel the intense perusal of his stare. "Why—why wouldn't I be?" Unable to maintain eye contact, she whisked her gaze across the room, and nearly jumped when he linked his fingers with hers, and stroked his thumb over her palm, sending tantalizing shivers zipping through her body.

"I do not know." Stefano tucked his finger beneath her chin. "But you appear…nervous. Do I make you nervous, Sofia Burska?" he murmured. "Do not be nervous. I will keep you safe." And with maddening slowness, he lowered his lips to hers in a kiss, gentle, devoid of passion, a friendly exchange.

Safe? Hardly!

Not when Sofia felt the impact of his kiss all the way to her toenails.

CHAPTER 7

Sofia looked at him with no small measure of alarm.

No kidding, Stefano thought with more than a little inner sarcasm and a whole lot of guilt burning in his gut.

He had stepped out of line. Way out of line. He was a prince tasked with the duty of showing his charming island nation to this visitor. The job description of a tour guide did not include kissing his visitor.

He should not have kissed her. He had no right to touch her, never mind press his lips to hers in a kiss. But he could not help himself and gave in to the temptation and kissed her. When he lowered his mouth to claim hers, he had every intention of keeping the kiss light and friendly.

He just wanted to assuage his fascination. He wanted to discover what secrets her lips held. Though he had a desperate need to know if she would respond to him, like he had come to fantasize, he felt certain he could manage to keep the kiss light and friendly.

But when his lips touched hers in that light and friendly kiss, he had felt a hot flush of *something* course through his veins.

What exactly that something was he had no way of figuring it out. Not when his brain seized up in his head, relinquishing its ability to function. His heart, on the other hand, appeared to have no such problem. It functioned, all right, beating in his chest. At an alarming rate.

He told himself his heart should not be thudding so

want more. No other woman had made him want more from his life.

Dio mio.

The new revelation rocked through him.

He—he was in love with this woman.

He had only known her a handful of days and he had fallen in love with her.

How was it possible? While he had witnessed family members finding true love, he had never believed in it for himself. No woman he had dated in the past elicited such an emotion from him, so he had not expected it, had not looked for it, had not dared to believe in it.

But now he realized every woman he'd dated had served as a placeholder for the real deal. For Sofia Burska.

But what could he offer her?

If he asked her to marry him, it would mean her life would never be hers to own. She would lose all she held dear to her. Her family. Her country. Her career. Her identity.

It was too great a sacrifice to ask of her.

It was an impossible future.

The morose thought kicked him in the chest hard enough he winced.

Stefano had no choice.

He loved Sofia enough to set her free before she found herself entangled in royal life and had *her* very life sucked out of her until not even the shadow of the woman existed anymore. He would hate to see the light of her life extinguished from the demands and duties of being a royal. Not everyone could survive beneath the daunting pressures. And he could not allow her to die a slow, painful death just because he needed her with an overwhelming desperation. That would be too selfish, too inconsiderate, too greedy.

No, Stefano would exercise control and self-restraint and not think about the lonely, loveless future looming before him.

With those reminders in place between them, he should

be able to douse this insatiable need for her, he should be able to conduct himself like a gentleman, he should be able to withstand a few hours—hours? Try minutes!—in her presence without hauling her into his arms and covering her mouth with his in a kiss.

Not a light and friendly kiss.

But a kiss with all the passion of a dying man who needed the very breath in her lungs to breathe, to remain alive. Alive and contented and fulfilled. And purpose-driven.

"Yes," Stefano managed, his jaw tight, his voice hard, unyielding. He closed his eyes for a moment, fighting to find that control, that self-restraint, to remind himself of impossible futures.

* * *

He was a prince. She a pauper.

How many times did Sofia have to remind herself of this?

She followed the prince along the lengthy, wide hallways, down the marble-step staircase, through private ornate doors, to one of the side entrances of the palace, all the time crazily conscious of his nearness, his body's heat, his all-male scent.

The two of them, no matter how her heart flipped and her lungs flapped all over in her chest, were never ever going to enter into an exclusive, I'm-yours-you're-mine kind of a relationship, with a happy-ever-after, the kind where the prince carries his princess back to his castle and they make a whole bunch of little princes and princesses.

Never.

Ever.

Not. Going. To. Happen.

At least, not in the real world she inhabited. Her imaginary one… *Get real. Stop dreaming.*

At their approach, a white-coated guard swung the door wide, then clicked his heels together smartly.

So letting herself get all rattled and breathless and jittery around the prince was ridiculous.

It was ludicrous.

Injudicious

Don't act like a total nerd.

With a nod of his head and a *grazie* from his mouth in acknowledgment, the prince walked out into the morning sunshine, confident she followed him, his signature fluid and dignified gait taking him to where an unmarked black car with tinted windows waited discreetly.

It wasn't until he'd stepped away from her personal space that Sofia could finally draw in a full breath. She was an adult, a mature, levelheaded adult, she reasoned, following him to the waiting car at a slower pace. For a few hours, she could handle being alone with the prince, being in close proximity to him without letting herself get all weird, without letting things between them get all complicated.

The uniformed chauffeur stood at attention, holding the back door stiffly. Another man, in dark civilian clothes, wearing a chiseled countenance partially hidden behind dark sunglasses and sporting a don't-mess-with-me build, stood near the front passenger door.

The prince approached the car, transmitting a silent message to the obvious bodyguard who received it with a barely noticeable inclination of his head. Stefano stopped in front of the driver, turning toward her, and after indicating to her with his hand to precede him into the backseat, he slid in beside her. Despite the roominess in the back of the car, his thigh inadvertently brushed against hers and remained pressed against her, and sinking her teeth into her lip, Sofia bit back on a frustrated gasp.

Okay, just because she knew with her head she could handle the up-close-and-personal with the prince it didn't mean her heart received that transmission. Doing her best to look unflustered, she slid half an inch away from Stefano's leg while screaming a silent order to her flipping heart and flapping lungs to stop this nonsense.

She needed to chill out. She needed to be calm. She needed to be careful.

She could be all those things. She could chill out. She could be calm. She could be careful. She could be all those things, if for no other reason than she *had* to be all those things while she found herself in Stefano's company today exploring his island country. Besides—she almost croaked when the prince leaned back into the soft leather and extended his arm to rest it on the seat behind her head—she was practically at the airport awaiting her flight home.

"W-will your, um, your driver and, um, guard—I mean, will we, um, be sightseeing…" Sofia let whatever she was trying to say drift into a mortifying silence. *Oh, yeah, I'm really chilling out, calm, and careful.*

The mischievous twinkle already in Stefano's eyes tugged at the corners of his mouth. Sofia watched, mesmerized and forgetting to draw in much-needed oxygen, as a smile, slow and sexy and seriously lethal quirked his lips. And she knew, without a doubt, at that very moment, she was a goner.

"My chauffeur will take us to the marina and leave us there to begin our sightseeing." Stefano sobered. "I apologize, Sofia, for the intrusion into our privacy, but unfortunately, my personal bodyguard will be accompanying us today, keeping a discreet distance, I hope."

Her breath caught in her throat. His gaze seemed so intense, a shiver ran up her spine. She barely had enough breath left in her lungs to ask, "You have need for protection?" She barely had enough wherewithal to tack on, "Your Highness." *Keep him in perspective. Don't forget he's not a regular guy, but a prince.* She drew the corner of her mouth through her teeth and struggled to imagine what it must be like to never be able to take two steps without a security shadow.

"The citizens of Mondoverde are loving and peaceful. They would never commit a violent act against any member of the royal family." Though he lifted his shoulders in a casual shrug, he watched her like he tried to gauge her innermost thoughts. "However, threats, rarely risks, are always part of the job. And the job is twenty-four-seven. A royal is always a royal and always on duty," he said in a thick-toned voice. "Even when sleepwalking." This last remark lightened the moment, brought on a slight smile that loosened his tight lips a little, but did not quite dispel the gravity of his gaze.

"But surely you must have some down time, Your Highness." If she made a conscious effort to call him *Your Highness*, sooner or later it would become second nature to her and fall from her lips without any prodding from her brain. "You must have some place to escape to, some close friends to hang out with." Her hand shot out to emphasize her words. "To renew your mind, recharge your heart, refresh your spirit, rejuvenate your body." Sofia shifted in the seat to better look at his face. What she saw there made her blood heat up with fury. She dropped her hand to her lap, curling it into a fist. There was a hint of weariness in the shadows under his eyes. "Surely you can't be expected to keep on going like the EverReady battery."

A frown wrinkling his forehead, Stefano reached for her clenched hand and unfurling it, held it between both of his. "EverReady battery?"

"You know." She made an impatient gesture with her free hand. "The commercial on TV. The Energizer bunny—the pink toy rabbit wearing sunglasses beating a bass drum bearing the EverReady logo—who keeps on going and going. You're not that bunny."

"This is true." His words made it sound like he joked, but his expression wasn't quite all the way there. He seemed to undergo a private, internal war. Then on a sigh indicating his inability to resist, he kissed her knuckles. When he lifted his head, he gave her a half smile that made her stomach do flip-flops. "I am not a pink toy rabbit."

Working overtime to get her brain to click back into gear

on the issue at hand, she was about to ask "So what *do* you do to chill out?" when she looked down at their hands, still linked together, his wicked thumb making wicked circles on the sensitive skin of her palm.

"My life is good, Sofia. I cannot complain. I have many compensations," Stefano said, his voice diplomatic, but his eyes held a different viewpoint. It seemed as if a faint dissatisfaction with life tried to rear its ugly head. The sensation was fleeting. For all Sofia knew, it may never have existed because in the next instant, with the stoic poise learned from the cradle, the man sitting beside her transformed back into the reserved and cool royal. "It is a fair quid pro quo."

"Quid pro..."

"Exchange, Sofia, exchange." Releasing her hand, he turned his face to stare at the passing scenery of stone houses with red-tiled roofs, but even from his profile, she could see he had set his jaw. "Having title and position in exchange for being public property."

A privileged lifestyle in exchange for the incessant demands of the citizenry.

His mission in life was to serve his subjects.

A privileged lifestyle in exchange for the loss of a personal life, personal dreams.

His duty in life was to ensure the House of Graziani continued.

A privileged lifestyle in exchange for the relentless pursuit of the story-hungry reporters.

His aspiration in life was to somehow not lose his peace and his joy and his sanity while he juggled his mission, his duty, and his aspiration.

The stress. The pressure. The bone-deep weariness.

The weariness of the mind, the body, and the spirit.

The prince had no one to lean on, to draw strength from. Oh, yeah, he had his family, and from what Sofia had seen the previous night, they appeared to be a close-knit family.

But the prince had no special person, a woman, a wife to partner him, to encourage him, to help carry his load.

To insist he limit his official duties so he could enjoy some well-earned rest and relaxation.

To take him in her arms, hold him tight, and whip back anyone who tried to tax him to his limits, to sponge up his final breath, steal his last bit of stamina.

Sofia's fingers spasmed. She fought the urge to stretch out her hand and caress her fingertips over his bristled jaw to smooth out the tension locked there.

To protect him. To honor him. To love him.

To love him unconditionally.

To love him through the good times and the bad. To love him till death did them part.

Sofia's eyes widening, she intercepted the squeal of alarm by slamming a palm over her mouth, and sprung backward into the seat, pressing splayed fingers of her other hand to her pounding heart.

Oh. My. God.

How had this happened?

Ohmygod. Ohmygod. Ohmygod.

How had she…?

Sofia whipped her gaze off the prince and spun her face to the window and with unseeing eyes, stared out, then lowered her eyelids on a silent moan.

How had she fallen in love with Stefano?

She knew how.

Not only was he a prince, and a gorgeous-looking prince, but he was a man who loved his family. She saw that last night. She saw how his eyes, lit by an inner smile, slanted toward his mother. She saw how his teasing his father moved the smile from his eyes to his lips. He saw how he threw mocking glances at his brothers and exchanged sardonic banter with them. She saw how he would do anything, anything at all, for his family.

She saw how he would do anything, anything at all, for

his people. She saw the prince who labored unceasingly for their affection, respect, and trust, and had earned their affection, respect, and trust with his time and energy and hard work. She saw how he labored tirelessly for the good of the principality, promoting his micronation abroad, heading charities, and sitting on hospital boards. She saw how he endeavored to advance the well-being of the people of Mondoverde by wanting to encourage trade and tourism, by improving education, health, and employment, and as the commander-in-chief of the military, he endeavored to keep his countrymen safe and secure.

She saw how the man beneath the prince would not squawk at his duty, even if it meant a part of him, a large part, his heart, would die a silent death.

Oh, how she wanted to be the woman to save him. How she wanted to be the woman who had the right to love him. How she wanted to be the woman to bring him peace and joy and happiness.

To touch him. To taste. To have. To hold.

Impossible thoughts.

Sofia recognized these for the impossible thoughts that they were. She also recognized she had to be pragmatic and practical. She had no choice.

* * *

"Your Highness?"

Stefano shifted his gaze from the side window to Sofia and had to forcibly restrain himself from stretching out his arm and rubbing the frown lines off her forehead with his fingers. And then maybe let his fingertips brush down her cheek, slide to the back of her neck, apply a little pressure to bring her face toward his, and then lower his mouth to hers, branding her as his. He coughed to clear his dry throat and settled for lifting a brow instead. And found it to be not nearly as satisfying.

"You're so quiet. Are—are you feeling okay?" She moved her hand, perhaps intending to touch his face, to feel his skin, to see if he felt warm to her touch, but when she decided against it and slipped both her hands beneath her thighs, imprisoning them, forbidding them to reach out to him, he felt a sharp stab of frustration, a pain so abrupt, so acute, he had to work hard to plaster a smile on his lips and ordered his eyes to shutter down any visible emotion. "If not, Your Highness, we can cancel today's excursion."

"There is no need, Sofia, to cancel today's outing. I am fine." He was not fine. He was all wired up. Tension claimed every muscle.

He had been quiet because it took all his restraint to keep from pulling this woman into his arms. He had been quiet because he had been meditating on ways to pull this woman into his life.

"I will feel better, however, if you dispense with the *Your Highness* and call me by my given name." His smile felt a little more genuine on his mouth, a little more relaxed. He spurned his restraint and touched his forefinger to her chin, tilting up her head. "In case you have forgotten, *cara*, it is Stefano."

He had been quiet during the drive to the marina because he had been occupied with the burning need to convince this woman to remain in Mondoverde.

As his princess.

Somehow he had to convince this woman they belonged together. Forever.

Not because his father and his advisers had been pressing him to do his duty.

Not because he believed in love at first sight.

But because he felt a powerful connection to this woman. A powerful need to touch her. Taste her. Have her. Hold her. Forever. It was madness. But it was exquisite madness. Delicious madness. Compelling madness.

And he had all day to convince her she wanted this madness, too. His smile broadened. He would not waste one single opportunity. He barely refrained from rubbing the palms of his hands together. He definitely refrained from shooting down the wattage of his grin. Staring at the reflection of his face in the darkened glass, he realized for the first time in a long time, he felt energized. Excited. Exhilarated.

Sofia Burska is a commoner and a young one at that. The thought, hinting at a fast deflation of his pleasure, invaded the euphoric cloud cushioning his brain. *And she's a foreigner. A career-minded journalist. Why should she surrender her life to you and live in your gilded prison?*

Stefano's smile wobbled off his mouth.

She does not love you, his brain snarled. *She wants a write-up on you to further her career, but she does not love you.*

A jagged tear ran through the middle of his heart.

But she could learn to love the future ruler of Mondoverde. Stefano could persuade her to love the future ruler of Mondoverde.

There is prestige in being a princess. There is relief in never having to worry about money. There is the joy of wearing fine clothes and even finer jewels.

His heart admonished, *Not every woman is a mercenary gold-digger, a greedy, grasping opportunist.*

His brain screamed for him to have more control and not make a fool of himself over this overrated emotion called *love. If love is real, why has it eluded you for twenty-six years?*

His heart agreed for him to have more control and not mess up the chance to nurture the precious, fledgling, but *real* love that had been placed within the palms of his hands. *And if it has appeared to be delayed in coming, it is because it comes on God's appointed timetable. And it is here now!*

"We are here." Stefano pushed the words up through his throat and past his lips and sounded more brusque than he had intended. He felt confused, discouraged, enflamed.

At his scalding tone, Sofia jerked her chin up and faced him.

Love? What did he know about love? He'd seen it in others. But he had not experienced it himself.

Until now.

But was love enough to weather the life of a royal?

His was a difficult life. A demanding life. A public life.

Did he really have the right to pull her into what would be for her an arduous life?

And perhaps come to resent him. Despise him.

Peace would not settle on his apprehensive spirit.

Stefano would not be able to handle Sofia hating him.

He scrubbed both hands over his face, pressing his fingertips, hard, into his forehead in the hopes of pressing the turbulent thoughts down, down, down. The moment the car came to a stop at the marina, he threw open the door, and alighted, and slamming his fisted hands to his hips, he gulped in mouthfuls of air.

Tuned to her presence, or at least, her scent, Stefano dropped his hands and turned. She still sat in the back seat of the car, her hands no longer caged beneath her thighs, but clasped on her lap. His behavior was deplorable. She deserved better. *Rein in your wayward emotions and act like a gentleman.* He walked back to the open door, held out his hand to her. She hesitated, remaining silent, her expression skeptical.

"Please, Sofia, come," Stefano said just above a whisper, his throat raw, his words hoarse. He was supposed to convince her to love him, not give her reasons to hate him. Five years without any serious dating had obviously rendered him rough and unrefined. Or maybe it was a simple case of nervousness. He'd waited all his life for her. The real one. And now that she had come, now that he had recognized her as the love of his life, he felt like a nervous teenager. Clumsy. Klutzy. "Please allow me the honor to show you my beautiful country."

119

The begging worked.

Ignoring his outstretched hand, Sofia slid out of the car, circled her hands around the top of the door, and leaned toward him. "Your Highness, honestly, if you don't feel like showing me around, I understand. It's okay. Really."

"I do want to show you around, Sofia." *I want to show you my heart.*

"You—you seemed a little—little upset."

He nodded, then dropped his hands over hers on top of the door. "Not at you. Never at you. Please believe me."

"Okay, but if you have pressing responsibilities and you want to cut this short, it's okay, Your Highness. I understand."

He considered her words while holding her hands beneath his. "The only pressing responsibility I have at the moment is to be your personal tour guide." *And your future husband.* When his fingers tightened on hers, she dropped her gaze to them. "Let us go aboard *La Principessa*."

"*La Principessa*?" Sofia's voice shook, but she managed to curve her lips into a smile as she pulled her hands free and took a step away.

"My boat." He leveled a stare at her. "We will be alone." He could not help it. His voice came out gruff. "Undisturbed."

She almost missed a step and needed to grip his arm to steady herself. "Oh." Her grin faltered, her cheeks flushing before she shook her head, laughed and released her hold on him.

And since he had surrendered his restraints, Stefano surrendered to his desires, and brought her hands, first one, then the other, to his lips for a kiss. He smiled against her skin when he heard a half-smothered moan come out of her.

* * *

"Watch your step." Stefano held out a bronze hand and a sexy smile.

A quivering began in Sofia's stomach and radiated out in pulsing waves, the circles of current ever increasing until her entire being trembled.

Moments earlier when he'd taken her hand and then kissed her fingers, she had just about suffered some kind of spontaneous combustion.

It was the European way, she reminded herself. To kiss a woman's hand. It was gallantry. It was chivalry. It was good manners. It was nothing personal. But such reasoning didn't stop her from remembering how she reeled and razed beneath the super-hot feel of his lips on her skin.

Still trying to douse the sweltering inferno firestorming from the crown of her head to the tips of her toes and leaving every nerve ending sizzling in its wake, she felt a powerful reluctance to let his warm, strong fingers slide around hers to help her step onto the gleaming white boat. Understandable, her fears. If she allowed herself to be touched by him, again, however impersonal for him, it would have critical consequences for her.

She would resemble the unfortunate block of ice meeting the hot blast of the sun. Splat. She'd melt into a scorching, if not shaming, puddle at his feet.

Her survival instincts screeched their warning. *Don't touch him lest you die.*

Ignoring her survival instincts, Sofia chose to imprint this entire day and all its experiences to memory. Memories that would have to last her a lifetime. Memories that she would recount to her grandchildren some day. And if, in the meantime, she should emerge from this encounter a little worse for wear, a little bit frazzled, a little charred around the edges, so what?

Would it not have been worth it to have this one day with Prince Stefano of Mondoverde? Yes! For one day, she wanted to pretend that she, an ordinary person from Canada, a working girl with a humungous debt to repay, was princess material. For this one day, she wanted to pretend she was a very real Cinderella with her very own Prince Charming who loved her as much as she loved him. She wanted this one day, selfish or stupid.

Sofia let her hand be enveloped in his. And felt the immediate jolt shudder through her system. She thought she spied a flash of surprise cross his face, like he'd felt it, too, before his expression smoothed out, his eyes gentled, his mouth relaxed. But more than likely, she'd just wished it, wanting to believe he'd felt the same rush of blood, the same rush of excitement, she had.

"Welcome aboard *La Principessa*, Sofia." Stefano shifted, releasing her hand, and offered her a courtly bow.

"Thank you." She folded her arms to her waist to stay calm. Pretend she was Cinderella? *Yeah, right. Get real, girl. Enjoy the blessing of this day. File away the memories to be taken out at a later date to ruminate over. Relive the dream even. But don't forget who you are. Who* he *is.* "This is a beautiful boat, Your Highness." She watched his regal brow arch.

"It is not as extravagant a vessel as the other European royalty own." Prince Stefano let his easygoing gaze skim over the boat. "The House of Graziani—I—do not expect the good citizens of Mondoverde to pay for neither the upkeep of my indulgence nor for the flotilla of service boats required to assist a larger, more ostentatious yacht," he added, a grim expression of annoyance on his face. When he turned to her, his countenance was calm, his shrug sedate. "I have simple needs, Sofia, and *La Principessa* more than suffices those needs."

With a gentle rocking beneath her feet, Sofia took in the glossy wood deck and wide windows that let the natural light shine through. "Do you entertain...friends—or dignitaries here?" She stood and waited, trying to ignore the faint whisper of jealousy drifting through her. It was none of her business, she told herself, if Stefano brought women, beautiful women, beautiful and titled women aboard his boat for quixotic cruises over the Adriatic Sea, or quiet, candlelight dinners for two on deck, or… *Stop it! It's none of your business!* She had her gaze hopping everywhere but on her host.

"No."

"No?" she repeated, whipping her face to him with such ferocity she marveled she hadn't snapped her neck. He didn't bring *any* of his lady friends here to…? *Yes!* On the heels of her mental high-five, a knot of guilt and embarrassment constricted her chest. She had no claim on this man. She had no reason to rejoice.

"This is—how do you say?—my getaway transportation. Yes?" A boyish grin touched Stefano's lips.

Sofia's breath clogged in her throat. Stefano was a good-looking man, whether in a conservative dove-gray suit with a darker gray tie bearing the royal crest of the monarchy in silver, or in a tailor-made tuxedo with the black jacket cut to display his royal purple sash, or in the form-fitting blue jeans and chest-hugging black T-shirt he'd donned this morning. But when his face lit up with such infectious amusement, dispelling the shadows of stress marking the space under his eyes, she felt herself falling for him, harder, deeper than she already had.

"It is a small enough boat I can man by myself," Stefano explained, "when I feel the necessity to—"

"Get away."

"By myself." Stefano touched a light hand to her shoulder. "Excuse me a moment, Sofia."

By himself.

There was so much for him to deal with here. Twenty-four-seven.

The stiffness and the protocol of royal life. The obedience to a rigid schedule, a highly structured and carefully planned schedule. The enormous burden of duties and responsibilities toward the micronation. The never-ending media scrutiny and the nonstop flashing of cameras.

The mounting pressure from all quarters to choose the

right wife with the clock ticking and the weight of a country on his shoulders.

No wonder he needed to get away. If only for a few hours on his boat. To regroup, recharge.

Sofia's heart burst wide open, took Stefano all the way in, enveloping him within the folds of her growing love. Her desire to protect him, to buoy him up with her strength, to ease his overwhelming obligations from off his shoulders and carry them for him for a while, giving him time to rest his body, to renew his mind, to revive his spirit, blasted up within her.

She watched him walk to the stern of the boat and heard him call out something in Italian to his chauffeur who executed a deferential bow before climbing in behind the steering wheel of the car, and reversing it, drove away from the marina. Next Stefano exchanged a few quiet words with his bodyguard who frowned, shook his head in a vehement indication in the negative, rapid-fired back something in their native language, frowned deeper as he listened to the prince, gave one curt nod of his head, and with his mouth thinned to a white line, he disembarked, his long-legged pace taking him down the gangway while his hand jerked his cell phone from his pocket.

"What's going on?" Sofia asked a well-pleased-with-himself Stefano.

The car that had brought them to the marina had long disappeared. The bodyguard, still visible, parked his impressive body on the cement, legs spread apart, one hand fisted on his hip, the other hand pressing the cell to his ear, his face a mask of worry and fury.

"Oh, nothing." He grinned down at her, noted her narrow-eyed stare, and laughed. A spontaneous and carefree sound that melted her insides. He looked so young. So lighthearted. "I told the driver to come back for us tonight. And..." He tossed an amusing glance at the still-upset bodyguard, who now sat on a cement bench, gazing at the sky through his dark shades, his cell plastered to his ear. "And I dismissed my disgruntled guard, who is right at this moment, no doubt, calling in Mondoverde's air force to scramble into the airspace, without delay, and overshadow us with their airborne protection."

"Was that wise?"

A regal brow rose. His lips turned down. "Wise?"

"Well, you're a prince."

"Yes, this is so." Another grin came.

"You're a part of the royal family. You need protection. That's why you have a security force. To keep you safe."

Stefano's hands landed on her shoulders. "*Cara*, I have told you my people would never hurt me." His fingers began a gentle message.

"Not the Mondoverduvian people, no, of course not." Sofia could not check the flow of panic inundating her voice, freezing her blood, stalling her heart.

There were crazies out there. Fanatics. Overzealous extremists. In these turbulent times, it wouldn't take much for a radical on the other side of the world, obsessed with his petty grievances, to bring his crusades to Mondoverduvian soil. His lofty aspirations, not motivated by a sense of patriotism or duty or honor, but by the spotlight-is-on-me recognition, would inflame him to assassinate Stefano just because he represented the royal family, the ruling government. Stefano wasn't taking this serious. The danger. His possible death.

Her fear carrying her, Sofia poked him in the chest. Hard. With luck, she would leave a bruise. "But you don't live in an island unto yourself."

"Mondoverde is an island."

She made a snarling sound, then struck her forehead against his chest, once, twice, three times. She could feel his grin without needing to look at him. And it fueled her anger. "Your Serene Highness," she said, her tone terse, "this is an upside-down world in which we're living in. Violence, worldwide, is escalating. You are not immune. Murder and mayhem can easily invade your backyard."

"I do not have a…backyard."

Detecting a tongue in cheek edge to his words, she growled, "Stefano," and whipped up her head to slap him with a glare.

"I wondered when you would remember to use my name."

His eyes lit with humor, the perfect combination of teasing and testing, safe and sweet, and he conquered all the corners of Sofia's heart.

CHAPTER 8

"Let me show you *La Prinicpessa* before we set sail." With the palm of his right hand pressed to the small of her back, Stefano guided Sofia gently but firmly to the companionway. "Watch your step," he warned, reaching for her hand and preceding her down the four steps to the galley.

Sofia came to an abrupt halt, elongating their arms and forcing Stefano to stop also. And smile. "Oh. My. Goodness."

Glossy wood floors and cabinets and gleaming steel appliances made her forget she stood on a boat. A twin refrigerator/freezer, a three-burner propane-fueled stove and oven, and what looked like a state-of-the-art microwave. A chef's paradise.

"We will have some refreshments on the main deck in about..." Still holding her hand, Stefano glanced at his gold watch and made a cute, little side-to-side move with his head. "A half hour." He lifted his gaze and gave her a smile. "I want to put out to sea first. Lunch will be served an hour or so later. If that meets with your approval, Sofia?"

His aquatic agenda met with her approval. No problem there. What did not meet with her approval was his smile. Slow and sexy and super-charming. Or the way his blue eyes seemed to tunnel down to the furthermost reaches of her soul, searching for secrets, secrets she didn't want him discovering. Or the tantalizing brush of his thumb across the pulse beating erratically at her wrist.

"That's fine." A few hours on the boat. Alone with Stefano. Sofia tamped down on a moan careening its way up from her chest and into her throat. How would she be able to suppress her growing feelings for the man and keep him from guessing she'd fallen for him? She didn't want to embarrass him. Or make him uncomfortable. Or— Her eyes widened. She didn't want him thinking she would pretend feelings for him so she could inveigle an interview from him. Her ears tingled with horror.

"Something is wrong, Sofia?"

"No. No, not at all," she lied.

And hoped God would show her mercy and compassion and overlook her deliberate misrepresentation of truth. She prayed God would not ask her for an accounting for breaking the ninth commandment, *You shall not bear false witness*, but she had no idea how else to have handled a delicate situation, given Stefano's distrust and abhorrence of the media and she being a member of the infamous faction.

Lord, I don't want anything to spoil this day, my day for making memories. Memories of this day will have to last me the rest of my life. I know that. I know that's all I can have.

"I was just wondering," she made up the words as she went along, "how lunch would be served if you have no chef on board."

He threw a furtive gaze to his right, volleyed it to his left, then leaned in as if to share a secret. "Don't tell anyone," he began sotto voce, "but I can cook."

"You? Cook?" Her tone implied disbelief.

"Such impertinence," he complained with mock irritation. "We may not have any dungeons at the *Castello di Bellaterra*, but that does not mean I will not throw you in the brig," warned a stern-faced Stefano.

"You don't have a brig," Sofia singsonged.

"Do not be so certain, *cara*," he cautioned, working his facial features into the best display of inscrutability she'd ever seen.

"I'll believe you when I see it." The jovial banter did not relax Sofia. Not one little bit. It only served to up her estimation of the man who would one day rule his country. He was a complex person. The serious and reserved prince. The friendly and playful man. A combination designed to increase her apprehension. Increase her apprehension because it made her love him all the more.

"Then let us continue with the tour." Stefano caught hold of her elbow and stopped her as she began to move. His grasp was gentle but firm. "Should we discover my brig, Sofia, I will have no choice but to order you in." He sighed, loosened his hold on her arm, slid his hand to close his fingers around hers. "You will then have to remain in my custody, indefinitely, as my prisoner."

Sofia would stay willingly in his custody. "And if we find no brig on this fine boat? Then what, Your Serene Highness?"

"I should throw you in the brig just for that," he muttered, bringing them to a standstill. "I order you to stop calling me that. I have a name. I want you to use it."

If she didn't know any better, she would have believed he gritted his teeth. She went for a placating tone. "I don't think that's a good idea. Your Highness," she added softly.

"Why?" he bulleted the one-word question, exasperation rolling off him in furious waves.

"Because you're a prince—"

He cut her off with another word delivered with equal ferocity. "So?"

"And I am—"

"Do not dare to say you are a commoner."

"But I am." Sofia looked up into his face, so fierce and loveable. "We're on opposite poles of the status spectrum." This day would be more difficult than she'd anticipated. "There has to be some...some...distance between us." She wanted to rise on her toes to kiss his scowling mouth. "I may not be a Mondoverduvian citizen, but I still must show my respect for your office, your position, your—"

129

She attempted to speak, to give him some reasonable explanation why it felt imperative they maintain their respective stations in life, but he casually placed his finger in the air and shook his head.

"If you want to show me your respect, *cara*, you will do so by honoring my wishes," Stefano murmured, and the timbre of his voice sent shivers cascading down her spine. "For as long as we are together, and alone—" His voice dropped several decibels into the seductive zone. "—you will forget I am a prince." He trailed the back of his hand over her cheek. "We are simply one man and one woman enjoying each other's company on this beautiful day." With one hand still captured in his, he threaded the fingers of his other hand into her free one and tugged her closer. "Agreed?"

At that moment, she would have agreed to anything he wanted, and gave him a robotic nod.

A radiant smile curved his lips.

Oh, yeah, she was definitely a goner. No doubt about it. None at all.

"*Bene*, let me hear you say it," he asked in a hoarse voice.

"S-say what?"

"Say my name," he whispered, his blue eyes glittering with some emotion she couldn't decipher.

She felt a shiver vibrate her body from head to toe. "Stefano." Her voice was barely above a whisper.

"Again," he ordered.

"Stefano."

He closed his eyes, and releasing one of her hands, he steamrolled his now-free fingers through his hair, and expelled a loud sigh. "*Bene*." He drew in a deep breath, opened his eyes, and smiled a smile that made the sun outside diminish by comparison. "Let us continue with our tour." And Stefano led her three steps down to the saloon.

Lord, everything has been moving too fast here. That's no excuse, I agree, for not spending time in prayer with You, seeking Your face, Your guidance. But I'm here, now, Lord, and I need You. I really, really need your wisdom. I need to understand how best to deal with this afternoon with Stefano. You know the craziness going on in my heart. Help me, by the power of Your Holy Spirit, to not disappoint You with my character, conduct, and conversation, or hurt Stefano. But I don't want to be hurt, either, Lord. And at the moment, that's all I can see. Me getting hurt. He's sending out some signals. I don't want to read more in them than there really is. I know he wants to pretend we're two ordinary people having fun, but...

Once again, she halted, and gaped.

A plush carpet covered the floor of the saloon. The mid-morning sunlight filtered through the two walls of wide windows and shone its benevolence on the glossy wood cabinets and tables with leather stools. Cushy leather sofas lined one wall, while comfortable armchairs sat across from them.

"Wow." The word came out of Sofia's mouth on a reverential whisper.

Looking sheepish, Stefano admitted, "If I'm going to spend any time on *La Principessa*, I might as well be—"

"Comfortable," she quipped, wondering when she would awaken from her dream and be hurled back into reality. "There's more?"

"I have left the best for last." He seemed a little too pleased with himself.

Seconds later, after descending five more steps, Sofia understood.

* * *

Anyone who knew Stefano would not be surprised by his visibly calm facade. It was part of the persona he had nurtured and nourished since birth. But inside, where no one could see except God and no one could feel except himself, his bones rattled and clattered with pulsing and pounding nerves.

Showing Sofia this room was part of the tour, but he wondered now, pushing open the glass and wood door to his personal inner sanctuary and motioning her to precede him, if he had not made an enormous error in judgment.

Not only could she feel uncomfortable to find herself in such a personal room and in such close proximity to him—the owner of such a room, but watching her advance, slow and cautious, into his sanctuary, a delectable and adorable pink flush flowing into her face when her widening gaze ran over to the queen-sized bed in glossy wood tucked into an alcove in the same wood, he knew she not only could feel embarrassment, but did feel embarrassment.

"This is my bedroom," he announced, unnecessarily, and closed his eyes briefly at the huskiness of his voice. "It—it has an ensuite—equipped with an electric toilet and separate walk-in shower—with a door." He closed his eyes again. *Shoot me now.*

As next in line to the throne, Stefano had had to assist his father in running the complex affairs of their principality on a daily basis. As the Crown Prince of Mondoverde, he had had to entertain many dignitaries and heads of state. As the State Secretary and Minister of Internal Affairs, he had had to discuss and debate issues of concern with the ministers of his government and with the corresponding ministers of other countries. As a popular orator of the royal family, he had had to attend approximately four hundred events a year—that was, at least, one affair a day—where he has had to give a speech, attend openings, christen institutions, and promote the general welfare of the country. How could it be this one woman—and only her—could render him into a babbling fool?

"This is quite the stateroom." Sofia's voice was soft. "Very…comfortable." She could not seem to tear her eyes off the bed.

Too late Stefano realized his monumental miscalculation.

He scrubbed the pad of his thumb over his lips.

He had not taken into account that when he would escort Sofia into his room, he would always and forever imagine her in his room. In his arms. In his bed.

He had to get her out of his room. Before he dragged her into his arms. Into his bed.

"Come," he said, his tone curt. He did not mean it to be so snappy and snippy, but when a man battled to stay sane, safe, when a man sensed his own defeat, destruction, keeping the pitch of his voice steady and soothing did not rate very high on his to-do list. Maintaining honor, integrity, respect did. At all costs. "Let me show you the guest cabin." And he literally dragged her from of his room. "The setup is similar, but on a smaller scale. It has a private bath." An internal groan shook his body. Private bath. *Dio mio.* Now he had to wrestle from his brain the image of her in the bath. His grip on her hand tightening, he whizzed her by the cabin, intent on getting them back on deck. Away from intimate rooms. Where he could breathe. He hoped.

"What is that room?" Sofia's words came out a little wobbled. Probably because she had to hustle to keep up with his agitated gait.

"My office." He slowed down to throw open the glass and wood door for her to peek in. "I have a wireless printer and copier. Laptop. Phone. The usual office paraphernalia."

"But this is your boat," Sofia exclaimed.

"Yes, this is my boat." Amused, Stefano grinned. "I have already told you that."

"But this is a pleasure boat."

His grin broadened. "Yes, this is true."

"A pleasure boat means rest and relaxation. What do you need with this—" She waved a hand at the desk in gleaming wood, the flick of her wrist clearly indicating her displeasure.

"*Cara.*" Using her hair wrapped around his fist, he gently but firmly turned her face to his. "As the hereditary prince, I am not allowed to rest and relax."

"But you have to rest, to relax. Everybody has to. You need

a time-out from your duties." Her concern for his well-being became more and more zealous.

His love for her became more and more profound. Stronger. Intense. He had to. He had no choice. He captured her lips in a sweet, tender kiss. The sweet and tender kiss left them trembling.

"Do not worry about me, *mia bella* Sofia," Stefano murmured against her lips. He pressed a kiss to her forehead. Was it possible she had feelings for him? Hope began to arise in his soul.

"*You* obviously don't worry about being *human*."

He heard the heat of anger edge her voice. Lifting his head, he saw the heat of anger paint her face.

Stefano released a sigh. He released Sofia. He straightened the curves of his spine and stood at attention.

As the future ruler of Mondoverde, he was always watched, always judged. He had to mold himself into a man who was always calm, always controlled in every situation. Because his life was public, his demeanor had to be circumspect. Always. No room existed for living a normal life as Sofia would define normal. No room existed for him to enjoy the luxury of emotional outbursts, like Sofia just did. He had to always present himself as rigidly correct. His training inspired the confidence of the government ministers, the Mondoverduvian people, the House of Graziani. The citizenry could trust him. Trust his leadership. Trust he would always be at the helm taking care of the country's welfare. As the future ruler of Mondoverde, he did not enjoy the privilege to rest, to relax. He was on call. Every minute of every day of every week of every year. Until he would breathe his last breath.

"This is who I am," Stefano defended stiffly. "This is what I was born to be." He held his hands together in a tight ball. "I am Prince Stefano Alberto Emmanuele Alessandro Graziano, Crown Prince of the Principality of Mondoverde." He was a man destined to rule his island nation. A man destined to produce the heir to the Graziani throne. A man destined to love this woman who was only now beginning to realize his life was not his own.

And she hated the realization.

And if this woman would become his princess, her life would not be her own.

She would always be on display. Always watched with eagle-alert eyes. Always forced to submerge her birthrights.

Marriage to a ruling royal always trumped birthrights.

His jaw ached from gritting his teeth. How could love, now that he had found it, be this difficult? This challenged? This uncertain?

"And I am Sofia Burska, a commoner from Canada," Sofia responded in a soft voice, her fingers clasped in front of her in a death-grip.

And there it was. The impasse.

He felt his heart nose-dive.

She lived in one world. He in another.

She lived by one set of rules. He another.

She lived with freedoms. He with restrictions.

Two lives. Two very different lives. Different upbringings. Different hopes. Dreams.

Stefano held her gaze for long seconds, furious at the futility of this argument. There must be a way to forge the two polar-apart lives into one smooth, fluid joining of two souls. Two soul mates.

Be strong and courageous. Do not be afraid; do not be discouraged, for the Lord your God will be with you wherever you go.

The words from the Book of Joshua, the words Stefano had chosen for himself as his life scripture, the promise of God to lead him as he would lead the people of Mondoverde, filtered through his raw emotions. *Do not be afraid; do not be discouraged, for the Lord your God will be with you.*

Stefano inclined his head slightly. Closed his eyes briefly. Forcing himself to release his jaw muscles, he made himself…relax. It was not over until Jehovah God said it was over. And his relationship with Sofia was far from over. It was just beginning.

"Sofia," he said softly, "we agreed, did we not, just for today, we would forget our stations in life and enjoy this warm and sunny day God has given us?" He slid the knuckle of his forefinger beneath her chin and lifted her face so their eyes could meet and hold. "For today, I am a simple, but eager tour guide. Allow me to introduce you to my beautiful country." He moved his finger from her chin to feather a caress along her jaw and rest his palm over her cheek. "I so want you to love my country." His words were a whispered plea.

He so wanted her to love him. The man. To forget he was a prince and to love him, the man.

Sofia raised her hand to press it against his face. "I already do," she breathed.

Stefano relished her touch. The soft skin of her fingers resting against the stubbled skin of his cheek. He could have remained standing like this forever. A connection. Not just a physical connection. But an emotional connection.

But all of a sudden, Sofia became aware she touched him and tore her hand away, cupping it in the palm of her other hand. Embarrassed, nervous, apprehensive, she spun away, her intent obvious. To establish a safe distance between them. Stefano mourned the distance. The physical distance. The emotional distance. Once again he wondered why love had to be this complicated.

"You read that?" A hushed awe filled the office.

Submerging his disappointment and frustration with the subsequent uneasiness swirling around them, Stefano followed the direction of her fascinated gaze.

The Bible on his desk.

Running his thumb across his bottom lip, it occurred to Stefano he had no idea where Sofia stood on matters of the faith.

Did she have a personal relationship with Jesus Christ or did she just give the Lord lip service?

Did she attend church on a weekly basis or did she grace its door only when nothing more interesting came along?

Did she believe in the fundamental truths of the Word of God…Father, Son, and Holy Spirit—the three Persons of the one Godhead; the immaculate conception of Mary through the power of the Holy Spirit; the Savior of the world, Jesus Christ—fully God and fully Man; the atonement work of His death on the cross—paying for the sins of mankind with His life and the shedding of His blood; His resurrection from the dead and His ascension into heaven—sitting at the right hand of His Father and making intercession on behalf of men, women, and children; the coming of Jesus for his believers—the Rapture of the church; the seven-year tribulation period with the Antichrist, empowered by Satan, ruling the world; the return of Jesus with the saints of all ages to fight and win the final battle of good versus evil—the battle of Armageddon; the judgment of Satan, demons, and unbelievers and their consignment into an eternity in hell; the resurrection of the new earth and the eternal reign of the Lord Jesus Christ as the King of kings and Lord of lords, with His believers, who have confessed Him as their Lord and Savior, living forever in His presence on the new earth or did she consider the contents of the Bible to be a glorified collection of fables and not God's inspired and prophetic words?

Stefano sighed. Anyone in his circumstances would find it tough to acquire the right wife with the clock clanging and the weight of the country on his shoulders. But he had complicated his situation by not only insisting he had to be in love with the wife-to-be, but she had to share and uphold his spiritual beliefs.

They had to be united in the spirit. Their foundation had to be solidified in the faith. Otherwise, a house divided against itself would not stand.

He had not only his personal happiness at stake, but he had to ensure the continuity of the House of Graziani, and safeguard the welfare of the Mondoverduvian people. The Mondoverduvians were rock-solid conservatives. Divorce would not be allowed. So it was imperative he choose the correct woman to be his princess.

And he had plenty of examples recorded in the Bible of the murder and mayhem of a divided house, where the ruler worshipped the one and true and living God and his spouse, who did not, led him astray into rebellion and anarchy and idolatry.

Besides, as a Christian, he was commanded by the Word of God to "not be yoked together with unbelievers. For what do righteousness and wickedness have in common? Or what fellowship can light have with darkness? Or what does a believer have in common with an unbeliever? For we are the temple of the living God."

Stefano had to discover if Sofia was a believer. Their future together hinged on it.

"Yes, Sofia, I read the Bible," Stefano answered with no apology and studied her reaction. "Daily."

"Really?" Sofia glowed like a pair of headlights on high beam. "I wouldn't have thought someone in your position and power would feel a need to read the Bible."

"Sofia, it is *because* of my position and power that I *need* to read the Bible." Stefano moved to the desk and picked up the black leather-bound Book. "In the Book of Deuteronomy, the king is instructed when he sits on the throne, he is to always keep a copy of the Word with him and to—" He rifled through the pages, stopping when he reached the 17th Chapter of Deuteronomy. "'—read it daily as long as he lives. That way he will learn to fear the Lord his God by obeying all the terms of these instructions and decrees. This regular reading will prevent him from becoming proud and acting as if he is above his fellow citizens. It will also prevent him from turning away from these commands in the smallest ways. And it will ensure he and his descendants will reign for many generations.'"

Stefano lifted his head, looked at Sofia, his heart pumping at an accelerated pace. "My father taught me as his father taught him and as he was taught by his father that wise rulers recognize allegiance to God is the number one requirement of an ideal ruler. The reading of the Bible, the understanding of the Scriptures, and the submission to God's Word will ensure the right spirit of humility and obedience in the ruler and safeguard the promise of a continuous dynastic succession and guarantee God's blessings upon the country and its citizenry."

Sofia's beautiful face became marred with a frown. He wanted to make her understand. He needed her to understand. He rushed in with his heart flapping in his chest. "Sofia, I am but a man. A human man. To rule my people fairly, righteously, honorably, I must conform to the righteous standards set forth in the Word of God. Without His precepts written in my mind and heart, my mind that I may recall them, my heart that I may perform them, without His wisdom and grace, His power and presence, I can never be an effective ruler of Mondoverde." *Or a godly husband. A godly father. A loving husband and loving father.*

He watched her approach the desk, frown lines still marking the skin between her eyes, and his heart flashed to his throat, threatening to choke him. She reached for the Bible in his hands and his nerveless digits relinquished it. She flipped through it, the frown lines disappearing when she located what she searched.

Raising her face, Sofia locked gazes with him. "My parents taught me God has a plan and a purpose for each person. He has called us, and if we trust Him, He will enable us, to fulfill whatever task He has appointed to us. In the Book of Esther…" She glanced down at the Bible in her hands, then fired her eyes back at him. "…Chapter four and verse fourteen, Mordecai tells Queen Esther—" She lowered her gaze to read. "'And who knows but that you have come to your royal position for such a time as this.'" She looked up, smiled, a shy, tentative smile.

"It's obvious to me—to anyone who's looking—you have a heart for your people. A generous heart. A caring heart. And you want to rule them wisely. Benevolently." She laid the Bible on his desk. "It's a very crucial role you have been called by God to embrace, to fulfill." She hesitated. "So many people depend on what you do," she said softly.

Stefano leaned his backside against the desk, rested his hands on the desktop on either side of him, tilted back his head, and stared at the ceiling. A leader was never to show anything but strength.

Could he share his heart with Sofia? Could he make the confession? Could he reveal his vulnerability?

"So many times," he admitted on a deep-chested sigh, "I have felt weak and inadequate and…" He lowered his gaze to her. "Frightened."

Closing the gap between them, Sofia rested her palms on his shoulders. He tilted his head backward. "I'm sure the pressures and stresses will only increase when you ascend to the throne." She probably was unaware of it, but she massaged his shoulders with her fingers, although he was aware of the calming effects of her ministering fingers on his emotions. "Nevertheless, you have the promise of God's presence." She kissed the top of his forehead. "It won't minimize the enormous task you face in governing your people, but God's presence will make all the difference." She tensed when she realized she had kissed him and withdrew her hands. Took a step back. Then another.

"J-Joshua, I'm…I'm sure felt the same…same way," Sofia stuttered, a slow flush sliding over her skin. He fought down the urge to pull her into his arms for a real kiss. She coughed to clear her throat and continued. "When he took over the reins of leadership from Moses, he must have felt overwhelmed at times. He probably considered resigning before the conquest of the Promised Land even began. But God told him three times to be strong and courageous. And God urged him to not be afraid or discouraged."

His gaze whipping up to capture hers, his eyes widening in surprise, Stefano rocked to his feet and took her hand, his grip warm and firm and crushing. "It is interesting, Sofia, you said that." His voice sounded awed and wobbly and hoarse. "The scripture I have chosen to be my guiding principle in life is Joshua Chapter one and verse nine. 'Be strong and courageous. Do not be afraid; do not be discouraged, for the Lord your God will be with you wherever you go.'" He realized he crushed her fingers and loosened his hold. "I guess I needed confirmation." He brought her knuckles to his mouth for a kiss. "Thank you," he murmured against her fingers.

She reached out to put her hand on his chest, on his breastbone, beneath which his heart beat hard, fierce, excited. She must have felt the erratic beating under her fingertips because her brown eyes darkened, her blush deepened, her breathing quickened. She lifted her fingers a fraction of an inch, stopped, then pressed them back to his chest.

"Stefano." Sofia stumbled into silence, a little look of confusion furrowing the skin between her eyebrows. She had lost her train of thought when he had flashed her a grin. "What? What?"

"I am delighted you have remembered to address me correctly, *cara*." He loved the sound of his name falling from her lips. He nibbled on her knuckles. He loved it when he flustered her. She was absolutely adorable, all pink and precious. He planted one more kiss, this one on the middle of her palm, and smiled when he felt her shiver. Progress. They made progress, albeit slow progress, but progress nonetheless. "You were saying?" he asked, and taking pity on her rattled state, he let go of her hand.

Her frown lines scored deeper into her forehead. "I was saying?" Making a strangled sound in her throat, she wrenched her hand from his chest and made a hasty retreat of a few feet.

She was delightful this creature and Stefano vowed, no matter what it took, he would make her his. "We were discussing Joshua. About being strong and courageous. Not afraid or discouraged," he prompted with a hike of his brow.

"Oh. Oh, yeah."

He grinned at her Canadian vernacular.

"Um." Sofia performed a cute, little head-shake as if juggling her brain back into place, and hopefully, back online. It must have worked because her vision cleared. "Like Joshua, you, Stefano, are charged to be strong and courageous, to not be afraid or discouraged. And like Joshua—" She bolted toward him, grabbing his upper arms. His automatically came around her to hold her to him. "—you have God's assurances which are sufficient to last your entire life." She gave him a shake to underscore the importance of the comments she was about to impart. "You have God's promise that you will sit on the throne of Graziani and rule Mondoverde. You have God's power to enable you to rule effectively and with grace and justice and integrity. And, Stefano, you have God's presence; He will never, ever leave you nor abandon you." The tips of her fingers dug into his flesh as if by the sheer force of her will she could make him believe. "Believers of every age can be inspired and encouraged by these same three assurances."

A silence descended, enshrouded them. For long moments, they stared into each other's eyes.

Sofia Burska was the woman Stefano Graziano would marry.

He had the urge to shout his love for her. He controlled the urge for fear he would frighten her. He still had to convince her she was his princess—the princess he had been searching his entire life.

He did not control the urge to run his knuckles down the side of her cheek. When she shivered beneath the stroke of his hand, he did not stop the caress or pull his hand away. His eyes holding hers, he brushed the pad of his thumb over her bottom lip, displacing her nipping teeth. She again shivered in his arms and her breathing sped up.

Stefano was a goner.

He lowered his head to press his mouth to hers. His intention was to keep the kiss soft and simple, similar to the one he had given her in her room. Just a friendly, non-fear-provoking kiss. But when his lips touched hers, he felt like he had come home after a long, long absence in the desert, so parched and thirsty. And she was so sweet, so supple beneath his hands, his plan for the soft and simple kiss was captured in the wind and carried out over the Adriatic Sea. On a moan, he tilted her face to give himself a better angle on her mouth and heard her gasp of pleasure. Encouraged, he slid one hand down from her face to settle it on her spine and drew her closer against his chest.

Time stood still. The world vanished. The sightseeing forgotten.

The kiss endured.

Her hands crept up to encircle his neck. His hands settled more firmly, pulled her more closely. His heart pounded against hers. Her breath mingled with his. Blood heated up. Brains fogged over. Muscles liquefied.

Shocked, horrified, Sofia pulled back against his arms, breathing heavily.

Breathing heavily, Stefano pulled back, but did not release his hold.

He'd felt the kiss all the way down to his soul.

Judging by her reaction, she had felt the kiss all the way down to her soul.

"You okay?" he rasped out.

She opened her mouth, but no words emerged. She closed her mouth. After a moment, she tried again to push out an answer. "Yeah." She swallowed. "Sure." Her cheeks were deeply flushed, her breathing erratic.

Well, at least, one of them was okay. He was nowhere near to being okay after that kiss.

He wanted another kiss. And another. And then another. Stefano wanted to keep on having her kisses until he died. And what a way to die.

CHAPTER 9

The sea purred and lapped against the boat. The wind was kind today, a caress instead of a slap. The noonday sun overhead shone its brightness and warmth. Stefano sat, his wrist relaxed over the top of the steering wheel. Sofia took the seat beside him, wishing she felt the same cozy tranquility. She didn't. She felt ravaged by conflicting emotions.

She felt ravaged by his kiss.

The kiss had forced the air from her lungs.

The kiss had ignited her senses, setting them on fire.

The kiss had broomed aside, for the duration of the kiss, any impediments she had raised to maintain a respectable *emotional* distance from this man.

Sofia knew better than to succumb to the powerful emotions Stefano evoked within her.

She knew nothing could come from it. Nothing lasting. Nothing fulfilling.

But, the need. Oh, the need.

To cherish him. To treasure him. To love him.

The kiss had blasted a direct line to her heart…and soul, and had dropped its anchor.

And ruined her for any other man.

This man could never claim her as his own. Not in public. Not as his wife. And sensing, perhaps knowing, she would never accept the clandestine crumbs, he couldn't offer her the secret life of a mistress. She saw something broken lurking in his eyes when he'd let them both come up for air. Part regret, part shame. Part guilt.

Nevertheless, she belonged to this royal prince forevermore, heart and soul. When she would return to Canada, she would be leaving her heart behind in Mondoverde.

Her mood somber and stressed, she battled back the descending depression by whipping her gaze to the shoreline disappearing behind them. "Belleterra is the capital of Mondoverde, isn't it? It's so beautiful. Seeing the stone houses with the red-tiled roofs from this spot on the sea, I mean. I'd only gotten a glimpse, really, from the air when I landed." Her sentences rambled from her mouth.

She prayed he didn't notice.

He did.

Lifting his sunglasses to prop them just above his hairline, he slanted her a musing quirk of the lips. "Bellaterra is beautiful no matter how you see her. By air. By sea. By automobile." A pause. "By day." Another pause. "By night." His voice had lowered to a husky timbre.

Her mind beginning to spiral out of control, Sofia ripped her gaze off his killer blue eyes, right now glinting with amusement, seduction, and something else her frazzled brain couldn't identify, and stared straight ahead with visions of all the things they could do at night attacking her mind. She felt her cheeks grow hot.

Stefano must have possessed the uncanny ability to read her mind because she heard his hoarse chuckle drift her way. Or…he had correctly interpreted the tomato-red stains on her face. Either way, he had an accurate picture of the state of her messed-up mind. Out of the corner of her eye, she watched him drop his sunglasses back over his eyes. She sighed a little, knowing she didn't have to turn her head and glance back at him to see him still grinning.

How was she to hang on to what remained of her sanity — and not make a fool of herself — if he used that supersoft, supersexy voice on her and flashed that super-confident, super-charming grin at her? Did he know he made her heart skitter? she groused in silence, snapping her eyes shut.

"Sofia."

She opened her eyes and saw him turned toward her, leaving one hand on the steering wheel and touching the shoulder closest to him, both firmly and tentatively. His expression staid and pressing, he waited for the signal. She gave him none, but looked into his eyes and stayed silent.

"You and I, we will need to talk." Stefano lifted his hand from her shoulder to shove it through his hair. When he whipped off his sunglasses, she saw a burning intensity appeared in his eyes. "I want to—"

Sofia didn't want to hear it. She tried to shrug off the quick hit of panic. However he wanted to say it, she didn't want to hear there could be nothing more between them than attraction. She'd save him the embarrassment. She'd save her the humiliation.

She sling-shot the question to derail him. "So, Stefano. Tell me about the principality. How did your family come to establish their throne on Mondoverde?" She felt his frustration. His annoyance. They fairly rolled off him. Hands folded on her lap, she maintained a kindly countenance to his tight-lipped expression.

With exaggerated slowness, Stefano perched his sunglasses on his nose. A second passed. Then two. Then three. He drove the boat along the shoreline in a silence of fury. Judging by the stiff, white line of his lips, he seemed like he worked, hard, real hard, to douse his irritation.

Finally, when he probably thought he could speak without shooting fiery darts at her, he sighed in admission of defeat, and said, "In June, 1946, following the Second World War, the Kingdom of Italy came to an end when

147

the Italian Constitution Referendum was held. The people had spoken, and the then king, Umberto II, had no choice but to transfer his powers to the Prime Minister of the Republic of Italy, Alcide de Gasperi."

Fascinated with the history, Sofia twisted in her seat, slipping one leg under her, and gave Stefano her full attention. "I guess the Italians must have been ticked off big time with the king to vote overwhelmingly for the abolishment of the monarchy."

Stefano smiled at her vernacular. "Yes." He slowed down, dropped anchor. "Umberto di Savoia was Italy's last king, reigning just slightly over one month."

"One month?"

Stefano's shoulders lifted in a what-can-I-say kind of shrug. "In an effort to repair the monarchy's image after the fall of Benito Mussolini's regime, the unpopular King Victor Emmanuel III transferred his powers to his only son, Umberto II, in 1944, but kept the title of king. When the referendum was being prepared, Victor Emmanuel abdicated the throne to Umberto in an unsuccessful attempt to gain support for the monarchy. It was too little, too late for the Italians. After only one month on the throne, Umberto was forced to step down because of the referendum, and was exiled, never allowed to return to his native country, not even when he was dying."

"That is harsh," Sofia judged.

"That is called consequences," countered Stefano. "The ruler of a country must function effectively as the vice-regent of Jehovah God. The responsibility, as the leader of God's people, weighs heavily upon his shoulders. He is given those people to be a steward over. To bless them. To protect them. Not abuse them." His face took on the defensive lines of a mother lion standing guard over her cubs. "It is imperative he request wisdom and a discerning heart tuned to the voice of the Holy Spirit so he can lead the nation as God wants the nation to be led. He acknowledges his dependence on God. If he does not, he is a fool. He is God's servant, putting the needs of his people above his personal desires for aggrandizement."

Staring back at the coastline of Mondoverde, he murmured, "To whom much is given, much is expected. God's servant will stand accountable to the Lord for what he does and does not do with what or whom he has been entrusted." When he dropped his attention to her, she saw the weight of his responsibility sculpted in the austere lines of his mouth. She could guess what lay in the eyes shielded by the sunglasses. A ferocity, an intense determination to do right by his people. "The Lord Most High appoints rulers and He deposes rulers." A casual shrug of the shoulders. A smoothing out of the tense muscles. A calming of the facial features. "The di Savoia dynasty was judged and deposed."

"What about forgiveness for mistakes?"

"If we repent of our mistakes, we are forgiven, but that does not mean the consequences of sin will not play out. They will. They cannot be stopped. And many innocent lives will be affected."

"'Love covers over a multitude of sins,'" Sofia quoted from the forth Chapter of the first epistle of the Apostle Peter.

She saw his lips curve before Stefano crooned, "Love," and though she could not spy out his screened eyes, she felt mesmerized by his mouth.

"*Amore,*" he repeated the word in his native tongue and somehow the word 'love' sounded more potent in Italian than in English. "This spot here where we have anchored," he explained in a low, husky voice, "is called *Baia di Amanti.* Lover's Bay. It is well-named, is it not?" He removed his sunglasses and gave her an amused look, with a single eyebrow raised.

"W-why is it called…" Sofia stuttered.

His amusement never faltering, he motioned with one hand toward the shoreline.

"Oh." Heat raced up into her neck and spread into her cheeks. "Oh…yeah, well, um…" Words failed her. Her brain failed her. Her heart was about to fail her.

On the shoreline, stood a stone and marble sculpture of a man and a woman, in all their glory, locked in what looked like a kiss hot enough to melt all that stone and marble. It certainly raised the internal thermometer of Sofia's body to a perilous temperature. While these Italians lived their lives, at ease with their hot-blooded passion, neither offering apology for their fervent ardor, nor restraining from demonstrating their fervent ardor, in private or in public, she, on the other hand, was about to incinerate from the inside out.

Stefano chuckled.

"How—how about you…um…continue with—with…"

Continue what? What had they been talking about? Why had her brain jumped ship and left her abandoned? Why couldn't she tear her eyes off that statue? It was only an inanimate object. A hot, very hot, inanimate object. She heard Stefano's laugh again. It was the impetus she needed to rip her gaze off the lovers. And slammed it on her tour guide. And almost suffered one of those spontaneous combustions. His lips still curved in a grin, but his eyes… His eyes burned with an intensity she had not seen before.

"How…how about you…you continue with the story of your…your family." Sofia stood, and though she made a deliberate move to turn her back to the…kissing couple, she felt the sizzle of their embrace scorch her spine. Ignoring the blatant lovemaking going on behind her, she folded her arms across her chest, and said, "You still haven't told me how your family came to rule Mondoverde."

"I will prepare us some lunch," Stefano responded, casting a cursory glance at his watch, then looked up and smiled one of his devastating grins. "And I will continue with the history lesson as we eat," he promised, making his way to the galley. "We will take our meal on the main deck, yes?"

Twenty minutes later, they were seated at the table and chairs on the main deck, enjoying the simple dish of *spaghettini in bianco,* a pasta tossed in olive oil and coated with a number of spices including black pepper, garlic, oregano, and basil.

"I'm not a connoisseur of wine." Sofia chuckled, slipping her hand under the bowl of the glass. "But this is awfully good."

Her comment pleased Stefano. He beamed with pride. "It comes from the Italian peninsula, from the vineyards of Abruzzo where Giovanni Graziano grew up." He pointed a green olive at her before popping it into his mouth.

"Giovanni Graziano?" Sofia questioned, her finger making a lazy loop around the rim of her glass.

"My great-grandfather." Stefano picked up the bottle and angling it over her glass, he topped it up with the white wine, then filled his own glass. He took an appreciative sip, his eyes laughing at her over the rim. "Yes, *cara*, I shall continue with the history of the House of Graziani."

He tipped his head back, resting his neck on the back of the chair, and let his eyelids drop half-mast. Lost in his reflections, he stared at the few white clouds dotting the blue firmament. The afternoon sun offered unusual warmth for early May. Even so, a slight breeze blew across the Adriatic Sea, ruffling his hair, crisscrossing the brown strands with untamed abandonment, giving the Hereditary Prince of Mondoverde a seriously uncultivated, disheveled appearance.

Sofia rather liked *this* prince. He was...down to earth, approachable, friendly. Sexy.

"Sofia, would you like to hear the rest?"

The sound of Stefano's voice jolted her. He had caught her off in thought. With her guard down. Daydreaming. About him. The grin playing about his lips and glinting in his eyes affirmed he knew, or at least, suspected her thoughts. Squelching a moan, she tried to regain her rattled senses, tried to project a calm, sophisticated persona. "I would. Yeah." She brought the glass of wine to her lips, took a hasty sip. It went down the wrong way. She began to cough and splutter. Her eyes watered and overflowed with tears. She felt foolish. Graceless. So unprincesslike. No kidding.

Stefano surged to sit up straight and gently patted her back with one hand while he took the glass from her fingers with his other. "You are fine, yes?" He set the glass on the table and began to move his palm over her shoulder blades in round, soothing circles.

"Y-yeah," she croaked, drying the moisture beneath her eyes with the tips of her fingers. "I'm not much of a drinker." She didn't drink at all. She'd only taken that sip to bolster her sagging self-confidence.

She'd bolstered it all right.

Right into a humiliating silence.

"Would you care for some iced water?" Concerned and solicitous, Stefano dipped his head to catch her gaze, the palm on her upper back sliding up to massage her neck.

"I'm fine, Stefano." Sofia desperately wanted to jiggle her chair a little to the right to break the connection. His hand at the back of her neck warmed her as he lazily manipulated her muscles with his wicked fingers. "Really I am." *No, I'm not! Not with those fingers turning every single cell of mine to mush.* "Please continue with your story," she whispered.

He gave her a searching stare. It could only have lasted a second. Two at the most. Three, if she really tried to stretch it. But it was long enough to hold her captive, enough to paralyze what was left of her brain, enough to dry up an already dry throat. She longed for a sip of wine to soothe the aridness building in her mouth. She dared not.

"Let us go and sit on the cushioned bench seats, shall we?" Pushing back his chair, he stood, pulled out hers so she could stand, then he reached to pick up both their goblets. He strolled to the bench seat, set down their glasses, and waited for her to sit, curling up in one corner of the seat before he took the seat beside her, leaving maybe three inches of pulsing space between them. "Now. Where was I in the story?" he wondered.

"Umberto was exiled and died without returning to Italy."

"That is correct." Stefano reached his arm across the back of the bench seat and patted her shoulder, then left his fingers lightly resting against her. "Sadly, the Prime Minister failed to live up to the high expectations of most people, including my great-grandfather."

"Prince Giovanni." Sofia did her utmost to disregard the warm flesh of his fingers stroking the sensitive skin of her neck.

"He was not a prince at that time," Stefano corrected, smiling. "He was a simple farmer," he pointed out in a sobering tone, "disillusioned with the status of life on the mainland and dissatisfied with the oppressive laws and restrictions imposed on the populous by the new *regime*." His wicked ministering fingers delved further into her hair at the back of her head, sending a quick shiver to move through her.

"How did he become a prince?" she choked out.

"Hmm?" He seemed distracted. With her mouth.

"Prince Giovanni." Her voice sounded breathy. Her palms felt sweaty. He was going to kiss her again. He was going to plant another of his devastating kisses on her mouth.

She didn't think she would survive it if he did. Not this time. She should move. She ordered her body to move away from him. Move? No. Bolt. She ordered her body to bolt away from him, far, far away from him. But to what city of refuge could she escape a complete meltdown?

She sat on a boat, anchored in the *Baia di Amanti*, of all places, alone with the sexy and charming prince—well, not exactly alone, she amended with an ironic twist of the mouth. They did have that stone and marble sculpture for chaperones. Some chaperones. She could almost hear the kissing statues pry their lips apart in order to bring their stony hands together in exuberant applause, pleased their vibrant presence encouraged — what else? — *amore*.

She needed an army of angels to rescue her from certain deadly temptation, not a sculpture of a man and woman locked in…in… She wheezed out a breath, closed her eyes, clasped her fingers. Sizzling lovemaking. The man and woman were locked in sizzling lovemaking. Her limbs felt weighted down, like marble from the ardent statue had been liquefied, poured into her body, and then allowed to solidify. Her heart, however, was anything but marbleized.

She stayed put.

"How did he become a prince?" Sofia ordered her squealing heart to stand down. It squealed all the louder with gleeful anticipation.

For a second, his eyes flashed to hers, held for one, long pulsing moment, then releasing her, shifted to study the rippling waves. All her breath siphoned out of her lungs, collapsing them. That was good, she mused, wilting in the seat. It made for more room for her squealing heart. It was expanding exponentially in her chest and demanded more space.

Could a person be so lost to another by a simple look?

She could have sworn she heard the female component of the statue let loose on a shout of victory. Almost afraid to look, she cautioned a glance over her shoulder toward the shore. She would not have been at all surprised to see the female high-five her male partner. Her eyes widened. Did the man part of the sculpture just wink at her? She gave her head a vigorous shake and looked again. No. The two were still in a lip-lock.

She hallucinated.

It was the lover-like atmosphere created by the statue. It was the romantic name gracing the bay. It was the quiet isolation of this spot in the sea.

It was the wine. Yeah, that was it. It was the wine. Sofia didn't drink and her system was unused to the wine filtering through her veins, intoxicating her blood, sedating her brain, blitzing her vision.

No wonder she hallucinated. She was inebriated.

No.

It was the look in Stefano's eyes.

The look of love.

No.

If anyone wore the look of love in their eyes, it was her. She'd better smarten up, she castigated herself, deliberately slicing her gaze off the sculpture. Right now!

No more foolishness. No more wishful thinking. No more pretending she could be a princess.

She didn't have the correct shoe size, so the glass slipper would never fit, no matter how much she wanted to shove her foot into it. No matter how much she wanted it, the prince would never come looking for her foot. It was too no-frills. It was too pedestrian. It was too un-royal-like.

"When my great-grandfather was thirty-five and disillusioned," Stefano interrupted, rocking Sofia back to the present, "he packed up his family and left his home in L'Aquila, Abruzzo. Using International Law, he moved his family to the island, renaming it Mondoverde, and created his own dynasty, the House of Graziani."

Intrigued, and her journalistic mind going a mile a second, Sofia asked, "International Law?"

One corner of his mouth curving slightly in a sort of half smile, Stefano reached a hand to smooth out the wrinkles scoring her forehead. "You really did not do any research on us before coming here, did you?" He leaned close, close enough for her to feel his warm breath fan across her flushed face, close enough for her to see his amused eyes, the color of forget-me-not petals ringed with deepest sapphire, stay focused on her, and murmured, "You do have internet capabilities in Canada, do you not?"

She ignored the words and the amusement tugging at his lips. "Tell me about this International Law," she ordered in her most prim and proper voice.

His smile turned genuine. "International Law is the Law of Nations, a set of rules generally regarded and accepted as binding between nations and the law proclaims if the island was *res derelicta*—"

"*Res derelicta*?"

"You did not study Latin when you were in school?"

"No. Why should I? It's a dead language. Extinct."

"Extinct?" He chuckled, tapping a playful index finger on her nose. "How can a language be dead, *cara*, if it is still in use? Legal terms, medical terms, religious terms are all in Latin. And Latin is used in science and pharmacology, even in forensics."

"Fine. Fine. Fine." Sofia performed her best eye roll. "So my education has been sadly lacking." Her body language muttered, *So what?*

He read her body language correctly and vindicated, "People all over the world are studying Latin with enthusiasm and energy. It is gaining new popularity among modern Italians. Conventions of Latin speaking people are becoming a regular occurrence in Europe. So you see, *cara*, Latin is anything but a dead language."

"If you say so," she singsonged.

He put his hands on her shoulders and looked into her eyes. "I do say so."

"Mmm. Hmm."

Her skepticism made him all the more resolved. "I will teach you the language that was brought to Italy about 1000 BC."

"You can't."

"Why can I not?"

"Because I don't have an aptitude for learning languages."

Another reason Sofia wasn't princess material.

A prerequisite for being a royal was to be able to converse fluently in several languages. She was fluent only in English. She disgraced her Polish roots by knowing not one word of the Slavic language. Even her parents had given up trying to teach her the most rudimentary of phrases. So how could Stefano teach her Latin? Impossible.

"I can teach you," he affirmed with all the arrogance of his position, accustomed as he was, to always getting what he wanted, when he wanted.

His ego would not be able to suffer failure, Sofia reasoned, even as a part of her wanted to protest with herself, but he would suffer failure trying to teach her a dead language. She would disappoint.

Stefano dropped his voice to a soft croon. "*Ego sum in amore cum vobis.*"

Sofia went still. She had no idea what he'd just said, yet a sharp bite of pain had her gasping.

* * *

I am in love with you. Stefano had spoken his declaration in Latin, but now he appealed to Sofia's subconscious without speaking. *Look into my heart,* cara. *See my love for you. Look into my eyes,* amore mio. *See the truth of my love for you.*

Sofia looked into his eyes and flew off the seat, jerking to the other side of the boat. He had read confusion in her gaze and what might have been despair, hopelessness, misery. Pain. Now she stood, like a stone wall, as far away from him as his boat allowed, letting the wind rage through her hair, over her face.

Stefano held back the curse words that immediately sprang to mind.

He had skillfully sidestepped the matter of marriage. He had circumvented royal and governmental pressures on the subject of procuring the heir. He had resolved and resigned himself to the fact he would not marry for love, but for duty. But now that he had found the most important person in his life, a partner he truly loved, he felt invigorated, animated, more capable to direct his energies in positive directions.

Not just personally, but for the good of Mondoverde. But especially, most especially for himself. And the woman, this woman who had made herself indispensable to him, this woman who was the source of the pulsing power fueling his high spirits, would not allow him to tell her he loved her. Why? *Why?*

Tension crept through him, but he ignored the tightening in his shoulders. He would not permit this blessing to slip through his fingers. He would determine the specifics of her problem with him, solve the dilemma to his satisfaction, turn her into his arms, lock his hands on the small of her back, pull her close to his chest, press his thighs against hers, claim her lips in a kiss as hot, if not hotter than the statue couple engaged in, and before she would be able to come up for a hit of oxygen, he would put a ring on her finger, sealing her to him forever. However, right now, he needed to bring her back from the brink of alarm. He did not want his future wife to jump overboard in her haste to abscond.

Grabbing a deep breath, Stefano faked it. He faked it because he knew he could fake it. He had been trained to effortlessly mask any rioting emotion and fake it. He crossed his legs, settled his knotted fingers on his knee, made his facial expression neutral, and kept his body relaxed. But inside, he alternated between feeling slack-jawed and strung-out.

"My great-grandfather heard of Mondoverde," Stefano began, relieved his voice came out steady and even and completely disguised the internal upheavals catapulting within him. Thank God he had had his training. Thank God he had learned how to fake it. "It was not called by that name at that time. In fact, it had no name at all. He learned the island was *res derelicta*, abandoned property," he explained, forcing the grip of his fingers to slacken.

"It was also *terra nullius*, land belonging to no one." He watched piqued interest overrule hopeless pain on Sofia's countenance and his feigned relaxation began to turn real. "Mondoverde was founded as a sovereign Principality in 1946 in international waters and the newly designed flag was raised by Giovanni Graziano who styled himself as His Serene Highness. The constitutional, hereditary monarchy was created. As head of the House of Graziani and as sovereign ruler and head of the Principality of Mondoverde, not to mention, as head of the government, he established a certain, shall we say, edict for all future Crown Princes to follow."

The journalist came to life. "You mean the expectation to marry by the age of twenty-five and produce the heir—and spare—for the Graziani throne as soon as possible."

"That would be the one," Stefano drawled, sliding down to slouch in the seat, and crossing his legs at the ankles, he slipped his hands into his pockets.

"Your father—"

"Prince Alessandro," Stefano supplied with a quirk to his lips.

"Prince Alessandro married Princess Cristina when he turned twenty-five?"

"He did." He waited a beat, then added, "I put in the royal appearance one year later. My parents were, shall we say, committed to the cause."

"Uh…yeah…right." Sofia fumbled with words, fumbled with her hands, like she had no idea what to do with them. "And…and your grandfather, he…he, too, he…" She turned an enchanting shade of pink as her words drifted into the Adriatic sky and were carried away by wind across the Adriatic Sea.

Stefano wanted to jump up, stride over to where she stood looking so flustered, pull her into his arms, and hold her tight. He wanted to cup one hand, firm but gentle, under her chin, tip her face up slightly so their gazes would lock, bend his head toward her, and kiss her until they sizzled in the same passionate embrace the statue couple demonstrated. He sat up but stayed put. For now.

"Yes, *cara*, my grandfather, Prince Stefano I, also married when he turned the magic age of twenty-five."

"And let me guess." Sofia lifted her hands, hairbanding her flying hair. "A year later your father put in a royal appearance."

"Not exactly."

"Not exactly?" Surprise lit her eyes. "You mean your namesake broke with royal protocol, too?"

"Not exactly."

"Not exactly?" Expressions chased each other across her beautiful face. Irritation leapfrogged over interest. Inquisitiveness hurtled over both. "What do you mean 'not exactly'?"

The moment proved too good to pass up. Relishing her reaction, Stefano cleared his throat. "My father was born the same year."

Sofia did not disappoint.

"Your father was…" She froze, her mouth still open like she intended to continue speaking. Then her jaw dropped. The color in her cheeks deepened. Her eyes widened.

Stefano could not hold it in. His laughter rang out. When his laugh had downgraded to a chuckle, he intoned, "My grandparents did not put the baby carriage before the royal marriage." Time was up.

He stood up, slow and sure. He strolled in her direction, slow and sure. He stopped in front of her, slow and sure.

She had crossed her arms at her chest, defensive mode, her gaze locked on him, daring mode.

He was at ease with her body language. He excelled in offensive maneuvers. He had served in the military, after all, and knew how to overcome the opponent.

He reached for her shoulders, pulled her to him, slid his hands down her spine to rest at her hips, slow and sure.

He needed to talk with her. But there was a season for talking, and now was not the time for talking.

He dipped his head, slow and sure, pressed his mouth to hers, slow and sure. He moved back and forth a couple of times before settling in. He felt her stiffen for a moment, then felt the stiffness flow out of her body, and he smiled against her lips. He broke off the kiss to nibble his way along her jaw, aware of her soft skin against his lips, then over to her ear, aware of her soft scent teasing his nostrils. He drew her lobe into his mouth and then bit down gently. He felt the shivers race through her and he tightened his hold and reclaimed her mouth in a searing kiss that could rival any the statue couple could put on view.

Without warning, Sofia severed the kiss, severed the embrace, and taking a step back, she glanced around with wild eyes, like she expected the walls of a trap to close in on her.

Stefano would have laughed at the absurdity of the closing walls image given they stood on the open deck of his boat with nothing but air and water around them, if not for the fact he could not laugh. He could not laugh, he could not speak, he could not breathe because a wall of bewilderment closed his throat.

CHAPTER 10

Sofia felt trapped.

Her frantic gaze darted here, there, everywhere.

Trapped on the boat, there was no safe haven for her to run to escape the intoxication called Stefano, unless, of course, she wanted to slip over the side of his boat and walk on water, like the Apostle Peter did on the Sea of Galilee.

But she suspected her level of faith lagged way, way behind the apostle's, and if she were to try the walking-on-water stint, she had no doubt she would sink into the cold blue waters of the Adriatic Sea. Yeah, Peter began to sink, too, when he took his eyes off the Lord and fastened them on the spirited elements whipping up, encasing him, threatening to pull him under, but he had the Lord mere feet away to reach out to and grip His hands.

All Sofia could do was to step back into Stefano's embrace and feel the warmth and strength of his body. And settle. Settle for a flirtation.

That she couldn't do. Wouldn't do. Light and meaningless flirtations were out of the question. Not that what she felt for Prince Stefano was light or meaningless or flirtatious.

She found herself out of her emotional depths with the prince, and all the figurative thrashing of her arms and legs in an attempt to keep her afloat, alive, unscathed, proved to be woefully ineffective.

She loved this man. Wanted this man. Couldn't have this man, this prince of Mondoverde.

She wasn't his type. She didn't fit into his world the same way a circular object couldn't fit into a triangular aperture.

She felt a sense of sadness swarm her. Like she'd lost. Lost something important. Lost something important she'd almost had the chance to grasp, but it somehow slipped through her fingers, leaving her feeling deflated, depressed.

She had always planned to concentrate on her career. To become the best journalist. To touch people's souls with her news articles and somehow make a difference in their lives. Marriage, children, they had never entered into the scheme of things, her scheme of things. They had never been a priority with her. They had never made it onto her to-do list.

Now that she'd had the opportunity to meet Stefano, her world felt strangely out of whack. Like all her priorities, her goals, her aspirations had been turned upside down and inside out. Now that she'd had the opportunity to meet Stefano, she *wanted* marriage, children, even at the expense of her career. Her career? She was actually willing to chuck her career?

She who had vowed to pursue the profession of journalism with tenacity and grit, she who had defined her world by her stubborn determination to prove she could report on the real, soul-stirring news events of the day, she who had prided herself on establishing her life map which had zero tolerance for a husband and children, she would now consider chucking her career, the career for which she'd amassed a whopping student debt to achieve? Her breath caught and her world spun before settling.

She wouldn't have to chuck her career. She felt a tightness in her chest. She couldn't have Prince Stefano.

But life had to go on. Sofia dragged in a quaking breath. Her heart might be shattered, the ache in her chest intolerable, but life had to go on.

The sense of sadness swelled as pain slipped in. The pain of what might have been if Stefano had not been born a prince and she a commoner. Would she be able to go back to being the person she'd been before coming to Mondoverde? Would this pain ever go away? How could she make this pain go away?

"Sofia."

Her gaze spun to his face.

His eyes softened, Stefano moved toward her.

She swallowed, attempted to hide her shaking hands in the pockets of her jacket.

Lord, I know it was Your will that I come here on assignment and meet this prince. Her breath began to hitch. *But was it also Your will I fall in love with a man I can never have? How will I survive the rest of my life without him?* Her chest began to heave. *Reading snippets about him in magazines or catching glimpses of him on TV will never be enough for me. I want to believe, deep in my heart, You are in control here. I want to believe, deep in my spirit, Your presence and power will sustain me. I want to believe, deep in my soul, You will be with me, but…my faith is…weak.* She pressed her crossed hands between her breasts to try to control the tears rising within her.

Stefano reached out to rest his palms on her shoulders, his hands warm, his grip gentle. "Sofia," he said, and she thought his voice sounded hoarse, nervous on her name. "You know I am expected to marry." It was a statement of fact, but his dark eyebrow shot up in query. At the sluggish up-and-down movement of her head, he took a deep breath and continued. "I never expected to have the chance to marry for love even though God calls us to declare what we want to happen in our lives." He took one hand off her shoulder to swipe it through his wind-tossed hair. "I've been so busy praying for God's guidance and wisdom to perform my duties and responsibilities I never thought to ask Him for a love-filled marriage. But He wants to answer my prayers. He wants to grant me the deepest desires of my heart." His smile appeared. "You showed up in the foyer of the *Castello di Bellaterra*. Remember?"

How could she not remember? She had unwittingly mistaken the sexy prince for palace staff. A groan escaped from her mouth. "Yeah, I remember." Heat leached into her cheeks. "You conveniently forgot to introduce yourself." Annoyance edged her words.

"This is so, *cara*." Amusement tugged at the corners of his mouth and brightened his eyes. "You made it so easy for me to have some fun." He did not wear the countenance of remorse.

It only fueled her annoyance. "So glad to have been of service, *Your Serene Highness*." With the limited space his nearness afforded her, she executed an awkward curtsy.

"You will not be angry with me, *Miss Burska*."

"And why shouldn't I be?" Sofia asked him, her foot tapping on the deck, a clear indication her annoyance escalated. Her annoyance and her love. He looked so cute. How could she do battle against cuteness? And yet, it was imperative.

"Because I am Prince Stefano, the Crown Prince of Mondoverde." The words held a serious, autocratic tone. Therein lay the ammunition to defend herself in battle as long as she ignored his eyes that held a glint of blue devilment and his mouth that held the sexiest curve of a grin.

He was a royal prince, she reminded herself.

She was… She was Sofia Burska, a working girl. An in-debt-to-her-eyebrows girl. An insecure girl from across the Atlantic Ocean, from another continent. From another world. A world so far removed from the privileges and pleasures of Bellaterra Castle. When reality punched its way to center stage, clouds of discouragement brushed darkness across her mind and heart and soul.

Misinterpreting her melancholy, Stefano took her face in his hands. "Sofia, it was not my intention to hurt you, you understand, yes?" His worried gaze raced over her face. His features turned remorseful. "I am sorry."

Her palms came up to hold his wrists. "You have done nothing to apologize for, Your Serene Highness." She dropped her hands to her sides. It wasn't his fault he was born a prince. It wasn't his fault she had fallen in love with a prince. It wasn't his fault she ached something fierce because of this prince. Her fingers clenched.

"Your Serene Highness?" Stefano repeated, a smile on his lips that did not quite reach into his eyes, as though he had trouble figuring out if she teased or tormented. "Are we back to formality again?"

"It would be best," Sofia answered woodenly.

"Why?" He shot at her the one word missile, losing the smile and gaining a tick in his jaw from clenching his teeth.

To the degree his hands would allow, she dipped her head, lowering her gaze to study her shoes, because maintaining eye contact with him was not an option. Not if she didn't want to read a world of aching confusion in his eyes. "Because you are a prince."

A red-hot silence crackled in the air following her statement. One pulsing second burst into two, ignited into three. Sofia chewed down on her bottom lip, feeling his razor-sharp stare raze the crown of her head, but she dared not look up. She felt too afraid he would read the longing in her eyes, the need, the love.

His hands dropped to her shoulders. They felt as heavy as a great river of ice. And as cold, sending a pained chill up her spine. His voice, when he spoke sounded strained, his words clipped. "After the last few days of getting to know each other, of—" He knuckled up her chin with barely restrained impatience. "—*kissing*," he hissed, balls of frustration shooting from icy blue cannons, "why are you hung up over my title? *Dio mio*, it is only a label to identify me." He released her chin to slice the air with an angry hand. "Nothing more."

"Your Serene Highness—"

"You call me that one more time and I *will* build that

dungeon, throw you in it, and toss away the key," Stefano growled, his fingers digging into the bones of her shoulders, his lips settling into a line of white-hot fury.

"It's who you are," Sofia argued back. "You can't deny your station in life."

"I am not."

"Then what is your problem?"

Flabbergasted, he stared at her. "*I* do not have a problem." He raked all ten fingers through his hair, making a visible attempt to calm down. "But *you* appear to have a problem."

"I don't." Not unless Sofia counted the uneasiness spiraling through her from not knowing where this conversation headed. Not to mention the tension settling in her neck from trying to keep Stefano from guessing he owned her heart.

"Sofia," he said her name softly, changing tactics and sending tingles rippling down her spine. "Will you do me a small favor?"

She stared at him with no small amount of wariness. He held her gaze levelly. She nodded.

"*Bene.*" A quick smile flashed on his face. "For a moment, will you forget I am a prince? Can you do that for me?" The smile had been stolen by the seriousness of whatever thoughts scampered around in his head. "So I can tell you something?" His palms came to cup her shoulders again, gentle yet resolved.

She was held immobile as much with the hands as with the eyes. They were solemn, intense. Nervous.

* * *

A chunk of that ice must have slid from her shoulders to lodge in her throat because her answer froze in her mouth so all she could manage was another nod of the head.

"Sofia, from the first moment I met you—in the foyer—" Stefano's eyes grew intense with every word he spoke. His hands remained gentle, warm on her shoulders. His voice dropped in decibels, grew raspy. "There has been something between us. Some connection. Some spark of awareness."

Sofia felt her mouth start to drop open. She carefully closed it. She could ignore the shiver running through her at his words, but her rapidly beating heart insisted on recognition. She inhaled a deep breath to pull some oxygen into her lungs and she took in his scent instead. Pure and clean and all-male. Her heartbeat ratcheted higher.

She would have liked to deny his statement, if for no other reason than to provide protection for herself, but honesty would not permit her to do so. She would have liked to dispute his statement, but she wasn't stupid enough to argue. Not when his statement fell right on the mark. She'd been feeling those sparks, too. Only for her, her heart had become engaged. And his was not. His remained intact, uninvolved.

She could not allow herself to surrender and act on those sparks lest they ignite into flames that would reduce her heart to ashes. To return home with a heart with more holes than Swiss cheese was one thing. To return home with a gaping hole in her chest where her heart had once resided was another. She had to return home with some dignity.

And spend the rest of her life nursing her holed heart.

"I want you, Sofia."

"What?" She couldn't keep the breath from whooshing out of her lungs and out through her mouth when his remark hit her right where it hurt the most. In the center of her softest, most vulnerable spot. Her heart.

"I want you," he repeated, his voice low and throbbing with some emotion. "I want us to—"

"No!" Sofia splayed her hands over his chest, intending to push him away, but got sidetracked feeling the beating of his heart, so fast, so strong, through her palms, her fingertips. She sensed his hot breath on her upturned face. She felt his fingers grip harder. She saw his eyes, so dark now, the blue appeared almost charcoal-black, and for a moment, just one moment, she found herself mesmerized, confused. Needy.

Then a wave of self-preservation mingled with a healthy dose of anger surged in to make the save. She would not accept the role of a plaything, a dalliance, a place-warmer until his preferred princess came along. Dignity. It was a matter of dignity. Hers. "No!" she cried, pushing with all her might against the hard rock of his chest until he loosened his grip on her. Her stomach clenched, her breathing furious, she stepped away from him, and clapped her arms around her midriff.

"Sofia, you do not under—"

She cut him off with the crispest tone she could manage. "I am not interested in what—*who* you want. *You* concentrate on getting yourself a poised, beautiful princess bride."

Stefano's frustration rumbled over the deck of his boat, tidal-waving straight for her. "Sofia, let me explain—"

Her heart shattering into a zillion pieces, she intoned, the pitch of her voice cold, "I don't want to hear it." She couldn't bear hearing his cheap words about having a cheap affair. "*I* will concentrate on—"

She almost said she would concentrate on living life without him, loving him for the rest of her life until she died an old maid with a broken, if not, dead heart. Instead, she lifted her chin, frosted her eyes and clipped out, "I will concentrate on my career in journalism, becoming the best journalist in the field." Let him believe she was career-focused and not in the least bit interested in him. She called it desperate survival tactics.

She spoke slowly and succinctly when she added, "Take me back to the palace, Your Serene Highness. Now." He made no move, just watched at her. "Please take me back," she whispered, agonized, all the zillion pieces of her heart disintegrating to dust and blowing away like chaff in the wind.

Stefano slowly backpedaled. His cheeks began to twitch. His jaw began to quiver. His cold stare filled the deck as a barren silence filled the air. "As you wish, *Signorina* Burska," he mimicked her earlier cold tone. Holding her prisoner with his dark gaze, he glared at her, his fury tangible. With a controlled movement, he withdrew his cell phone. His face set like granite, he punched in some numbers, then growled something in Italian. Shoving the phone back into his pocket, he hit her with one final hard look before flying off in a fiery rage heading for the upper helm station to pilot the boat back to where they'd left the car.

Sofia felt relieved, she told herself. And she was. She felt relieved she hadn't made a fool of herself. She felt relieved she hadn't capitulated to his sexy charm. She felt relieved she hadn't allowed him to guess how much she loved him. Yeah, she felt relieved, she thought, fighting down the overwhelming need to cry. Unfortunately, she also felt like she'd been the victim of a hit-and-run by a dump truck and left alone, splattered on the pavement, to die.

* * *

When the boat drew near the pier at a reduced speed, Stefano's bodyguard approached the mooring with a purposeful gait and his regulation sunglasses perched on his nose. Once the boat docked, he quickly tied the boat to the dock, then helped Sofia disembark, his touch on her arm firm but impersonal.

After she gained the pavement, she spotted the chauffeur standing by the car, and not bothering to wait for Stefano to alight, she headed for the sanctuary of the car. Avoiding making eye contact with the driver, she let him open the back door for her. "Thank you," she managed, her voice thick with unshed tears, and slid into the back seat, twisting her fingers together, and staring blindly out the window.

The drive back to the palace was marked with a sustained stony silence. Every few minutes, the chauffeur would lift his troubled gaze to the rearview mirror to frown at them. The bodyguard sat in the front passenger seat, just as quiet and probably just as curious. Neither of the palace employees would dare to overstep their boundaries and question the prince about the screeching silence. Neither of the palace employees would want to be cited for impropriety and fired by the prince.

The moment the car pulled up by the side entrance to the castle, Stefano didn't delay in opening his own door. He swung it out and stepped down, almost like he couldn't wait to be rid of her, but instead of marching off, he twisted around and remained motionless. For a second, something dark and dangerous flashed in his eyes when she stepped out of the car, and then his face went completely blank. It was like looking at a statue. Not like the one they'd seen on their boat ride. That one showed emotion.

"Thank you, Your Serene Highness for the excursion." Her voice was low, but remarkably steady under the circumstances. "I appreciate you taking time out of your busy schedule to show me Mondoverde." Now all she had to do was make a graceful and polished retreat to her room, pack up her belongings in a quick and efficient manner, and escape Bellaterra Castle as fast as she could arrange it.

"Not so fast, *Signorina*." Stefano's iron grip around her upper arm detained her. "When you return to your country and concentrate on your…career," he said, his mouth curving up slightly, then twisted, "remember the Graziano royal family is off limits to your…journalistic endeavors." The last two words were delivered with a healthy dose of distaste.

Anger knocked out the agony and the grief from her and made her forget her insecurities, made her forget she addressed the Crown Prince. "Journalism is a perfectly legitimate profession and as honorable as your own, Your

Serene Highness." The last three words were delivered with the same healthy dose of distaste.

"I never said your vocation was not legitimate or honorable, *Signorina*." He looked austere despite his casual attire. "But in my personal experience with the media, some reporters like to advance their careers by using the royal family for fuel, even if it means slanting information, stretching truths, and exaggerating headlines."

A hot-tempered flush heated her cheeks. "Using the royal family for fuel?" Sofia sputtered. Hot-tempered daggers had to be shooting from her eyes. "How dare you insinuate I would slant information, stretch truth, and exaggerate headlines to advance my career!" Hot-tempered adrenalin for sure zipped through her bloodstream.

Stefano held up an impervious hand, his fingers lean, long, and compelling authority. "*Signorina*, I wish to make certain you understand I will tolerate no maligning insults directed at either myself or any member of my family. I do not wish to see any *articles* written by you about the Graziano royal family. Do I make myself clear?"

She heard the steel in his words. But she had just as much steel in her, she discovered. "Perfectly, Your Serene Highness. But allow me to make *myself* clear." She paused long enough to gasp in some air, and from the corner of her eye, she noted both the chauffeur and the bodyguard make a discreet withdrawal. She had forgotten all about them. It was unfortunate they had to witness this very public argument. It resembled more like the Battle of Armageddon, she mused, gritting her teeth.

"You did not have me sign any such stipulation." She straightened her spine. "You knew I was a journalist when you invited me out today." She threw back her shoulders. "You, therefore, understood the risks involved." She raised her chin, aiming it at a defiant angle. "It's too late now to worry about your lack of discretion." She crossed her arms at her chest, her fingers digging into her flesh. "And, Prince Stefano, allow me to also say it's definitely too un-prince-like to try to control citizenry and circumstances to serve your purposes by using intimidation."

On that pronouncement, Sofia whirled around, making an exit as good as any actress worthy of an Oscar. Seething and steaming, she made her way up marble stairs and along carpeted corridors, her footfalls brisk and bothered. After she stepped into her room and closed the door behind her, the adrenalin vanished, and sagging against the door, she buried her head in her hands.

What had possessed her?

Why had she acted in such a horrible manner?

What was the matter with her?

Need you ask? queried her hurting heart. *Unrequited love,* her heart enlightened.

Unrequited love made a woman crazy? A moan ground out passed her lips. She had to leave, right now. She had to get away from here, right now, before who knew what unrequited love would make her say, make her do. Something foolish. Something humiliating. She clamped her mouth, lest she say something else to Stefano. Like...she loved him.

On a whimper, she pushed off the door, inched to the bed. Without meaning to, she paused at the window. She crooked a finger to pull one of the drapes aside by a couple of inches, and looked down, knowing her bedroom window overlooked the parked car and...Stefano. He still stood there, legs spread, hands fisted on his hips, staring off into space. The man she loved with all her heart. She kissed the fingertips of her right hand and pressed them lightly against the glass before turning away on a bit-back sob.

Stefano hated her, Sofia realized with a dark hit of pain. The knowledge grabbed her gut and twisted it hard. And

173

the tears she'd been bottling up fizzed and hissed. She sank onto the side of the bed, dabbing her cheeks with the back of her hand, and wishing she had never come to Mondoverde.

CHAPTER 11

Just as the sun sank in the western sky, a knock rattled the door to Stefano's palace office. Lifting his eyes, he scowled at the oak-paneled door, scowled at the fated intrusion, the inevitable disruption. His gaze slammed back on the papers strewn across his massive desk, critical reports from the various ministers of the Crown Council, reports he was supposed to have been studying in anticipation of his meeting with the ministers in the morning, but he had only seen blurred white for the past several hours. And when he had been able to concentrate, pockets of minutes here and there, he had seen black-inked words bleeding into one another, incomprehensible and uninteresting.

He scowled at the papers. Scowled at the only excuse he had for his inability to carry out his duties to the realm with reasonable proficiency, with purposeful consideration. Sofia Burska. "Come." His voice filled the room when he roared the one word and stood. He scowled at his father when he elbowed open the door since both hands were full.

And he scowled at Micia who wove back and forth in front of his father with breathtaking disregard for safety as she led the way to his desk. When she pawed his leg, Stefano refused the request with a shake of his head. The cat sent him a long, shrewd look, then hopped lightly onto the surface of the desk, sniffing the papers. Finding them

175

un-sniffworthy, she cast them a look of disdain and plopped her body on them with the contempt only Micia could demonstrate.

Stefano swore and dived in to rescue the now-crumpled but no less critical reports, and tossing them onto the corner of his desk, he thought wistfully of the bottle of amaretto he had stashed in the cabinet of the credenza. A glass of the amber, bittersweet almond tasting liqueur would pair nicely with the coffee his father carried. He could use something to take his mind off—

His vision was snagged by a pair of green eyes. *What?* he asked the cat via telepathy. When Micia remained silent, watching him, waiting patiently, he demanded, *Did you come here just to attack me with your ray gun vision?* The cat gifted him with a knowing stare, curled on the desktop, stood, made a tight circle, and laid herself down again, one eye closed, the other clamped on him.

"Stefano." Prince Alessandro advanced into the room, having pushed the door shut with a cheerful thrust of one Armani heel. "We missed you at dinner tonight." He set a cup of coffee before Stefano and sipped from his own after pulling up a chair facing him. "You have been conspicuously absent from all family meals for the past week," his father added, his tone understated, with nuances of teasing. "Scrupulously avoiding all family contact." He took another sip of his coffee, studying Stefano over the rim of his cup with the all-seeing eyes of a wise and loving parent.

Huffing out a beleaguered sigh, Stefano sat. Of course, he had been ducking family contact. He was in no mood to stand in the crossfire of questions and parry the shots. He was in no mood to discuss Sofia and her abrupt departure from the palace. He was in no mood to *think* about Sofia. But that was exactly what he had been doing for the past week, since she had hastily packed her suitcase, made a frenzied call for a taxi, and drove away from the *Castello di Bellaterra* without a backward glance. He should know. He watched her leave.

Abruptly, Micia stood, comforted him with an extended paw, a sympathetic purr.

But his temper continued to rise, close to erupting, from the frustration, from the exasperation. From the pain. The slightest tremor could set off the dormant volcano.

Reminding himself to not crush it with the strength of his storming fingers, he reached for his cup. Bringing it to his lips for a mouthful, he felt instant and profound appreciation the coffee had been doctored with a shot of amaretto. He savored the sip, allowing it to course through his iced-over veins, thawing, just a little, the frozen blood trapped there.

With careful deliberation, he set the cup down, but kept his fingers wrapped around it, absorbing its warmth, and hoping, soon, the glacier encasing his heart would melt and he would be able to resume being a live human being instead of going through the motions of life like the walking dead.

Holding his father's gaze, Stefano said, "I have had much work." He grasped onto the quasi-truth. "All of it required my immediate attention." The words held a note of impatience bordering on testiness.

Micia released a sorrowful meow that had Stefano grinding his teeth. His cat did not believe him.

"You could not delegate to your aide?" A smile covering his diplomatic face, his blue eyes giving nothing away, his father, the ruling monarch of Mondoverde, leaned into the chair, crossed his legs, and balancing his cup on his knee, he looked amiable, relaxed, like he had all the time in the world to have this conversation.

Stefano's tongue sizzled. "No, I could not." Why couldn't his father take the hint that he wanted to be left alone? Feeling the sharp pang in the center of his chest, he forced out, "Let it be." The direct approach would work.

Or not.

Prince Alessandro lifted his cup to his mouth and over the rim, his eyes sparkled blue mischief. "You are testy, yes?"

"Fine." Stefano gathered the reports together with a savage grasp. "Yes." He tapped the edges of the papers on the desktop with none too gentle hands. "I am testy." He shoved them into the folder, unread. "So?" He slapped the folder down on the desk, barely missing the cup of coffee, not caring the reports remained unread, or that he had almost knocked the contents of his cup all over his desk and his cat who yowled her complaint, and scowled at his father. He knew he was overreacting. He knew he should reach deep inside him to pull out his usual, *learned*, calm and quiet demeanor. But he had no will.

"That is what happens when you miss meals." His father's lips twitched once, then firmed. "You become testy."

"That is not why—" Stefano's mouth was hammered shut by dismay that he had almost let loose on the real reason he acted like a furious lion with spearing quills caught in his paw. Most smart people would slowly walk away when confronted with an angry lion.

Not his father.

His father believed in disregarding a lion's strong and compact body, in disregarding a lion's strong and powerful legs, in disregarding a lion's strong and menacing teeth, and grab the roaring lion of adversity by its shaggy mane, and like Samson of the Old Testament, filled with God's presence and power, rip it apart with his bare hands.

"What happened with you and Sofia Burska?"

His father also believed in the direct approach.

Micia sat, alertly listening to the conversation and watching him with wise green eyes.

"Nothing happened with me and Sofia Burska." And was that not the truth? Nothing happened. Nothing that he had planned, had hoped for. He realized he held the cup with such a fierce grip, he wondered it had not snapped into a million jagged pieces in his hands, each fragment spearing his skin. Slowly, he inhaled one deep-chested breath. Slowly, he blew it out through his mouth. Slowly, he unfurled one stiff finger at a time. He would be calm.

Slowly, he leaned into the back of his chair, thrust the hands, newly formed into fists, into his pockets, and arranged his facial features into a deadpan expression.

With the dainty surefootedness of a cat, Micia stepped onto the arm of his chair. Sensing therapy was needed—the unconditional love only a Calico cat can give, willingly and enthusiastically—she settled on his lap and began to purr.

"*Figlio mio*, be grateful it is I who speak to you," Prince Alessandro said in a dry voice. "If it is your mother, you know she will climb the highest peak of the Gran Sasso d'Italia mountain, all 9,554 feet of it, if it will mean she can get it out of you." A laugh rasped out of his mouth. "She is a formidable force." His whispered words were full of awe and love.

And Stefano's gut constricted.

To have a marriage like his parents. His grandparents. His great-grandparents. Full of awe. Full of love. What a legacy. His top lip pressed into the bottom. His upper teeth ground into the lower. His marriage was not to be the same for him. His would be…duty-bound.

"Any progress on the matter of marriage?" His father asked, his expression innocent, his gaze piercing.

Stefano experienced mixed feelings about the abrupt change in topic. He felt relief they no longer discussed Sofia. He felt hounded by the ever-present pressure to marry. He felt a black fog of depression approach, hover overhead with menacing intent, land with precision on his shoulders, digging in its talons of trepidation, reaching their poisonous points all the way down to his chest. He flinched.

"No. There is not." Like thistles of violence, the words catapulted from his mouth, causing the cat to commiserate with a sorrowful meow. "Feel free to make a search for a suitable wife for me," he ground out. What did he care? If he could not have Sofia, the love of his life, his forever mate, the keeper of his soul, what did he care whom he wed? He would do his duty. He would marry for the throne of Graziani. He would provide the heir for the Principality of Mondoverde. And no one, *no one*, would ever suspect, that inside, in his heart, where it mattered most, he had died.

Micia raised herself on her hind legs, rested her front paws on Stefano's shoulders, and stared at him. To Stefano, it seemed the cat was able to see into his soul and he wondered if Micia could see all the pain and frustration lurking there.

"Sofia Burska is a journalist, is she not?" Prince Alessandro set his empty cup on the desk, and leaning forward, he rested his elbows on his spread knees.

His father's lightning-swift change of subjects rattled Stefano. Especially the subject of Sofia. He wanted to avoid the subject of Sofia. Ignore it. Deny it. But the intensity of his father's expression—and that of the cat's—made him exhale a "Yes."

Prince Alessandro remained silent a moment, studying Stefano, who tried to ignore the humor in his father's eyes and the challenge in the cat's. "I understand from your mother, Sofia was sent here on assignment." His eyes crinkled slightly as he smiled and straightened. "To get an exclusive with you." His voice sounded far too reasonable for Stefano's comfort.

"She tried, yes." Stefano mirrored his father's reasonable tone perfectly, but his stomach churned.

"Yet...she left without procuring one," his father mused, settling into his chair, his fingers curled around the arms in an easy clasp, his expression quizzical, with shades of tender amusement swirling through it.

Somehow Stefano got his shoulders to move in an approximation of a shrug. "While I did not agree to a formal interview, I am certain during her brief stay on

Mondoverde she amassed enough information on the House of Graziani to write a novel for publication let alone an article for her newspaper." His words were sharp with pain and anger he did not bother to hide.

"That is possible," his father acceded, crossing his legs and resting his folded his hands on his thigh. "But it has been a week since her abrupt departure and my aides tell me they have seen no such article in *The Polish Alliancer*."

"Perhaps her editor did not wish to print her babblings." The shrug came easier to Stefano. Practice made perfect, even though he found himself subjected to slit-eyed feline observation. "Perhaps her newspaper feared a lawsuit from us."

"I do not think so." Prince Alessandro shook his head from side to side. "If her information was researched and found to be accurate—even if it was not," he said with a wry twist of the lips, "the newspaper would have been quick to print it. You know royal headlines guarantee an instant increase in circulation which means an influx of revenue for the paper."

"I have no idea why the story is not out there." This time the lift of Stefano's shoulders did not come with ease. It was a jerk up and a jolt down.

Why had Sofia's editor not printed it? His brow puckered, his eyes narrowed. It could have brought financial benefits to the paper. It always brought financial benefits to any newspaper carrying stories on the royal family. His gaze wavered to the window and locked on the pane of glass. It could also have launched Sofia's career, the career she so valued, to great heights. It always launched any journalist who did a write-up on the royal family into immediate respect and demand. It could have garnered both her newspaper and her with profitable recognition in the world of the media. Royal headlines always did. So why—

A philosophical sigh from the cat caught Stefano's attention. Micia looked at him, then gurgled a throaty purr.

"In not allowing the article to run," Prince Alessandro interrupted in a low voice, "Sofia has demonstrated wisdom, discretion. Compassion."

Stefano's vision circled back to his father, but he made no response.

"Excellent qualities for a princess of Mondoverde, would you not agree, *figlio mio*?"

Stefano gave a slightly harsh laugh. "*If* the lady in question is interested in being a *principessa*, married to *me*, and embracing the idea of *bambini*. Of *amore*," he added in a tight voice, jumping to his feet, and poured the cat into the chair he vacated. Raking all ten of his rigid fingers through his hair, he stormed to the window. Shoving both hands, clenched into fists, into his pockets, he stared out without seeing anything except Sofia's image reflected in the glass. "The only thing important to Sofia is her career." He thrust up a hand to give the knot in his tie a brutal tug, to rip open the top three buttons of his shirt without thought to ruining the silky material with the vicious pull. What did he care? His shirts were replaceable. His heart was not. Another laugh shot into the room. His. And it held bitterness.

"Stefano." His father waited for him to turn around and face him. "If that was true, if Sofia was only interested in her career in journalism, she would have had her story in print by now." He paused to let the words sink in. "Because she has not is indicative her loyalty to herself, to her own goal in life, has been tested during her stay here, and has begun to erode as her commitment to the advancement of her career has been displaced with a new goal. You."

Gripping the window ledge behind him, Stefano felt the color in his face fall away.

"Stefano, the girl was probably overwhelmed." Prince Alessandro waved a hand to indicate the palace, them. "She probably felt inferior. So she bolted."

Stefano stumbled to the chair, lifted the cat, depositing a protesting Micia on the floor, and sank into the chair.

"If I did not misinterpret the...chemistry...between the two of you, I would say *amore* is very much alive and felt by the both of you." His father stood, reached for both cups. "If you love her, fight for her. And when it feels like you are the only one in the relationship doing the fighting, remember who you are fighting for, remember love and family are worth fighting for, and fight all the harder. Fight until you have the victory. Graziano men do not give up. They never give up. It is not in their genetic makeup to even consider giving up. Especially on *amore*." He came around the desk, laid a fatherly hand on his shoulder. "I would encourage you, Stefano, to pray for guidance and strategy." He patted the shoulder a couple of times before adding, "An optimist sees an opportunity in every calamity while a pessimist sees a calamity in every opportunity. Which are you, *figlio mio*?" His father's face struck a benevolent smile, then with Micia following, he left, closing the door behind them with a quiet click.

Stefano sat, allowing the seriousness of the moment to rest on his shoulders. His father's sage words circled his mind. He breathed a prayer to the Lord of Hosts, asking for help to rely on His strength to wage this battle. With the humble and heartfelt prayer concluded, a slow smile formed on his mouth.

* * *

"My office. Now."

Sofia still gripped the receiver when she heard the heavy-handed click followed by the drone of the disconnected line. A shiver trickled down her back.

Her boss. Her used-up-all-my-patience-with-you editor.

She'd been expecting the summons. Each day that came and went she'd been expecting the summons. She hadn't been fooled into any false perception of a reprieve by his silence regarding her failure, so she'd been expecting the summons.

The day had dawned dark and foggy, a perfect reflection of the way her insides felt.

And in this perfect reflection, the expected summons—the moment of accountability—had finally burst onto her scene.

Would her boss express his disappointment in her with dissatisfaction carved in his gaze and displeasure etched in his voice? Would he express his feelings of betrayal, that after he'd given her a chance to prove herself, following her myriad declarations to the fact, she'd let him and the newspaper down? Pushing back from her desk, she stood, paused, and though she gulped in a stabilizing breath, her nervousness spiraled.

Or would he simply bellow, "You're fired!"?

She thought about her student loan.

She thought about the disgrace at being terminated.

She thought about Prince Stefano of Mondoverde.

Sofia couldn't keep the moan from spilling out of her mouth. A swift glance around her assured her none of her colleagues paid any attention to her, their concentration focused either on the computers or on the phones.

It had been two weeks since returning from her fruitless and flopped assignment. Two weeks since she'd fled from the beautiful island nation of Mondoverde. Two weeks since she'd left her heart in the royal hands of the Crown Prince.

During these two weeks, she'd managed to evade questions. Questions from her editor. Questions from her colleagues. Questions from her family. She'd evaded them by making herself scarce. Unavailable. Until she could trust herself to speak without eliciting more questions she didn't want to answer.

It had been two weeks. There still was a giant hole where her heart used to be, but at least, she wasn't crying anymore. She was thankful the gnawing pain in her chest had weakened to something she was going to be able to endure. She was also thankful during the days the prince had edged into her mind every other second, rather than every single one. The nights, however, still proved challenging. During the nights, when she lay in bed, alone, with sleep eluding her and the bed sheets scrunched in her fingers, the unabashed prince moved into her mind with his fluid grace and inherent dignity and sexy grin.

Outside the closed door to Walter Kostecki's office, she paused again, released her bottom lip from the mutilation of her teeth, drew in another gulp of desperately-needed oxygen into her lungs, and worked on her smile. On a winged-up prayer for guidance, wisdom, and words, she lifted her hand, fisted it, and rapped her knuckles on the door.

On the terse command of "Come!" the already tightened screws in her stomach squeezed harder, making her flinch, but she made the heroic effort to tamp them down and pushed open the door. "Sir?" she asked, not advancing from the doorway. Dissatisfaction was carved in his gaze.

"Sit." Her editor had been leaning in his chair. Now he brought it down with a thud. "Close the door behind you." Displeasure was etched in his voice.

"Sir?" Sofia took the seat in front of the editor's desk. "You wanted to see me?"

One eyebrow spiked up, and resting his elbows on the desk, her boss leaned in. "Need you ask?"

Betrayal hung in the air in the office like the fog clung to the air outside.

She swallowed and shook her head.

The moment of accountability.

His gaze skewered her. "Explain." He threw out the one terse word.

"I…" She stalled at his rough-edged command. Unable to hold his accusatory gaze, she dropped her eyes to her hands on her lap, clenched so tightly that the skin on her palms was shredded by her nails within microseconds of her sitting.

"Burska." His low voice thrummed over nerves stretched taut. "I want you to explain to me why you came back from a simple assignment with nothing." The words steadily grew in volume until the last word was shouted. "I thought I made it clear we needed that article?"

"Yessir."

"Look at me."

Sofia raised her head.

Her boss gripped the pen, ramming the top end onto the desk with each word he spewed out. "I want to know what happened over there that *The Polish Alliancer* does not have our scoop." Steam practically spurted from his nostrils.

"I…"

"You've said that already. Out with the rest." His expression turned volcanic. "Now."

"I can't—can't write the—the article, sir."

"Why?" The one-worded demand stormed from his mouth to slug her in the chest, hard.

Sofia felt her mouth opening, then closing on the words she didn't know how to say. "I—" She shook her head, tried again. "I—"

"Burska." Walter Kostecki looked and sounded like a man who had clearly lost every vestige of patience and was about to commit murder. Premeditated murder. Her murder.

"I crossed—I crossed professional lines. I didn't mean to," she added hastily on seeing he'd stop daggering the desk with the pen, but now he held it in his fingers, the grip so rigid, his knuckles had whitened.

"Explain," he ordered.

"I—" She concentrated her attention on the pen in his hands. She took in a steadying breath, then admitted in a soft voice, "I fell in love with Stefano—" She flinched at his muttered curse, the one harsh word echoing in the office. She braved raising her eyes to his. "And I can't see my way clear to write something that will contribute to his loss of privacy."

With a viciousness that caused her to wince, her editor threw down the pen and flung himself into the back of his chair. "Did we or did we not," he said through gritted teeth and thrashing his hand back and forth to indicate the two of them, "have this discussion before you left? The one where I clearly told you not to fall for the prince?"

"Yessir," she whispered.

"And what do you do?" He clutched the arms of his chair and leaned forward, the movement slow but menacing. "You disregarded my warning." He sounded incredulous. Then on a harsh expel of air, he threw himself into the back of the chair again. "So what now, Burska? You get to have one of those open-carriage rides to some fancy, old cathedral and marry the rich and handsome prince?"

"No." She felt like a thousand sharp-pointed spears harpooned into every inch of her body, with the heaviest concentration being on her chest. She licked dry lips. She swallowed in the hopes of generating some saliva to moisten her dry throat. Both lips and throat remained dry. "No," she croaked out. She wanted to say she finally met a man who could make her dream new dreams, but... Her eyelids fluttered shut on the pain of loss. She wasn't princess material, she wanted to add, but she couldn't make her mouth to work, couldn't get the words out it hurt so much.

"So, you have no prince and you have no story." Her boss looked at her with a disappointed shake of the head. "I'm sorry, Sofia," he said after several tension-filled seconds, his voice as soft as it was regretful. "I don't have a choice." He raked his fingers through his hair, spiking it and amplifying his usual tousled veneer. "You knew how important it was for us to run that story." He paused. "We needed, desperately, the shot of new life in our media arm." He paused again, his expression turning apologetic. "You understood it would come to this."

"Sir?"

"I'm sorry, Sofia," he echoed, his tone quiet, tender. "But I'm afraid I am going to have to let you go."

"Sir?" Sofia forgot to breathe. "You can't mean this. Please. Please don't—"

"Sofia." Walter Kostecki rose to his feet, came around his desk to stop by her side, and rested a gentle hand on her shoulder. "I'm sorry, Sofia, but I don't have a choice. I don't have the resources to pay your salary. Effective now, you are off our payroll." He removed his hand from her shoulder to tunnel his fingers through the hair at his neckline. "I may have to let others go." He sounded defeated. "Our financial integrity is that fragile." He sighed, returned to his chair and collapsed into it. "You were our hope for survival." The lift of his shoulders was weary, his facial expression was wan. "We don't have the ability to compete in a rapidly increasing hostile economic environment." He moved his lips into what was supposed to be a smile. It never made it. "And I'm too old and too tired to keep up the fight." He picked up a copy of *The Polish Alliancer* and gave it a fierce study. "You have potential," he told her without looking up. "You have determination. You will land on your feet. Good-bye, Sofia."

The last three words carried finality.

CHAPTER 12

So you have no prince and you have no story.

Walter Kostecki's pronouncement thundered in Sofia's brain.

Her hands staying loose at her sides, her legs continuing to support her on her three-inch heels, she worked, desperately hard, at keeping her face emotionless while she snaked around her coworkers' desks back to her own. She gripped the back of her chair, hung her head, and closed her eyes on the burning forming there. She also had no job.

She had no job. She had no story. She had no prince.

Despite the barricade of her closed lids, tears filled her eyes and her throat got tight.

She had no Stefano.

Sofia had to breathe for a second before she could summon up the courage and strength to continue with what she had to do.

She had to pack up her meager belongings at *The Polish Alliancer* and head out into a lonely life that just got complicated with joblessness.

You have potential. You have determination. You will land on your feet.

She stifled a hysterical laugh.

Walter Kostecki had no idea—no one knew, not even her family, only God—how hard she worked to overcome her insecurities. How hard she worked to demonstrate her potential as a journalist. No one knew of her deep-seated need to prove her worth. It was stupid, this need. It had no basis for existing. Except she had three older, very successful brothers. And next to them, she felt mediocre.

And she wanted to make her parents proud of her.

No one knew what it cost her to reach deep, deep within her for that determination to do her very best regardless how she quaked inside. To find her niche in life. And to excel at it.

Land on her feet? No. She couldn't even see her feet. She couldn't see past the gaping hole in her chest where her heart should have been. How could she land on her feet? She didn't have what it took to reach inside, deep inside, and pull out the determination she needed to land on her feet and... And what?

She didn't want another job.

She wanted Stefano. Her prince. The man who owned her heart.

One of the tears she'd been working so hard to hold back leaked through her tightly screwed eyelids and slid down her cheek.

"Sofia?" The excited receptionist hurried toward her. "A courier just delivered this for you."

Sofia wiped away the runaway tear and blinked back the others. "What is it?" Her words sounded hoarse to her own ears, but the other woman didn't seem to notice. She was too captivated by the long, slender box in her hands.

"Open it up and see, but I think it's pretty obvious," the receptionist gushed, handing over the box. "You have an admirer."

"You've been watching too many romantic comedies," Sofia muttered, feeling a flush steal over her face when she noticed the other reporters had all abandoned their desks and computers and phones and formed a semicircle around her.

"I didn't know you were dating a guy." Hurt flashed in the receptionist's eyes. "How come you didn't tell me you were dating a guy."

Sofia thought of Stefano. "I'm not." Her words of denial sounded numb and lifeless. As numb and lifeless as she felt.

"Then who—?"

"I don't know." Each word came out heavy, flat. Sofia didn't care. She only cared about one man. She was a fool to want to be desired, to be loved by one man and one man only. A man she couldn't have.

"Don't keep us in suspense, Sofia. Open it up." This from one of the interested onlookers semi-circled around her.

Setting the box on her desk, Sofia tried to smile, but her lips wouldn't curve in the right direction. Her entire face felt stiff as if overlaid with cement. Even her hands felt stiff as she began to lift the lid off the box. Stiff and numb and lifeless.

When she worked the lid off, she froze.

Oh.

Oh, my.

One perfect purple tulip nestled in the tissue paper at the bottom of the florist's box.

"Is there a card?" the receptionist wanted to know.

"Hmm?" Sofia felt dazed staring at the beautiful flower.

"A card." The receptionist made a sound, part frustration, part humor. "Is there a card in there saying who the sender is?"

"A card." Sofia looked, but she didn't have to read a card to know the identity of the sender. "Um. No. No, there isn't." The color of the tulip gave it away.

Clapping her hands together, the receptionist almost hyperventilated when she screeched with glee, "So, it's a *secret* admirer."

Yes. Secret.

"I don't think I've ever seen a purple tulip," the receptionist mused, a thoughtful frown marring her forehead. "I've seen red, of course, and white and yellow, but not purple." The frown deepened. "Wonder what it means? Not that I haven't seen a purple tulip, I mean," she added quickly, "but the color. What does a purple tulip mean?"

"Royalty," Sofia supplied in a soft voice, lifting the tulip from the box with deferential fingers and bringing it to her nose. And the national color of Mondoverde, she added to herself. Why? Why would Stefano have sent her this flower? And it was Stefano she had no doubt.

"Forever love."

Sofia flicked her attention to one of her colleagues who stood leaning over his computer.

"Forever love," her coworker repeated, studying the screen, and then spun his gaze onto Sofia. "I looked it up on the Internet and it says a purple tulip means forever love." He walked back to take his place in the semicircle with an easy grace, a slight grin tilting up the corner of his mouth. "You're seeing somebody. Tell us. Every single juicy detail." The grin widened to a fleeting smile. "Ve have vays to make you talk."

"There's nothing for me to talk about." A jolting sensation brought a flush to her cheeks. "Like I said, I'm not dating anyone." That was true. "There is no card in the florist box." That was also true. "So…" She lifted her shoulders in what she hoped looked like a beats-me kind of shrug. It wasn't like she lied. She just withheld her suspicion of the identity of the sender. Why had Stefano sent her the tulip? "Since there is no card and no boyfriend," she dug herself in deeper in the withheld information arena, "perhaps it's a simple case of the florist sending the beautiful flower to the wrong recipient." The explanation sounded plausible.

The explanation would have been believable, except…

Except a fraction of a second later, a loud commotion took center stage, causing the earlier flush to Sofia's cheeks to be brushed off her face like a robust wind swooping in and sweeping the pavement clear of any loose articles. She sucked in her surprised gasp just before it left her lips.

The Palace Security, the elite segment of the *Corpo della Guardia*, responsible for the protection of the Mondoverduvian royal family, burst through the doors, fanning out with a controlled aggressiveness, storming the workplace, and securing every square inch of *The Polish Alliancer* office. No one moved. No one dared to breathe, let alone scream. Even Walter Kostecki scurried out from his office with a cutoff, "What the—" and had both words and movement immobilized when he saw the Palace Security ringed the office, their stance assertive.

A pulsing moment later, through the door left ajar by the Palace Security but not unmanned, Stefano, Crown Prince of Mondoverde, entered, dressed in a dark suit, impeccably tailored and very, very expensive, wearing thousand-dollar Italian shoes, and moving with controlled power.

Sofia laid a hand on her chest, fingers splayed, and widened her eyes. The sight of him, all arrogant and royal and gorgeous, here, here in Toronto, here in this office, was enough to shove the air from her lungs. *What is he doing here?* Despite the fog from outside had snuck in through the window to wrap around her brain, the words still managed to form in her mind, her sight still managed to stay focused on him as she watched him scan the office with a shrewd gaze.

"All secure, Your Serene Highness," one of his guards announced, standing by the door, with the same military stance employed by the other guards deployed throughout the office. Eyes forward, chin up, chest out, shoulders back, stomach in, heels together, toes apart. And if the situation warranted the action, hands at the ready to reach for their concealed weapons.

Stefano gave him a curt nod, his own gaze latched onto Sofia, and there was something disconcerting in his eyes, a steady, measuring expression. When his eyes released her, dipping to the tulip held in her hand, she gasped in a much-needed gulp of air, but it had no time to enter her lungs because when he snapped his gaze to her face again, that gulp of air performed a hasty U-turn and plunged passed her lips. Her poor lungs had no chance to try again to inflate with oxygen. Stefano came toward her, purpose in every step.

Though her breathing apparatus had not succeeded in inflating with air, her heart, which must have hitched a flight across the Atlantic Ocean with Stefano, had returned to active duty, thrashing against her ribcage with such force, she marveled her chest didn't suffer a massive perforation.

He came to stand mere inches away, his blue eyes holding a tight focus on her, yet his sexy mouth remained silent.

Sofia would have said something, something cordial like, "Good afternoon, Your Serene Highness," or something affable like, "Welcome to Toronto, Prince Stefano," or something mirroring her twitchy state of mind, something more along the lines of, "What are you doing here, Stefano!" but her voice box had suffered a systems failure the moment he'd entered the office, and all she could do was gaze at his face, drink in his beloved features like a parched person who'd stumbled on a fountain of water after traversing the hot, arid desert.

Revived by the sudden sight of him, she wanted to reach out her hand. She ached to touch the tips of her fingers to his stubble-lined jaw, to caress the softness of his olive-skinned forehead, to stroke her fingers through the dark silky strands of his hair to wrap them around his neck, and pull herself to him until she could tuck herself under his arm and lean into him. She kept her hand forcibly at her side.

Stefano raised her free hand to his lips, but he didn't kiss it. He just held it against his lips for a long moment before he said, "I see you received the flower."

All Sofia could do was swallow. And maybe nod just a little bit.

His grin was a mile wide against her fingers, then he

caressed each knuckle with his lips. "Remind me, Sofia," he murmured, her name sounding like a prayer, a plea, a benediction, "to explain the story behind the purple tulip."

"It means forever love," the receptionist piped up in helpful mode.

Panic knocked through Sofia. Heat flamed on her cheeks. She'd forgotten where they were. That they weren't alone. Not daring to look in the direction of the rapt onlookers, she snatched her hand from Stefano's and jerked back a step. She tried for a smile, but her lips had a hard time moving up at the corners. Stefano, Sofia noted, had no such trouble. He watched her, his mouth settling in what could only be described as a wicked grin.

"We looked it up on the Internet," the receptionist informed the prince, not in the least bit uncomfortable she helped herself to some of the credit. "The meaning of the purple tulip." Flicking her accusatory gaze at Sofia, she said, hurt spilling from every word, "Sofia didn't tell us she was dating a prince."

"I'm not." Sofia didn't know how her voice could sound so calm when her insides did cartwheels.

"She is not," Stefano agreed, his dark head bent in an autocratic nod, but his dark eyes danced with a sort of somber amusement.

Sofia thought she heard him add, "Not yet," in an undertone, but shook her head at the wishful thought. She worked to draw in a breath. "What are you doing here, Your Serene Highness," she demanded, then saw the lines of strain and fatigue fanning from the corners of his eyes. She wanted to smooth away those hard lines. Not with her fingertips. But with her mouth. She took another step, backward and judicious.

Stefano held her gaze with his dark eyes and she felt the crackling attraction between them. "We did not conclude our interview, *Signorina*." He nullified the two steps she'd taken away from him by stepping into her personal space.

195

His fingertips stroked over her face, down her neck, to brush against her collarbone.

"We never started one to finish," she contradicted on a rasping breath.

He let his hand, lean and long-fingered and smoothly assured, slide down her arm to link fingers with her. "Then we must rectify the situation immediately, must we not?"

"No."

His autocratic brow arched. "No?"

"No."

"Why?" Stefano's gaze penetrated deep and she found it unsettling.

"Because I'm not writing the article on you. And because I won't..." The sound of her voice was broken but brave as Sofia continued, "I'm fired."

"Good."

"Good?" She glared at him with flooded eyes. The first splash of tears hit her smooth cheeks. "I've just lost my job. I've got a whopping student loan—"

"You have another job already waiting and it pays considerably more than your meager salary at this newspaper."

She pulled at her captured hand without success. Setting the tulip on the surface of her desk, she brought her hand to swipe at the tears. "What job? What are you talking about? I have no other j—"

A flash of his wicked grin was the way Stefano cut her off before he lowered his mouth to hers. "Besides, your presence is requested at a royal function."

"What royal function?"

"A wedding."

"A wedding?" She felt his mouth in her hair and then his kiss on the top of her head. "Whose wedding?"

"Mine." He cocked a thumb at himself to identify him as the person in question.

The disclosure of his pending nuptials with another

woman, a suitable princess-type woman, a woman who would lie in his arms, receive his kisses, and bear his children, had Sofia's stomach twisting, her chest clenching, her breath faltering.

* * *

"No."

Stefano heard the panic just starting to bubble up in Sofia's voice.

"I won't come with you. I can't come to Mondoverde."

A heavy cement block landed on his chest. Was his plan unraveling before he even started to execute it?

With a smile that never even came close to reaching her eyes, Sofia stammered, "I thank you, Your Serene Highness, but I cannot accept your invitation."

Invitation? Try a proposal.

This was not how he had played out the scene in his mind when he had made his plans one week ago. In his plans, he would come to Toronto, he would seek her out at her newspaper office, he would escort her to a secluded, but romantic spot, far away from the rapturous attention of her colleagues, he would tell her he loved her and intended to marry her, she would respond she loved him, too, and yes, she would marry him, and then he would whisk her onto his private jet, destination Mondoverde, before she would allow any reservations to rear up, implanting fears and doubts into her mind and heart, and preparations would then begin for their official betrothal ceremony and marriage.

He shoved splayed fingers through his hair. His plan was unraveling before he could even start to execute it.

Stefano had to work to keep his expression passive. He had to work to keep his voice placid. "You are refusing a royal invitation—a personal invitation from the royal family, *Signorina* Burska?" He had to work to uncoil the muscles twisting in his gut.

She wet her lips with her tongue. "Yes."

He knew they felt a strong, physical attraction to each other. He also knew there was more, much more, to it than just attraction. He felt it every time they kissed. Every time they touched. Every time they looked at each other. He knew she felt it, too. The connection. On all levels. The love. The love that could not be denied.

Stefano studied her now and realized just how right his father had been. Sofia, he now grasped, felt overwhelmed. Overwhelmed by his position. Overwhelmed with insecurity.

She looked pale, had shadows under her eyes, and her mouth was down-turned. Could it be… Hope began to arise within his heart and soul. Could it be Sofia had been as miserable without him and he without her these past two weeks?

The need to comfort her, to encourage her, to persuade her had him reaching out to stroke her cheek, then slipping his fingers beneath her chin and tilting her face up to his. "I do not believe, Sofia, you would refuse an invitation from Prince Alessandro and Princess Cristina after they so graciously entertained you at the *Castello di Bellaterra*, their home, and treated you like a member of their family, with respect and…love." He stroked his thumb over the soft skin of her jaw. "You will come with me, *cara*, because you are not mean-spirited."

Her big brown eyes filled with the slightest sheen of tears, which were blinked away.

"I can't come." She looked defiant despite the tears. She looked desperate.

Stefano took both her hands in his, lifted them to his mouth, and pressed a kiss to her fingertips, ignoring the oohs and ahhs and sniffles from the female observers. "We will talk. In private." Giving a nod of salutation encompassing the crowd of spectators, he released one of Sofia's hands, picked up her tulip, and offering it to her, he decreed, with his inherited air of confidence, "Come."

Minutes later, ensconced in the back seat of the Lincoln Town car and speeding away from the quaint neighborhood, Sofia demanded, "Where are we going?"

Stefano turned toward her and gave her a slow wink. "The airport."

"The airport?" Her words came out staccato. She sounded like she had trouble breathing. Then she choked out, "I told you. I can't come. I can't come and watch you get married."

"Watch me get married?" he repeated, frowning at her at first, then widening his eyes when her words sunk in. *Dio mio.* She thought he was marrying someone else? Emotion simmered just beneath the surface of her eyes, her mouth, her skin. She had set the purple tulip—the flower every Graziano prince gives to his princess—on the leather seat between them and now her fingers twisted in her grip. "It would appear—" He shook his head in self-disgust, his hands going to his hair, and not caring if he pulled his strands up straight into a highly undignified rendition of a royally bad-hair day. "—I am, how do you say it in English? Botching, yes? I am botching up my proposal."

Stunned, Sofia opened her mouth, but when nothing came out, she closed it again and swallowed.

"I will try again, yes?" Stefano took her coiled hands in his, staring down at their linked fingers. "Sofia, listen to me." He lifted his gaze, and unable to resist, he dropped his mouth to hers for a quick, hard kiss. "From the moment I laid eyes on you in the palace foyer and you had mistaken me for a servant—" He stopped, chuckling at the flush staining her cheekbones. "—you owned my heart."

He took her face in his hands. "I had given up believing I could marry for love. Most women see me only as a prince. A wealthy prince. They do not look beneath the title and position, the pomp and ceremony. They do not see the man." He dropped his head, forehead to forehead.

"I had resigned myself to marrying a woman who would never be my soul mate. She would just be a mother to my children."

He raised his head to stare deep into her eyes, to let her see the truth in the depth of his eyes. "But then you came along." He brushed a hand over her hair before settling both palms on her shoulders. "I fell in love with you—"

"What?" If she had appeared stunned before, she was passed panic now and well on her way to absolute terror. "You can't be. Not with me."

"Yes, *amore mio*, I am in love with you, and what is more, you are in love with me." He pulled her against him, buried the fingers of one hand in her hair and tilted back her head so he could look directly into her eyes. "Tell me." His whisper throbbed with emotion, with need. With worry. "*Ti amo.*"

He was a prince. Princes did not beg. He, Prince Stefano, Hereditary Prince of the Principality of Mondoverde, begged. "Tell me you love me, too. Please, *cara*. I need to hear the words come from your lips."

A charged silence followed his plea.

At the same time each second of silence, electrified with tension, dragged into another, Stefano fought to remain calm, cool, in control. He fought to reach deep within him for the inbred understanding and learned training so necessary to tamp down any emotional outbursts. He fought to remember, as the next-in-line-to-the-throne prince, he did not have the luxury to howl with fear. Or pain.

At this moment, he cared not for the privilege of being Prince Stefano of Mondoverde.

He cared not for the responsibility to always conduct himself in a circumspect manner.

He cared not for his plans unraveling before he had a chance to execute them and put a wedding band on her ring finger.

Right now, all he cared about was being a man, a normal, human man. All he felt, like a raging fire sweeping through him, was the terror of losing the one and only woman he had ever loved or ever would love. All he wanted in life was this woman, this woman sitting beside him, to be his royal princess wife, and sometime in the near future, for her to be the mother to his children.

He had to make her understand they belonged together. Forever.

Fear, pain provided the impetus. "Sofia—"

"I love you," she said in a soft, tremulous voice.

Sofia's sweet words landed straight in the center of his chest. Stefano closed his eyes and savored the relief flooding through him. *Grazie a Dio.* He dragged her to his chest. His arms anchored around her. His lips roamed her hair in a feverish dance of kisses.

"You might have mentioned that sooner, *amore mio.* Before I lost ten years off my life," he teased when he lifted his head to gaze down at her, but he heard the overtone of frustration beneath it. Stefano had never before felt such fear.

For a moment, her mouth almost curved into a smile, but a flash of something looking too much like the fear he had just suffered held the smile back from her lips. "I hadn't intended to tell you at all." She struggled against his arms.

His spine felt a cold wind move across it as frustration boomeranged back, bringing fear along for the ride. His heart took to pounding a ferocious tattoo in his chest. Warily, he loosened his grip, but did not set her free. He noted the pallor on her countenance, the sadness in her eyes. "Why would you not want to tell me?" His stomach clenched, but he allowed none of what he felt to show on his face. "What is wrong, Sofia?"

"What's wrong?" A laugh, if one could call it that, spilled out of her. "This is wrong—*I* am wrong." She pushed at his chest. He held tighter.

"Sofia, what are you talking about. You are perfect. I lo—"

With lightning speed, Sofia pressed her fingers against his mouth. "You're one of the wealthy royals in the world.

I'm just…me. A commoner. A strapped-for-cash one at that," she added in a furious undertone. Louder, she said, "A relationship—a marriage—with you, Stefano, can never go anywhere." She tilted her chin up a notch, daring him. "I'm not princess material. Your Serene Highness." The last three words came out in a fierce whisper as though she tried to convince herself, not him.

Stefano pressed a kiss to her fingertips before sliding his fingers through hers and lowering their hands to rest on his lap. He accepted the dare. "Sofia, my mother was a commoner. My grandmother was a commoner. My great-grandmother was a commoner. And so was my great-grandfather until he founded the Principality of Mondoverde. We have not forgotten our roots. We take nothing for granted. But in all things—our station, our titles, our privileges, our wealth—we give thanks and praise to the King of kings and continually seek His will and purpose for our blessings, to find the means to bless the citizens of Mondoverde whom He has given to us to be stewards over."

Then he put her hand, palm down, on his chest, over his heart. "I love you, Sofia. You are the princess I have chosen to be my wife, the woman who owns my heart, now and forever." He lifted her hand to his mouth for a kiss before planting it on his chest again. "You are stronger than you think, *cara*. You are dedicated, giving your all— heart, soul, and body. You have principles and you refuse to compromise them. You are kind and gentle. You understand pain and you have compassion for those in pain. You are loving. And every Mondoverduvian will be honored to call you their Crown Princess, and one day, their ruling princess." He paused, gave her a rueful grin. "I had planned this better, this proposal. A romantic setting. Me down on one knee. A ring box in my hand. I intend to correct this once we get home. But until then, will you believe me and put me out of my misery by telling me you will marry me?"

"Well...I don't know, Your Serene Highness." She tapped her fingertip to her lips, probably to indicate she gave the matter serious thought. More than likely, she suppressed a smile. "I don't see a ring."

He pulled her into his arms. "There is a ring, *amore mio*. It belonged to my great-grandmother, Princess Maria Elena. And it shall be on your finger shortly. I promise." With every sentence, he stroked one hand down her back, her hands trapped against his chest.

"I haven't said I'll marry you, Prince," Sofia felt obliged to say.

"You will marry me."

"You sound awfully sure of yourself."

"I am Prince Stefano, Crown Prince of Mondoverde. I am sure of myself," Stefano informed her before claiming her lips and sighing when her mouth was soft and yielding.

CHAPTER 13

"The behavior of a Princess of Mondoverde is more than cultivating good grammar. It is more than improving her posture. It is more than wearing tiaras and ball gowns and being a style icon. It is about loyalty more than royalty.

"A Princess of Mondoverde is a strong woman who uses her courage and intelligence to help make life better for the Mondoverduvian people she now serves. A Princess of Mondoverde, especially the Crown Princess, boldly faces her duties and responsibilities as a princess and yet allows her inner beauty to bring light and life and love to everyone around her. She will be kind, respectful, and humble. She will maintain excellent social manners and exhibit impeccable dinner etiquette. She will, at all times, be spotless, well-dressed, and look as perfect as a painting. She will never engage in gossip, nor will she reveal any news about the royal family that is not sanctioned first by the royal family. A princess, especially the Crown Princess, will never do or say anything that will reflect in an unfavorable manner upon the Crown Prince, his office, the government, the Principality of Mondoverde, or the Throne of Graziani.

"The Crown Princess of Mondoverde, as the wife of the Hereditary Prince, will immediately commit herself to performing the duty of the absolutely highest rank of importance as far as her obligation to the throne, and that is to produce the heir to the Throne of Graziani, and thus ensure the provision for dynastic succession."

The words of Tonino Masselli, the official representative of the royal House of Graziani, still echoed loud and clear in her ears. The words, carrying the weight of an entire country, had been echoing loud and clear in her ears for the past four months, ever since her return to Mondoverde with Stefano.

Now, on this momentous and fearful day, when Sofia, still lying on the satin sheets of her brass bed in the palace, opened her mouth, what flew past her lips sounded perilously close to hysteria. Panic swamped her in an instant. If she consented to be truthful, and she did, she'd have to admit panic had been shadowing her, hopping from one shoulder to the other like a demon spirit eager to corrupt the saintliest of saints, ever since she flew from Toronto to Bellaterra with Stefano and followed Stefano down the stairs from the royal plane to stand beside him on the red carpet, an honor guard standing at attention on both sides of them and flashbulbs flashing all around them.

That had been her first royal engagement as the future wife of the Crown Prince.

Others had followed. In rapid succession. A whirlwind of royal obligations and state dinners. So much so Sofia had been given a social secretary to teach her court etiquette and the Italian language. The sound, intended to be a laugh, rang out on a wail of hysteria. A virtual media frenzy erupted wherever she went, mostly with Stefano, sometimes alone. Pictures snapped. Her name chanted. Questions shouted. Mondoverduvian flags waved. A zillion eyes probed.

Always being watched. Always being judged. Always having to smile.

Always having to boldly face her duties and responsibilities as a princess-to-be and yet allow her inner beauty to bring light and life and love to everyone around her.

The demands. The stress. The tension.

The almost fanatical desire to be accepted by the populace. To earn the respect of the citizenry. To be loved by the people of her new country.

Always having to be spotless, well-dressed, and look as perfect as a painting.

Even when her stomach churned and her heart quaked.

Her stomach had churned, her heart had quaked for the past four months, more so since two months ago. Two months ago, marked the official start to her life with Stefano II, the Crown Prince of Mondoverde.

Sofia let her eyelids droop closed, and running a palm back and forth across her stomach, she let herself remember that day.

It had begun with the official portrait.

The local designer she had chosen had advised her on the correct attire for the occasion: a knee-length silk dress in a mauve tint, a nod to the color of the House of Graziani, fitted at the waist and flaring out at her hips, with a matching hat on her head, and the Mondoverduvian jewels hanging from her earlobes and circling her neck. Stefano had worn a dove-gray suit, white satin shirt and toned it with a purple tie that bore the royal crest of the monarchy in silver.

Together, her hand tucked into his arm, her heart thumping madly in her chest, a smile, a conservative one in comparison to the wicked ones he reserved for her in private, playing on his lips, they stepped past the four uniformed guards standing in pairs on either side of the double doors and walked into her second official royal function.

The Betrothal Ceremony.

The Palace Chapel was filled with family, hers and his, and because of Stefano's position, key politicians and important people were also invited guests. These guests, family and friends and government officials, had attended the palace dinner the previous evening, one with no formal speeches and no toasts, but hosted by Stefano, a relaxed occasion for everyone but Sofia, who'd been assessed by measuring eyes.

Those same measuring eyes followed Stefano and Sofia

as they were escorted down the aisle to the waiting minister, Carlo Adelardi, the spiritual adviser to the royal family, by a procession of choir boys who sang like angels. The short service involved a blessing, the ceremonial bestowal of the engagement ring, Princess Maria Elena's ring, by Stefano, the exchange of a kiss before the altar, and a brief sermon, an exposition of what was expected of them, by Carlo Adelardi, delivered in Italian. Following the conclusion of the ceremony, while the guests were shepherded out of Bellaterra Castle to return home, the family was marshaled into the grand drawing room to sit in gilt-decorated and ornate chairs to await the long-standing tradition that would cement the engagement in the eyes of the people.

The murmur of the crowd gathered in the huge square in front of the palace rose to penetrate through the windows and permeate the drawing room, curling and coiling around Sofia. She sat, too, because her knees suddenly wouldn't support her.

Would she ever get used to this? Would she ever get used to being on display? Would she ever get used to the fear swamping her that she would fall short of the mark?

And would the Mondoverduvian people scorn her, shun her, and shrink away from her because of their disappointment in her?

Would Stefano not be better off without her?

Where was the Crown Princess-to-be who would boldly face her duties and responsibilities? Where was the strong woman Stefano believed her to be? *Oh, Lord, what am I doing here?*

"Nervous?" Stefano asked, sitting beside her, his voice low and soft.

Her heart rose into her throat and pounded there. Blood thundered in her ears. "No," she lied and gulped. Her voice echoed strangely in her ears as though it belonged to someone else, someone on the other side of the world speaking through a faulty phone line.

Stefano took her knotted hands, and bringing them to his lips, he murmured against them, "You have nothing to be nervous about, *cara*."

"I'm not," she said a little too quickly and earned herself a quiet chuckle from him.

Untangling her fingers, he laid her palms flat on her lap, then cupped her cheeks in his hands. "They already love you, *amore mio*." He nuzzled her mouth, just once and lightly. "My people are smart. They understand you are the best *tesoro*, gift, for Mondoverde." He nibbled on the curve of her neck and she felt his lips turn up into a smile when she shivered and caught her breath on the delightful sensation of his soft lips and warm breath moving slow and superbly over her skin. Raising his head, he quoted his own guiding Scripture, "'Be strong and courageous. Do not be afraid; do not be discouraged, for the Lord your God will be with you wherever you go,' And so will I, *tesoro mio*. I will always be with you. I will always protect you. I will always love you." This time, heedless of witnessing eyes, he took her mouth again, kissing her until she was breathless.

Sofia entwined her fingers in his hair and held him to her, letting his kiss, his touch move over her, letting his belief in her, his love for her carry her.

I can do this. I can do this because Stefano loves me and has faith in me. I can do this because I have grit and gumption. I can do this because I can set my goal and work toward it and not give up even when the road to victory gets rough with obstacles and waist-deep ruts. I can do all things through Christ who strengthens me. Sofia gave herself the pep talk, accentuating it with the promise from Scripture, hoping to loosen the screws tightening in her stomach. *I can do this. I'm going to throw up.*

"Stefano, Sofia, it is time." Prince Alessandro's voice, low and accented, intruded.

Stefano lifted his mouth, but kept his arms entwined around her, and smiled at her.

Sofia didn't return the smile. She couldn't. Her mouth felt rigid like she'd just had surgery on it. "T-time?" She pushed the strangled word past stiff lips.

With one finger, Stefano smoothed the crease in her forehead. His grin was wry, a mere twist at the corner of his mouth. "It is time to go on display and greet our people and accept their joy at our betrothal."

No! I can't do this.

When Sofia remained speechless and had probably blanched enough to make Stefano think she might faint, he tightened his arm around her waist and explained in a careful, modulated tone, "We will step onto the balcony, Sofia, and wave to the Mondoverduvian people gathered below who wish to express their love to us. It is a tradition, *cara*. It will cement our engagement to them, as will the week of festivities that we are expected to attend."

She wanted to scream, *No! I can't do this*, but instead she swallowed down the words, and somehow managed a mechanical nod. *I have to believe, Lord, You have called me to serve You in this capacity, and therefore, You have anointed me with Your power to accomplish the tasks in life You have assigned to me.* She expanded her lungs with a deep breath. *But I don't feel anointed. I feel nervous. I feel overwhelmed. I feel panic-stricken.*

Stefano held her, brushed a light kiss onto her temple. Reaching for her hand, he rubbed it, and she wondered if he felt the dampness of her palm, if he could hear her heart pounding madly in her chest. "You are my chosen princess, Sofia. I love you," he murmured. "You have nothing to worry about. We are in this together, *amore mio*. Now and for always."

He stood, pulled her to her feet. He drew her close, clasping her to his rock-solid chest, his arms wrapped around her, as strong and sturdy, as steadfast and unshakable as the mighty Cedar tree, the tree known to surge toward heaven at a height of 130 feet, whose trunk expands to eight feet in diameter, and the roots plunge deep into the ground 230 feet, the tree which occupied a place of honor in the Mondoverduvian Coat of Arms. Such was the strength of his arms. A safe haven. A strong tower.

"Be strong and courageous," he whispered in her ear.

That was easy for him to say, Sofia mused, a little bit of the remaining hysteria chasing her as she let him guide her to the balcony doors. He'd had a life time of experience in going on display. He'd had a life time of training in being royal, with cameras flashing, recording his every expression, his every movement. All she'd had was a crash course in learning to navigate the new world of politics and wealth and royal etiquette.

Stefano stopped at the doors, tilted his head down to her, and smiled the smile that reassured her he not only loved her, but was proud of her. "Ready, *Principessa*?

Recalling Tonino Masselli's words, *The Crown Princess will never do or say anything that will reflect in an unfavorable manner upon the Crown Prince*, Sofia took in a deep steadying breath, gave her head a firm nod of acquiescence, and ordered her mouth to curl into a responding smile. She could do this and she would do this, not just for Stefano, not just for the throne, not just for the Mondoverduvian citizenry, but for herself. For Sofia Burska. It was one of those I-need-to-prove-to-myself kind of things. She would also do this as a love offering and a praise offering for her Lord and Savior, Jesus Christ.

And with the words of Queen Esther, the heroine of the Biblical Book bearing her name, the Jewish queen of the Persian king, Ahasuerus, *If I perish, I perish*, ringing in her mind and stiffening her spine, Sofia angled up her head and vowed to boldly face her duties and responsibilities as a princess.

Hand-in-hand, Stefano II, the Crown Prince of the Principality of Mondoverde, and his princess-to-be, Sofia Burska of Toronto, Canada, stepped onto the balcony to an immediate roar of approval. To the delight of the crowd of well-wishers chanting *Kiss! Kiss!* Prince Stefano kissed Sofia's temple, wrapped her in his arms and held her close against him.

* * *

A gentle knock on her bedroom door brought Sofia back to the present with a jolt. The knock brought her back to the reality of this day with a suddenness that left her feeling a swift sting of apprehension mixed with anticipation. Her cheeks throbbed with it as she called out, "Come in."

Sofia lay back against the pillow and rested her forearm over her eyes. Why was it so difficult for her to make this leap of faith? Why did she so vacillate between the concern of not being princess material and God's calling on her life to be the Crown Princess of Mondoverde? She bunched the sheets in her other hand. Why did she have such difficulty in reconciling her mind, heart, soul, and spirit to this compelling purpose of Jehovah God? And she knew it was the Sovereign God's purpose for her life to be intertwined with Stefano's because nothing, *nothing* happened by chance, but entirely by the decree of God who works out His own purposes.

"*Principessa!*" The maid, Lucia, bustled to the bed, trying to look calm, expressionless, but a note of worry echoed in the air after she said, "You are not ready."

Sofia dropped her arm from her face. "No, I'm not," she felt obliged to state the obvious. Biting down on her lower lip, she asked the maid, "Lucia? Do you believe in God?"

"Yes, *Principessa*, I do. How can one not?" The maid drew back the sheets. "A person only needs to look at the stars and moon, how they shine the light against the backdrop of night. Or the sun, how it shines and heats the land by day." She took Sofia by the arm, encouraging her to sit up. "Or the grandeur of the mountains like the Gran Sasso of Italia. The tranquility of our Adriatic Sea. How the earth perfectly rotates on its axis. How all clouds hang suspended high above us in the sky. It all appears so effortless, yet it is the mighty hand of the Lord God Almighty." Lucia regarded her in somber, measuring silence, then spoke in a reserved and somewhat chilly tone, "What is the matter, *Principessa*? You are having second thoughts about marrying our *principe*?"

The question carried an unvoiced warning. *You will not hurt Prince Stefano.* The royals may have been seen as reserved and cool, but Sofia had come to witness for herself they not only guard what—who—is theirs, but when they give, they give with their whole hearts and entire souls. And they earned—not commanded—but earned the loyalty and love of their staff. Any one of them would give up their own life for a member of the royal family. The stalwart Lucia included.

A chill, a sort of odd awe, rippled in the pit of Sofia's stomach when an intimidating frown puckered the flesh between Lucia's eyebrows. "No, it's not that." She could barely force the words out.

"What is it then?" Lucia held out the silk robe to Sofia and when Sofia stood, the maid helped her slip into it.

Concentrating her attention on tying the belt at her waist, Sofia answered in a low voice, "I know commoners are not unusual for the royal family, but…"

"But," Lucia prompted softly, yet still with a slight note of reservation.

Sofia took a deep breath, blew it out, lifted her gaze to the other woman, and probably breaking a royal rule in confiding in the servants, admitted, "But I sometimes wonder if God made a mistake. About me. Here." She waved a frantic hand to indicate the palace. "I love Prince Stefano." She let her eyes dip to the beautiful engagement ring on her finger. "But what if…what if I fail him? Fail the Mondoverduvian people? What if I'm all wrong?" she asked, her voice catching raw in her throat.

"*Principessa.*" The maid's face softened, concern filled her eyes. "You must not entertain such negative thoughts. The prince, he loves you very much. We all do," she said, her smile wide and genuine. A question lit her eyes, telling Sofia she wrestled with something. After a few seconds, she'd made a decision, Sofia knew, because the maid's eyes cleared, and with her mind made up, Lucia did what no palace employee ever did. She touched a royal. Or in Sofia's case, a royal-to-be. Lucia framed Sofia's face and said, "There is nothing wrong with you. You are the right person for the job."

"The job?" Her throat hurt. Sofia swallowed, but it didn't help, and her eyes suddenly burned.

"Yes, the job." Lucia reached for the box of tissues and handed it to Sofia who took one and dabbed at the tears forming in her eyes. "Being a wife is a full-time job, even more so when you are the wife of the next-in-line-to-the-throne prince. But nothing, *Principessa*, that happens to us is an accident."

Confirmation. The maid had just confirmed Sofia's earlier thoughts that nothing happened by chance.

Lucia palmed Sofia's shoulders and gently kneaded them. "Not the family we are born in. Not the home we live in. Not the setbacks that we experience. Not the sicknesses that attack us. Not even the victories that encourage us. Nothing is an accident, nothing is *wrong*, but everything rests beneath the powerful hand of Almighty God."

The maid took the tissue from Sofia's fingers and brushed it across Sofia's cheeks. "It is not an accident of birth that Prince Stefano was born into the royal House of Graziani. As it was not an accident that you were sent here on your newspaper assignment. And that the two of you met and fell in love. Or that you will give to us, very soon, our royal heir," she added with the merest flicker of mischief in her eyes.

Oh, yes. Sofia managed to stifle the grimace. Let her not forget she must perform 'the duty of the absolutely highest

213

rank of importance as far as her obligation to the throne.' Talk about pressures, stresses.

"The point I am trying to make, *Principessa*," the maid sobered, and taking Sofia by the arm, she walked her to the door of the bathroom. "Know in your heart God is in control, believe in your spirit in the presence and power of the Almighty, trust in your soul. He will be with you wherever you go."

Lucia reached over and squeezed Sofia's wrist lightly, her grin turning thoughtful. "Go boldly forward, *Principessa*, trusting in God's promise, 'Be strong and courageous. Do not be afraid; do not be discouraged, for the Lord your God will be with you wherever you go.'"

God certainly spoke and Sofia had better listen because that scripture kept popping up. With that scripture, God tried to reassure her. All would be well for her because He promised to be with her. What more could she ask? How could she not reach out and take hold of the peace and joy God offered her? All she had to do was stay focused on the Lord and obey His command to 'be strong and courageous.'

"Now." Lucia became officious. "Go take a shower and wash your hair. We shall do your makeup and then I shall help you put on Princess Maria Elena's wedding dress." She winged up one brow. "You know it is a tradition, an honor, actually, in our Italian culture, to pass on a wedding dress from generation to generation, yes?"

"Yes, Lucia, I know."

"You will make a beautiful Royal Princess Wife." The maid gently pushed Sofia into the bathroom.

"And Royal Princess Mother," they both pronounced at the same time and laughed, the maid joyfully, Sofia a little nervously. As far as Sofia knew, she should have no problems getting pregnant. But... Another what if surged against her heart. What if...she couldn't conceive? What if she couldn't 'produce the heir to the Throne of Graziani, and thus ensure the provision for dynastic succession?'

"Yes, with wisdom and love, God has weaved every circumstance of your life and of Prince Stefano's, the good and the bad, the ordinary and the remarkable, the painful and the uplifting, into this beautiful tapestry of life together." Lucia clasped the doorknob. "No, nothing is an accident," she whispered, pushing the door closed, and leaving Sofia to her privacy and her troublesome thoughts.

* * *

"You look...*bellissima, Principessa*." The awe in the maid's whisper reached Sofia before Lucia had advanced into the bedroom to come up behind her. Sofia, who stood staring at the vision reflected in the mirror, flicked her gaze to the maid's and saw moisture forming in the other woman's eyes. "You are the most beautiful princess I have ever seen." A reverent curtsy accompanied the words of praise.

"Thank you, Lucia." Sofia let her gaze be drawn back to her reflection, and she couldn't help the wave of wonder sliding over her. A laugh, full of astonishment, bubbled out of her mouth as she took in Princess Cristina's tiara sitting on her head, Princess Maria Elena's white lace mantilla— Sofia's very own princess-style wedding gown that one day she would pass down to either her daughters or daughters-in-law, and the white pearl earrings and necklace belonging to Stefano's grandmother, Princess Alessia. A vision of white beauty. Of royal beauty. "I can hardly believe this is me. That I'm going to become a real princess." She shook her head at the incredible miracle.

"Believe it, Princess Sofia."

Princess Sofia.

Would Sofia ever get used to the title? To the attention that came with the title? To the duties and responsibilities that came with the title?

As if she could read Sofia's mind, Lucia said, "The Apostle Paul told the Thessalonian church 'In every thing give thanks: for this is the will of God in Christ Jesus concerning you.'" She smiled a watery smile, sniffed back the tears, then transformed into the stiff-upper-lip palace employee, and said, "For this is the will of God in Christ Jesus concerning you, *Principessa.*"

For this is the will of God in Christ Jesus for me.

Sofia pondered the words in a reflective silence for a moment.

For this is the will of God in Christ Jesus for me.

Sofia felt, for the first time since becoming engaged to Stefano, like she finally grasped the awesome message.

For this is the will of God in Christ Jesus for me.

If the Lord God had called her to this high and highly important position, then He would ensure she be gifted with all she would need to be the very best princess she could be, a Christ-centered role model, providing leadership to her adopted country's people, especially the women, to encourage them to be all God had planned for them to be, to trust in the Lord—and wasn't that the country's motto? In God We Trust.

If she would embrace the House of Graziani motto—Seek Ye First The Kingdom Of God—she could rest in the confidence she could do all things through Him, Jesus, who would give her strength, as the Apostle Paul encouraged the Philippian church.

And if "Jesus Christ is the same yesterday and today and forever," then she could expect His unfailing guidance and everlasting love and infinite grace to sustain her. She would be the Lord's trophy of grace.

Yes, I can do this. I will do this. For God and country. For Stefano and the royal family. For myself.

With a magnificent burst of faith, she addressed the reflection in the mirror, "Yes, this is the will of God in Christ Jesus for me." She turned, careful of the dress, and smiling, said to the maid, "I have an appointment with my prince."

"Yes, Princess Sofia. Prince Stefano awaits you."

Minutes later, Sofia found herself outside the castle and

stared at her mode of transportation. "This is for me?" she murmured, asking no one in particular, ruefully amused and oddly dizzy.

Cinderella, you got nothing on me, she mused accepting a hand-up from her father, Ted Burska, into the white carriage drawn by six white horses that would deliver her to the cathedral.

"You look beautiful, Sofia." Her father's voice sounded gruff.

Sofia looked at her father, saw his love settled deep in his eyes. "Thank you, Daddy. I love you." She leaned close to press her lips on his cheek, then swiped her fingers over the smudged imprint her lipstick left behind.

"I love you, too, my little princess," he said, his voice raw with emotion. She watched him swallow, then he asked, "You're sure?" A frown of concern marred his forehead. "About this?" He motioned to the carriage. "It was all so sudden." The meaning was clear. Was she sure about marrying the Crown Prince of the Principality of Mondoverde?

"I've never been more sure of anything, Daddy."

A look of relief landed on his face. "Well then. Your prince awaits you."

"Yes, he does," Sofia agreed and the carriage started to move. Lifting her face skyward, she winked at God.

The sky was painted a stunning azure. The sun shone its benevolent light. The weather couldn't have been any more perfect. And the citizens of Mondoverde, her people, lined the cobblestone streets, throwing rose petals in front of the carriage. The petals floated through the air and were stirred up by the horse's feet. Their voices rang out, chanting her name. They waved flags, brightly colored streamers, flowers, and handkerchiefs. It was real. It was surreal.

After following a meandering route that gave the Mondoverduvians a chance to see the pomp and pageantry of delivering their princess to her prince, the carriage came to a stop in front of the old cathedral made of stone with a towering steeple topped with a cross. Christ Church Cathedral. Up those stone steps and beyond the double wooden doors, her husband-to-be awaited, along with family and friends, government officials and visiting dignitaries. For one brief moment, a slight shiver tiptoed up Sofia's spine. She squashed it.

On her father's arm, she entered the church. They stopped. "Ready?" her father asked.

She smiled at him through the veil covering her face. "Ready." The organ began to play the processional song and together, she and her dad began the long walk down the aisle formed by pews and filled with guests all gazing at her.

Stefano stood with the minister, Carlo Adelardi, and his best man, his brother, Prince Cristiano, but it was Stefano who held her interest as she walked toward the altar. Dressed in a white military suit with gold buttons and purple sash, with the Coat of Arms crest pinned to his right breast pocket and the Order of Mondoverde Seal over his left, white shoes on his feet and white military hat with the Coat of Arms badge on the front on his head, he looked impressive, masterful. Like the future ruler of Mondoverde.

The proud smile on his face beckoning her to him, Sofia felt such overwhelming love for her husband-to-be. Any remaining jitters vanished. Soon her father kissed her cheek, shook hands with Stefano, and handed her over to her prince, all with a Polish flourish. The ceremony began against the backdrop of expectant silence.

Determination and love reflected on Stefano's face. His voice remained as steady as hers had been shaky when repeating their vows. Rings, the symbol of a wedding dating back from ancient Rome, were exchanged. At the pronouncement they were now husband and wife, a loud roar of approval rose outside where massive screens had been set up to receive a live feed from the interior of the church. With a small sigh of welcome, Sofia opened her heart and her life to Stefano. His mouth found hers, gentle and firm, sweet and passionate. They kissed with a need that went so deep. After she and Stefano had signed the marriage certificate, the Wedding March sounded and they began to proceed toward the doors, stopping briefly before the royal family where Stefano bowed his head and Sofia curtsied. Once they reached the doors, the shouts of jubilation rose to a crescendo.

"Did I not tell you, Princess Sofia, they love you?" Stefano murmured in her ear.

"Yes, you did, Prince Stefano," Sofia replied with a huge grin.

An open-air carriage stood waiting to return the royal couple to Bellaterra Castle. Once Stefano sat beside her and closed the door, bells began to ring throughout the city of Bellaterra. They cued the people of Mondoverde and they went wild with excitement and celebration, waving hands and flags and shouting their names.

An hour later, Stefano and Sofia and their families sat in drawing room. The murmur of the crowd in the square below was heard, indicating to Stefano and Sofia it was time to move out onto the balcony. A wild roar of approval greeted them once Stefano and Sofia came out first and alone and moved across to the balustrade. When Sofia smiled at Stefano, a renewed burst of cheering was triggered. She waved at the excited mass of people gathered in front of the palace who seemed determined to let their prince and princess know they shared their happiness. When the rest of the family joined them on the balustrade, a chant went through the crowd for the prince to kiss his princess.

"With pleasure," Stefano said, his voice husky. He leaned down to cage her head between his hands.

Sofia twined a hand around his neck, and going up on her tippy-toes, she kissed him.

A frenzy moved through the people.

"If you two do not come up for air soon, we are going to have a riot down there," Prince Cristiano warned them from behind, his tone sardonic.

Stefano let Sofia come up for that air and matched his brother's sardonic tone. "He is just jealous—"

"Jealous?" Cristiano pretended outrage.

"Do not mind him." Stefano winked at his bride, his princess wife. "He will get his princess some day."

Cristiano muttered some unintelligible response and stepped away from the beaming couple.

A final wave and the family turned and filed back inside, adjourning to the private apartments where they would be served the wedding meal.

Flutes of champagne were passed around and Cristiano stood, clinking his glass with a fork. "Allow me to make a toast to the newly married and disgustingly happy Prince Stefano, and Sofia, Princess of Mondoverde." Sobering, he said, "May the fires of love keep you happy and warm. May your joys be as bright as the morning, your years of happiness as numerous as the stars in the heavens, and your troubles but shadows that fade in the sunlight of love. I wish you a life full of *amore* and—" He smirked. "—a castle full of *bambini*." Raising his flute, he said, "To you, Stefano and Sofia."

"To you, Stefano and Sofia," the gathered guests murmured before lifting their glasses of champagne to their lips.

The meal, in true Italian style, began with an antipasto of prosciutto, olives, stuffed mushrooms, and salami, and was followed first with the traditional Italian Wedding Soup, then with pasta, meat, salad, and roasted potatoes, fish and vegetables, and served with white and red wines brought in from the Italian peninsula, from the vineyards of Abruzzo where the first prince, Prince Giovanni, grew up.

After the meal, everyone was marshalled into the Grand Hall where an orchestra had set up, and Stefano and Sofia, hand-in-hand, walked onto the floor for the traditional first dance of the bride and groom. Applause shook the room. Whistles shattered the air. Tears streamed down cheeks.

Cristiano stood on the sidelines, watching the couple and feeling a twist in his gut. *It is* not *jealousy!* He was happy. He felt very happy his brother had found love, true love, his forever mate. He felt…melancholic. He tried to shake off the gloom that had attached itself onto him, darkening his mind, weighing heavily on his chest. When that failed, he marched to the open bar set up in one corner of the Grand Hall. He got himself a glass of wine, flipped a brief gaze on his very happy brother and happy sister-in-law, and deciding he needed some air, he veered off for the double ornate doors leading to the terraces, gardens, and courtyards, and the blissfully quiet outdoors.

The End

About Anna Dynowski

Anna's belief that love never fails (I Corinthians 13:8 NIV) and her passion for God, has led her to write what's in her heart—love—and what's in her soul—faith in God. Her heartwarming stories of love, romance, and Christian faith are designed to encourage and entertain.

She makes her home in Toronto, Canada, with her husband of 30 years, and her cat, Misha.

Readers may contact Anna at: annadynowski@yahoo.ca

Or you may visit her web site at:

www.annadynowski.com

Made in the USA
Charleston, SC
01 March 2015